~A Basket~
of Trouble

To Hell in

"Groundwater's second leaves the bunny slope behind, offering some genuine black-diamond thrills." —*Kirkus Reviews*

"An engrossing and entertaining mystery that keeps you reading until the final page." —Gumshoe.com

"The wait is over for the second title in the Claire Hanover Mystery series … Her page-turning style is welcome to any reader looking for a great read." —*For   as Coloradoan*

A Real Basket Case

An Agatha Award Finalist for Best First Novel

"A tense, exciting debut." —*Kirkus Reviews*

"This will appeal to *Desperate Housewives* fans and those who like cozies with a bit of spice." —*Booklist*

"*A Real Basket Case* and its author are a welcome addition to the mystery genre." —*Crimespree Magazine*

"An enjoyable mystery … *A Real Basket Case* should not be missed." —Romance Reviews Today, RomRevToday.com

"I really enjoyed this book. I can't wait to read the next!" —Mystery Lovers Corner, SleuthEdit.com

"A clever, charming debut novel. Her well-crafted characters comprise a nicely balanced cast, and she does a good job incorporating a blend of humor and relationship drama into a deftly twisted plot with the kind of surprise ending guaranteed to satisfy. Quick-paced and well written with clear and comfortable prose, *A Real Basket Case* is a perfect afternoon read for cozy fans." —SpinetinglerMag.com

"A gutsy sleuth, a fast-paced plot, and intriguing characters that keep you guessing. *A Real Basket Case* is a real winner! Don't miss it."
—Maggie Sefton, *New York Times* bestselling author of the Knitting Mystery series

"A crackling good novel with the kind of twists and turns that make roller coaster rides so scary and so much fun!"
—Margaret Coel, *New York Times* bestselling author of the Wind River Mysteries

"An impressive debut! Groundwater brings new meaning to the term *menopausal* in this flawlessly crafted mystery. Her gutsy, power surging heroine keeps the pressure on until the final chapter."
—Kathy Brandt, author of the Underwater Investigation series

"Like one of Claire's baskets, Beth Groundwater has put together the perfect mixture of humor, thrills, and mystery. A terrific debut!"
—Christine Goff, author of the Birdwatcher's Mystery series

BETH GROUNDWATER

A Basket

of Trouble

A CLAIRE HANOVER MYSTERY

MIDNIGHT INK
WOODBURY, MINNESOTA

First Midnight Ink Edition
First Printing, 2013

Book design by Donna Burch
Cover design by Kevin R. Brown
Cover illustration © Glenn Gustafson
Editing by Connie Hill

Midnight Ink, an imprint of Llewellyn Worldwide Ltd.

This is a work of fiction. Names, characters, places, and incidents are either the product of the author's imagination or are used fictitiously, and any resemblance to actual persons (living or dead), business establishments, events, or locales is entirely coincidental.

Library of Congress Cataloging-in-Publication Data

Groundwater, Beth.
  A basket of trouble : a Claire Hanover mystery / by Beth Groundwater. — First Midnight Ink Edition.
      pages   cm. — (A Claire Hanover mystery ; 3)
   ISBN 978-0-7387-2703-5
 1. Murder—Investigation—Fiction. 2. Colorado Springs (Colo.)—Fiction. I. Title.
 PS3607.R677B36   2013
 813'.6—dc23   2013025600

Midnight Ink
Llewellyn Worldwide Ltd.
2143 Wooddale Drive
Woodbury, MN 55125-2989
www.midnightinkbooks.com

Printed in the United States of America

DEDICATION

In memory of my two grandmothers,
Mary and Grace,
two women of indomitable courage, wit, and will,
who inspired me to try harder and reach higher.

ACKNOWLEDGMENTS

My readers know that I love to dive into research for my mysteries, and this book is no exception. Many thanks to Walter Hampel, General Manager of Academy Riding Stables in Colorado Springs, for answering my questions about how a trail riding operation works, from hiring wranglers to doctoring sick horses to managing clueless tourists. Also, thank you, Nancy Harrison, hippotherapist and co-owner of Mark Reyner Stables and the Colorado Springs Therapeutic Riding Center, for explaining to me how hippotherapy works and for allowing me to observe a few of those small miracles blossom in some sessions. Also, thanks for what you do to help disabled people live better lives!

Thanks to farrier Chris May for allowing me to observe him shoeing horses while I peppered him with questions and took photos. And last but certainly not least, thanks to Thomas J. Hurley, Attorney at Law specializing in immigration law, for patiently answering my naïve questions about the convoluted and complex provisions of immigration law. If I got anything wrong in this book on those topics, it was due to my own errors in thinking or interpretation of the advice given to me by these three patient souls and of the information I gathered from my own reading.

Just to give you an idea of what my own research included, other topics I read up on included names, breeds, and colors of horses; horse tack; the meanings of sounds that horses make; cowboy work wear; birds found in the Garden of the Gods; Down syndrome; autism; certification requirements for occupational therapists; human smuggling; and policies of the U.S. Citizenship and Immigration Services and the Department of Labor. One thing I enjoy about writing mysteries is all the learning that takes place as I delve into new topics!

Thanks to my critique group, Vic Cruikshank, Maria Faulconer, Barbara Nickless, MB Partlow, and Robert Spiller, for your astute feedback on the rough manuscript. Many thanks to my literary agent, Sandra Bond, who works tirelessly on my behalf and keeps me out of contract trouble. Thanks to Terri Bischoff, Acquisition Editor at Midnight Ink, and Connie Hill, Senior Editor, who made sure the book's prose was the best it could be. Thanks to Donna Burch for the book design and to Kevin R. Brown for the red-and-green holiday-colored cover that is ideal for a November-released gift basket designer mystery. Thanks also to all of the staff at Midnight Ink who toil behind the scenes to produce and market the books in my Claire Hanover gift basket designer series.

And lastly, I would like to thank the avid readers of the Claire Hanover gift basket designer series who take the time to write and tell me what they like—and don't like—about the books. I write them for you!

ONE:
THE OPENING

"Would you please stop fidgeting?"

Claire Hanover jumped, startled out of her troubled thoughts by the bemused sound of her husband's voice. She looked out the car window and saw they still had a ways to go. Then she glanced at Roger sitting beside her, his steady hands on the steering wheel.

"Sorry," she said. "I'm anxious about the stable's opening event. I want everything to go well for Charley's new business."

"Honey, I'm sure everything will be fine." Roger took his gaze off the road for a moment to eye her hands. "And if you keep picking at the cellophane on that gift basket, you'll tear it open before your brother gets a chance to."

She stilled her nervous fingers and pressed her palms against the sides of the large gift basket on her lap. She had taken a lot of care in choosing the contents and decorating it with vintage horse tack and a bow made from a horse-themed bandana. The last thing she wanted was to destroy the basket before Charley could even see it.

Claire took a deep breath to calm herself and slowly blew it out. "Okay, okay, I'll try to be still."

Roger reached over and gave her arm a squeeze. "We'll be there soon."

She peered at the cornflower blue Colorado sky where a few puffy white clouds floated on a light breeze. At least the weather was holding for the opening. Being early June, the summer monsoon season hadn't kicked in yet, with its afternoon thunderstorms. Claire wondered how the summer storms would affect the trail rides through the Garden of the Gods Park that Charley was offering at his stable. But, he had dealt with the same weather pattern in Durango before he relocated to Colorado Springs a few months ago.

In fact, her younger brother and his wife, Jessica, had managed his stable business in Durango very capably for quite a few years. But then the economic downturn had dried up tourism in Durango. After struggling to hold on, Charley had looked around for alternatives. Anxious to help, Claire had suggested he investigate Colorado Springs, where she and Roger lived, because summer tourism was still fairly steady there.

In a serendipitous turn of events, the owners of a large parcel of commercial land near the intersection of Garden of the Gods Road and 30th Street were happy to negotiate a lease with an option to buy. And, Charley was able to reach an agreement with the city to run commercial horseback trail rides down Foothills Trail through the adjacent Blair Bridge Open Space and into the scenic Garden of the Gods Park.

Thankfully, Charley had found a buyer for his property in Durango. That gave him the funds to make the move and buy a downsized home in Colorado Springs. They didn't need as much space because their son, like Claire's and Roger's two kids, was grown and on his own. An added benefit of the relocation was that Charley would be living closer to Claire. She hoped that would bring their relationship closer, too. They had been drifting apart lately, and that bothered her.

She needed to find out why.

"Here we are," Roger announced.

He turned his BMW X5 into the newly paved parking lot, taking the last open spot. People from other cars were walking under the brand-new wooden sign suspended between two huge peeled logs cemented into the ground. It proclaimed 'Gardner's Stables' and gave off an aura of strength and permanence. Claire crossed her fingers and hoped the aura proved true.

She unbuckled her seatbelt and reached for the car door handle, but Roger stopped her with a hand on her shoulder. "Maybe this will help calm your nerves." He leaned in and gave her a proper smooch and a hug.

By the end of the long sweet kiss, Claire was smiling. As Roger pulled back, she gazed into the puppy dog brown eyes behind his bifocal glasses. She raised a hand to caress the bald spot above his graying hair.

"I love you. You know that, don't you?" After their earlier troubles, she found every opportunity she could to remind him.

"Of course." Lifting a lock of her shoulder-length hair, dyed blonde to hide the gray, he inhaled the scent of her peach-lavender shampoo. "And I love you, too."

Claire ran a teasing finger up his arm. "And now you've got my mind on other things besides the opening!"

Roger laughed and gave her a wink. "Almost fifty, and I've still got it. Sit still and I'll come around to get the basket from you so you can get out."

While they walked up the path and under the sign, Claire surveyed the stable as if she were seeing it for the first time like the other attendees. A beige office trailer sat off to the left behind the sign, where customers went inside to pay and sign liability forms. Charley had bought it used from a housing developer who was downsizing. Some of the guests sat at the half dozen wooden picnic tables in front of the trailer. Jessica and Charley had planted a few new hackberry and crabapple trees among the tables, hoping they would eventually grow and provide shade. For now, a retractable awning over the trailer's wooden porch provided some shade for the built-in seating along its rails.

Charley had placed two handicap-accessible port-a-potties discreetly behind the trailer. Off to the right was a corral where wranglers watered the horses and matched customers to their mounts. Behind the trailer and corral stood the newly built barn. A large fenced-in pasture behind the barn provided an exercise area for the horses.

Gardner's Stables was small compared to many other local stables, especially the well-established Peak View Stables south of the Garden of the Gods that Charley would be competing with. But Claire thought it looked like a clean, well-run operation. She prayed silently that the move would turn out to be a good one for her brother. She could see him laying all of the blame at her feet for suggesting it if it went bad.

"Claire! Roger!" Jessica waved at them from the trailer porch and skipped down the steps to greet them.

Petite and athletic with freckled skin and red hair tied back in a ponytail, Jessica exuded energy. Her long Western print skirt swirled around her calves as she hurried toward them. Being in her forties hadn't seemed to slow her down at all. Claire felt gawky and slow next to her brother's wife, but she always enjoyed Jessica's lively spirit. Especially since Jessica had been able to retain that spirit after the early tragedy in her marriage to Charley.

Jessica hugged Claire and gave Roger a peck on the cheek, then looked at the large basket in his arms. "What's this?"

"One of my gift baskets for you and Charley," Claire said. "To celebrate the opening. It's full of local treats and a bottle of wine from Holy Cross Abbey. I hope you like it."

"Oh, wow, you managed to get Charley's favorite candy. Horehound is so hard to find." Jessica peeked through the cellophane at the other items nestled inside. "And are those chocolates from the Rocky Mountain Chocolate Factory for me?" When Claire nodded, she said, "This is wonderful. You didn't need to do this!"

"I know," Claire replied. "But I'm so glad you two have moved here, and I thought this was the perfect occasion to let you know. Now that construction is done and your business is open, I hope we can see more of you. I feel like I talked to Charley more often when you lived in Durango."

Jessica shot her a guilty look, but before Claire could say anything, Roger hefted the basket and asked, "Where should I put this?"

"How about on the food table?" Jessica pointed toward a cafeteria table set up in the shade of a copse of native scrub oak trees. It was covered with a bright red-checked tablecloth pinned at the corners. Two small bunches of balloons were tied to either end. "It'll be the centerpiece. Maybe some folks will notice it and ask you to make them a gift basket. Did you bring cards?"

Claire waved her hand. "No, this is your special day. I'm not going to advertise my business at your opening!"

Jessica shrugged and led them to the table, where people were helping themselves to lemonade, iced tea, and chocolate chip, sugar, and oatmeal-raisin cookies. She moved a couple of cookie trays to make room for the basket. Roger set it down, looking grateful to finally be rid of his burden.

Jessica stepped back, wiping her hands. "Perfect. Now, where's Charley? He needs to know you're here."

At that moment, Charley exited the barn with a family of five. He wore a crisp maroon Western snap shirt with white detailing and dark blue jeans with a crease. His cowboy boots had maroon-stained scrollwork on the toes, and he wore a broad-brimmed fawn-colored felt cowboy hat with a braided leather band. Claire wondered if Jessica had recently bought the whole outfit to gussy him up for the opening.

He made a sweeping motion with his arm toward the west, where the gray rock formations on the Glen Eyrie Castle grounds loomed. "It's a gorgeous location," he said with a proud grin. "Those grayish yellow chalk and shale hogback ridges come from the Cretaceous period. And the white limestone and red sandstone ridges in the Garden of the Gods Park date all the way back to the Triassic and Permian periods."

As the family stared at him with puzzled faces, Charley smiled. "Sorry, I let my passion for geology get away from me there. The formations are beautiful to look at, regardless of how they came about. You can ride your horse from here straight into the park and explore all the trails there."

He spied Jessica and waved her over. Claire and Roger followed her.

"Jessica, these folks want to board their horse with us. Could you take care of the paperwork?"

"Sure thing." She leaned over to Claire and stage-whispered, "I'm better at that sort of thing than he is. He always screws it up, then I have to fix it."

A frown wiped the grin off Charley's face. Claire realized both he and the family had heard Jessica's blithe, but still derogatory, comment. Jessica steered the family toward the trailer, turning to give Charley a thumbs-up before returning her attention to them.

Determined to restore Charley's smile, Claire gave her brother an enthusiastic hug. "Congratulations! It looks like your business is going to be a big success."

"Thanks, sis. I sure hope so." Charley pulled back and shook Roger's hand. He doffed his cowboy hat and ran a hand through his gray-flecked light brown hair, fluffing it back up. He slapped the hat against his thigh and surveyed the event attendees. "Wish more people had come today, though."

Claire turned to survey the twenty or so people wandering the grounds. She, too, wished there were more—a lot more. Was this a sign of struggles to come? Would Charley's investment in the business be lost? And Roger's and her investment? They had loaned Charley some of the money he needed for the move.

But their potential financial losses weren't what concerned her the most. She was afraid of what a business failure would do to Charley's self-esteem. He had always lived in his big sis's shadow.

Their parents had sent her to the University of Colorado for four years, to earn her, what Charley called 'high-falutin', degree in French and Fine Arts. But when his turn came to go to college, their parents' funds weren't as flush. They asked him if he would attend a community college for two years before transferring to Colorado State to finish his degree in Equine Science.

He had never made that transfer and never finished his degree.

The last thing Claire was going to do was expose any of her doubts about the business to Charley, though. She put on a brave smile. "They'll tell their friends about you. Spread the news by word-of-mouth, the best advertising there is."

Charley's brow furrowed over his light blue eyes, the exact same shade as Claire's. "And my successful big sis would know, wouldn't she?"

She knew the quip wasn't just a compliment, but a comparison—with him coming up on the negative side of the equation. Again. This perceived sibling rivalry in Charley's mind was their parents' fault. They always held her up to him as an example, and she had spent years trying to dispel it.

She gave his arm a playful slap. "Oh, please, my part-time gift basket business is nothing compared to this, Charley. You're the one in the family with the business smarts."

He snorted. "Yeah, smart enough to almost bankrupt myself before leaving Durango with my tail between my legs."

Oh, Charley.

"That was the economy, not you," Roger said.

Claire took his hand and squeezed it to show she appreciated his comment.

At that point, a red-faced gnarled little man in scuffed tennis shoes and khaki pants belted high over his protruding tummy stomped up to Charley. "You the manager of this fiasco?"

Charley reared back but kept a friendly smile on his face. "I own Gardner's Stables, yes." He held out a hand. "I'm Charley Gardner. And you?"

The man ignored both the question and the proffered hand. "What right do you have to ride your mangy beasts through city-owned open space?"

"I have an agreement with the city," Charley replied. "It allows me to run trail rides through there and the Garden of the Gods Park."

"And leave horse manure all over the trails!" Spittle flew from the old man's lip as he flung an arm in the direction of the Blair Bridge Open Space.

"We have a system for taking care of that," Charley said evenly, with an embarrassed glance at Claire and Roger. "One of my employees follows the horses in an ATV with a manure cart to shovel up any droppings on the paved trails."

The old man's eyes narrowed. "What about the dirt trails?"

"The City Parks Department told me to just leave the manure on them, because it packs down well and helps prevent erosion. Do you live near here? We mailed fliers explaining the arrangement to all the local residents."

"I'm only here in the summer. Came back from Arizona two weeks ago, went to walk my dog in Blair Bridge like I always do. Suddenly a noisy string of horses comes through, crowding us, stirring up dust and smelling up the place."

Charley stuffed a fist in his jeans pockets. "There's plenty of room for everyone. You can still walk your dog in the open space any time you want. But it's a good idea to hold him close on his leash when our horses come by, to prevent the dog from spooking a horse and getting kicked."

He dug a trifold flier out of a back pocket and held it out to the man. "Here's one of our fliers. It explains everything and includes a buy-one-get-one-free coupon for a two-hour trail ride."

The old man balled up the flier and threw it back at Charley. It bounced off his chest. "I don't want one of your stinking fliers. I'm calling the city council about this." Murder in his glare, he tromped off.

"Whew," Roger said. "Good job keeping your cool with that hothead. Have you had to deal with much of that?"

"Some," Charley replied. "Jessica and I met with local homeowners associations to show them the plan before we started construction. I explained that we would maintain the sections of the open space and park that we use, and repair any damage we cause. We've had a few complaints, some tense moments. I thought we'd gotten through the worst of it, but I guess the issue isn't dead yet."

Claire watched the old man stride away. "Can he cause problems for you, going to the city council?"

"They're the ones who approved the agreement," Charley said with a shrug. "Hopefully that guy won't get anywhere with them."

She worried her lip. "I hope so, too."

"Well, we'll cross that bridge when we come to it." Charley donned his hat and turned toward the barn. "C'mon, there's someone I want you to meet."

"You don't need to tie yourself up with us," Roger said. "Don't you need to greet people or something?"

"Nope." Charley pointed to a lanky, brown-skinned young man dressed in faded blue jeans and a blue-checked button-down work shirt with the sleeves rolled up to his elbows. He was talking and gesturing to a group of people. "I've got Kyle Mendoza there leading tours around. He's a real people person, and a great wrangler and trail guide. And since he's born and raised here, he knows his Colorado Springs history."

As if he felt Charley's gaze on him, Kyle waved at them and flashed a white-toothed grin before returning his attention to the group in front of him. "That's our owner and manager, Charley Gardner," he said to his rapt audience. "A finer man you'll never meet. Let's all give him a wave and yell 'Hi, Charley.'"

Dutifully, the group turned and greeted Charley.

"See, Kyle's got them eating out of his hand." Charley chuckled and returned the wave. "And he never misses a chance to butter up the boss."

"Great job, folks!" Kyle turned and set out for the trailer. "Now, let me show you around the place."

"I'll introduce you to Kyle later," Charley said. "But now, I want you to meet my right-hand man. Brought him from Durango with me."

He led them into the barn that housed enough stalls for the twenty horses Charley and Jessica owned and for ten more boarders. At the rear were a tack room, feed storage room, and a treatment area for a veterinarian or farrier to work on a horse. They walked past contented horses munching on green-smelling spring hay to the tack room.

A middle-aged Hispanic man sat there on an overturned plastic grain tub. He wore square-toed work boots, a long-sleeved olive shirt, and a pair of tan jeans liberally marked with stains and frayed at the seams. In one hand he held leather reins, and in his other hand a huge needle strung with thick waxed thread. He stabbed the needle in a rein and pulled the thread through.

"Jorge, I want you to meet someone," Charley said.

Jorge looked up, stood, laid his sewing repair project on the tub and turned to them. His legs were bowed as if he was still riding a horse. Permanent squint lines from years of working outdoors in bright sun fanned out around his brown eyes.

He wiped his hands on his pants. "Hello."

"This is my sister, Claire, and her husband, Roger Hanover," Charley said. "And this is Jorge Alvarez, my own horse-whisperer. If any of my horses develop a health or behavior problem, Jorge here straightens them right out."

Jorge smiled and shook both their hands. "Pleased to meet you," he said formally, with a slight Mexican accent. "But Charley is too free with his compliments."

Charley slung an arm around Jorge's shoulders. "No, I don't compliment you enough, my man." He looked at Claire and Roger. "Jorge worked for me for six years in Durango, came highly recommended by a friend who runs a stable in Las Cruces, New Mexico. I thank God he agreed to come here with me."

Curious about Jorge's accent, Claire asked, "Are you from New Mexico, then?"

"No, I was a *vaquero* in Oaxaca, Mexico, before coming to the United States eight years ago to work for Charley's friend. He taught me to speak good English, so I could work with the *touristas*."

"Did you bring your family with you?" Roger asked.

Jorge lowered his head. "No, I have no family."

"Not for my lack of trying to match him up, though." Charley gave Jorge a friendly slap on the back. "I'll let you get back to work while I show Claire and Roger around."

After he led them away, he said, "I found a small apartment for him, and Jessica and I have him over for dinner once a week. I hope he makes some other friends here. I'd hate for him to be lonely."

"Next time I have you and Jessica over for dinner, I'll invite him, too," Claire said.

Charley looked surprised. "That's really nice of you."

He approached a stall housing a well-muscled brown horse with a long black mane and tail. The horse came right to him, blew into his hand, and lowered his head for Charley to rub.

"This is Gunpowder, my favorite mount. He's an American Quarter Horse gelding. That's the preferred breed for rodeo competitions, and because of their even temperament, for taking tourists on trail rides, too. Gunpowder here, though, tends to be frisky. So unless we get a rider who can prove to me that he has a lot of experience, only the wranglers and I ride him."

"Do you have any stallions here?" Roger asked.

"Oh no, too dangerous. There's almost nothing that can keep a stallion from a mare in heat, so I only have geldings and mares. None of the boarded horses can be stallions either. Gunpowder still thinks he's a stud sometimes, though."

Charley gave Gunpowder one last pat, then led them back outside into the bright sunlight. "You two thirsty?"

Claire felt a trickle of sweat running down the middle of her back under her T-shirt. "I could use a glass of lemonade."

While they stood by the food table sipping their drinks, Kyle came over with three people. "Charley, you've met my brother, but I'd like to introduce my parents, Ana and Emilio." He swept his hand toward a couple who looked to be in their fifties. Both had dark hair and eyes and were impeccably dressed in khaki pants and soft Pima cotton polo shirts.

"Pleased to meet you." Charley shook the couple's hands then shook the hand of the short young man hovering beside his parents. "And how are you, Petey?"

"Fine!"

Claire realized that Petey was older than his height indicated, in his late teens or early twenties, and he had the characteristic almond-shaped eyes of someone with Down syndrome. When Charley introduced Roger and her to Kyle, his parents, and Petey, Petey enthusiastically shook their hands and grinned broadly.

"Petey is one of Jessica's hippotherapy clients," Charley explained to Claire and Roger.

Claire had been curious if Jessica had picked up many horse therapy clients after the move to Colorado Springs. She was happy to meet one of the people Jessica was helping. She smiled at the young man. "Do you like to ride horses, Petey?"

He bobbed his head. "Yeah, yeah!"

"Your wife has accomplished some wonderful things with Petey in just a few sessions," Ana said to Charley. "His balance is better, and his coordination. He's even talking more, though most of his new words have to do with horses."

As if on cue, Petey tugged on Kyle's shirt and said, "Daisy? Carrot?"

"He wants to give his favorite horse, Daisy, a carrot," Kyle explained. "I'll take him to the barn."

"I'll go with you," Emilio said. "I haven't met Daisy yet."

As the three walked off, Petey's hand in Kyle's, Ana beamed. "Kyle is so good with his brother. It's such a comfort to me to know that when Emilio and I pass on, Kyle will be here to take care of Petey." She gave a little sigh then turned to Claire and Roger. "It's because of Kyle that Petey can come for his horse therapy."

"He does extra work around here in exchange for the sessions," Charley added, "repairs, clearing brush, and such. He's staying late today to clean up after the opening."

"Has Jessica gotten many clients?" Claire asked.

"A few," Charley said. "She hopes to gradually build up more as the word gets out that a new occupational therapist trained in hippotherapy is in town."

"I've already spread the word in my Down syndrome parents' group," Ana said.

"And Jessica has a couple of clients who are kids with autism. Their parents said they would tell their friends, too," Charley said. "Speak of the devil, here she is."

Jessica exited the trailer with the new horse-boarding clients, said her goodbyes to them, then came over to give Ana a hug. "Where's my boy, Petey?"

"At the barn talking to Daisy," Ana replied. "I think I will join them. Thank you for inviting us to your opening."

"I'll see you Tuesday for Petey's next session," Jessica said.

Ana smiled. "He'll be anxious for it, since he's seeing Daisy today. I hope he can wait two days!" She gave a wave and headed for the barn.

"So you've got two businesses up and running here," Roger said.

"Only one business," Jessica replied. "The hippotherapy is a non-profit. We don't make any money from it. I only charge clients for my time and the use of the horse."

"Ah, I see," Roger said. "So that makes it more affordable for people."

"Some of the families can't even afford that, though," Jessica replied, "so I've already applied for a couple of local grants. If I can get some grant money, I can offer scholarships. God knows, I've been there, and I know how a childhood disability can financially strap a family."

Claire nodded and touched Jessica's arm. Jessica and Charley had lost their second child, a daughter, at the age of three to alpha mannosidosis, an incurable genetic disease resulting from missing an enzyme that breaks down sugar waste-products. Claire was sure that's why Jessica subsequently got her degree in occupational therapy, so she could help other sick and disabled children.

Jessica squeezed Claire's hand, acknowledging the unspoken offer of comfort, then pressed on. "I also try to keep costs down by using volunteers to lead the horse and walk on either side of it while the client is on the horse." She sighed. "Unfortunately, most of my volunteers are teenage girls, who aren't that reliable."

Claire had an idea, something that might bring her closer to her brother. "What about me?"

Jessica gave a little hop and clapped her hands. "That would be wonderful, Claire."

"It's been awhile since I've been around horses," Claire said, "but I took some Western riding lessons when I was a teenager. Remember, Charley?"

He nodded. "And I remember that fall you took that broke your arm."

Claire automatically started rubbing the spot above her wrist.

"I could start you out as a side walker," Jessica said, "which only takes one training session. Once you're comfortable with that, you can do some leading. Can you come Tuesday morning to train? Then you could help with Petey's session and a couple of others in the afternoon." Her face fell. "Or will you be too busy making and delivering baskets?"

Claire shook her head. "The poor economy has affected me, too. I've only got a few baskets to make this week, so I can come Tuesday. And remember, Roger and I are coming back tomorrow morning with our friends Ellen and Dave to take a trail ride."

"And we're only charging you for two—Ellen and Dave," Charley said.

"Oh no, we're paying customers!" When Charley opened his mouth to speak, she held up a hand. "No argument. We want to support your new business here as much as we can. Maybe you can give us a free ride later, after you're established."

Charley frowned, but when Jessica put a hand on his arm, he exhaled. "Okay."

Someone came up to Charley to ask a question, so Claire and Roger headed for the food table to grab some cookies. They chatted with a few other attendees then decided to head home. After saying their goodbyes, they walked back out to the parking lot.

While Roger started the car, Claire pursed her lips and surveyed the dwindling attendance at the opening. "I hope Charley succeeds here. He needs to so much. I'm afraid he's overextended himself to get this started."

Roger backed the car out of the parking spot. "Well, worrying about it won't help any. And speaking about overextending, what possessed you to volunteer for Jessica's hippotherapy?"

TWO:
TERROR IN THE STABLE

WHEN ROGER DROVE INTO the Gardner's Stables parking lot early the next morning, Claire spied Dave Redding's car. Dave was the ex-husband of her best friend Ellen, and the two had been working on getting back together. The profiles of two heads in the front seat leaned toward each other to share a kiss.

Claire let out a little squeal of delight and squeezed Roger's arm. "They just kissed!"

"Doesn't take much to excite you, does it?" Roger said with a grin. He pulled into a spot and turned off the ignition.

"I'm just so happy for Ellen and Dave. After all the troubles they've had, it's good to see them getting back together again."

"Just like us."

"No, not like us. We never got divorced—or slept with other people."

Roger reached over to tuck a curl of her hair behind her ear. "You're right, honey. We never stopped loving each other."

And her body had never stopped responding to his touch. She smiled at him and gave his arm a pat. Then she opened her car door, too excited about their upcoming ride to sit still.

"C'mon. Time's a-wasting. Today's going to be fun!"

She ran over to tap on Ellen's window, who hopped out of the car to give Claire a hug and a squeal of her own. They checked out and commented on each other's riding ensembles—Western shirts, jeans, boots. Ellen had even added a red bandana tied jauntily about her neck. The two men stood with hands in their pockets and rolled their eyes.

"And I love your hair," Claire exclaimed. "You're not a redhead anymore. You're back to your natural brunette."

Ellen smiled. "Dave likes it better this way."

"Me, too." Claire glanced at Dave, with his distinguished prematurely white hair. She gave him a wave, then leaned in close to Ellen. "So, you two looked pretty chummy there just then. Thinking of getting remarried?"

"Could be, could be." Ellen arched a brow. "We're just taking it one day at a time right now. Trying to ease back into each other's lives, have some fun together. And speaking of fun, what a great idea you had to go on a trail ride together. I haven't ridden a horse in years!"

Claire pointed at Ellen's shiny new red tooled-leather cowboy boots. "I can tell!"

Throwing back her head, Ellen laughed.

"I can't wait to introduce you to my brother and his wife." Claire linked her arm in Ellen's and pulled her up the path to the stable. "If you like the ride, I hope you'll tell everyone you know about their stable."

She shouted over her shoulder, "Follow us, guys, for a good time!" She wiggled her generous butt for emphasis, and Ellen joined suit.

Dave grinned and rubbed his hands together, elbowing Roger to do the same.

As they walked under the wooden sign into the yard in front of the trailer, a wiry young man with walnut-colored skin and long black hair tied back in a ponytail came high-tailing it out of the barn. He shouted, "*Señor* Charley, *señor* Charley!"

Holding a coffee cup, Charley stepped out of the trailer onto its porch. "What is it, Pedro?"

Pedro skidded to a halt, eyes wide in alarm. In between huffs, he said, "*Es* Kyle. He *muerto!*"

Claire gasped.

Charley dropped his cup. It shattered and splashed coffee on his boots. "What?"

"Gunpowder stomp him! *Andale!*" Pedro waved Charley toward the stable.

The two of them took off running, the hard soles of their leather boots crunching in the gravel.

Claire started after them, but Dave put a hand on her arm. "We should tell Jessica, get her to call 911."

She looked back at Ellen and Dave, apprehension tightening their lips and shoulders. "Yes, do that, but I know first aid. If Kyle's just hurt and not really dead, I should see if there's something I can do."

"I'll get the first-aid kit out of the car for you," Roger said.

"Good idea. Wait here," Claire said to Ellen and Dave then ran as fast as she could toward the barn.

When she entered, huffing to catch her breath, it took a moment for her eyes to adjust to the diminished light. A group of five men huddled outside Gunpowder's stall, speaking in hushed, urgent tones. The other horses snorted and shuffled in their stalls, obviously spooked.

One man made a grab for Gunpowder's halter, and the horse let out a chilling scream. He bucked and kicked the back of his stall with a resounding thump, making Claire and the others start.

"How long have you been trying to get Gunpowder out?" Charley asked.

"Not long," Jorge said. "As soon as we got here this morning, we brought the mares in from the pasture. I wondered why they were acting so *loco*, then I saw Gunpowder smashed against the side of his stall. I looked in and saw Kyle—and *sangre*, the blood. I yelled for Pedro to get you."

"We've got to get in there and check on Kyle." Charley directed the men to open the gate to an empty stall. He sent one to grab a blanket. "And someone call 911!"

"Our friend Dave's telling Jessica to call," Claire said.

"Good, good." Charley barely looked at her before turning to Jorge. "Can you calm him?"

"I will try." Jorge stood outside the bar gate across the front of Gunpowder's stall. He made calming "shush, shush, shush" sounds to the horse and held out a mini-carrot on his palm.

Gunpowder was having none of it. He high-stepped back and forth along one side of his stall, chafing his flank against the planking. Eyes rolled back in terror, he tossed his head up and down, whipping his mane against his neck.

Claire realized the horse was avoiding the other side of his stall, staying as far away as possible. She shuddered to think of what lay there.

"Okay, everyone," Charley said, "calm down and back away, unless I've given you a task. Gunpowder can sense our fear."

Overlying the sweet, dry straw smell and faint odor of horse urine were the ripe scents of human and horse sweat—nervous, fearful sweat.

Charley waved a hand. "Pedro and Gil, go calm the other horses."

The men moved to do his bidding.

Jorge continued to calmly shush and cajole Gunpowder until the horse stood still, snorting and tossing his head. As Claire held her breath, Gunpowder finally stepped toward Jorge and blew on the hand holding the carrot. Jorge ran his other hand along Gunpowder's neck, stroking it slowly, until the horse took the carrot. Then he stroked Gunpowder's neck with both hands. He put his face in front of the horse's and breathed in rhythm with him.

Roger came up beside Claire and gave her the first-aid kit. She put a finger to her lips.

After a moment, Charley asked, "Should we blanket him?"

Jorge shook his head, while continuing to breathe with the horse, then took hold of his bridle and took a step back. Gunpowder followed. While everyone in the barn watched silently, Jorge slowly backed Gunpowder out of his stall and into the empty one across the aisle. He gave the horse another carrot, then closed the gate.

With a collective sigh of relief, everyone moved toward Gunpowder's empty stall. Charley went in and knelt in the straw. Claire followed and leaned over his shoulder.

A bloodied body lay against the side of the stall, one leg bent at an unnatural angle. Flies buzzed around the blood-soaked hay underneath. A strong copper scent permeated the air. The body was clothed in the same blue jeans and blue-checked work shirt that Kyle had worn the day before. The face was bruised and the nose smashed, but Claire could tell that it was Kyle.

Charley felt Kyle's wrist. His shoulders drooped, and he turned to Claire. "He's cold." Utter dejection lined his features.

Claire checked for herself and glanced at the first-aid kit. *No need for that now.* She put a hand on Charley's shoulder. "There's nothing we can do for him. He's been dead for hours."

"*Santa Madre de Dios.*" Pedro crossed himself.

"God damn," Roger murmured.

"I'm sorry, Charley." Claire sighed. "All we can do is wait for the police and EMTs to arrive. We shouldn't touch or move anything."

Jessica ran into the barn. "The ambulance is on its way. Where's Kyle?" She stopped at the entrance to the stall and gasped. She put one hand to her mouth and flung another out, her body wavering.

Roger caught her around the shoulders and held her. "He's gone," he whispered.

Charley rose and moved out of the stall like an automaton. He stood with his back to the group, pinching the bridge of his nose. When he faced them again, his eyes glistened with unshed tears.

"I can't believe Gunpowder did this."

Jessica turned her head into Roger's shoulder and started sobbing.

Jorge shook his head and lined the toe of his boot through the dirt. One of the other men took off his hat and held it against his chest, then the others followed suit. Even the horses were silent, now that Gunpowder had calmed down.

By unspoken agreement, everyone in the barn bowed their heads in a moment of silence. When Claire raised hers, dust motes gleamed in the beam of sunlight streaming through the open doorway. She felt as if she were in a chapel, in the presence of mourners.

Charley looked at Jessica, pain etched in the lines of his face. "Oh, God, Kyle's family. What'll I say to them?"

———

A few minutes later, as Claire and Roger filled in Ellen and Dave on what had happened, a Colorado Springs Police Department cruiser drove into the parking lot. Two uniformed officers got out of the cruiser and approached them, then stopped and turned when a fire rescue truck and an ambulance drove up with lights flashing. They bypassed the parking lot and drove as far into the stable yard as possible. With a cacophony of slamming doors, the firemen and EMTs exited their vehicles. The two EMTs started unloading a stretcher from the back of the ambulance.

Claire walked over to them. "The person's been dead for awhile. The body's already cold."

They kept on unloading the stretcher. "We'll decide that," one said brusquely.

Claire nodded and waved a hand toward the barn. "He's in the barn."

The EMTs hustled toward the barn with the firemen following.

One of the patrolmen took out a pad of paper and pen. "What's the name of the victim?"

"Kyle Mendoza," Claire answered. "He worked as a wrangler here."

An unmarked gray Dodge Charger drove into the lot and a tall, large-boned man wearing a gray suit got out. As he walked toward them, head down, one of the uniformed cops called out, "Detective, this lady says the body's cold."

The man lifted his head, and with a shock, Claire realized she knew him. He was Frank Wilson, a senior detective with the CSPD. They had butted heads on a previous murder case in February. The male victim had fallen on Claire, shot through the chest while giving her a massage, and Detective Wilson had erroneously arrested Roger for the crime.

Wilson ran a slim-fingered hand through his gray-flecked black hair. "What do the EMTs say?"

Before the cop could answer, the two firemen walked out of the barn shaking their heads. When they reached the group, they said, "She's right. The body's cold. The EMTs are filling out the paperwork now."

"Hopefully they aren't disturbing the scene," Wilson replied then turned to the patrolman who had shouted. "Call the coroner's office."

While the patrolman talked into his shoulder radio and the firemen returned to their truck, Roger touched Claire's arm. When she glanced at him, he mouthed one word, "trouble."

She gulped, nodded, and focused on Detective Wilson, whose familiar, knowing gray eyes were now boring in on them. "What are you doing here?"

She took a deep breath and squared her shoulders. "My brother, Charley Gardner, owns this stable."

Detective Wilson's stone-faced gaze fell next on Ellen and Dave. "Stay right here. All of you. I'll need to talk to you later." He turned to the two patrolmen. "One of you stay with them and start collecting IDs. The other come with me."

After he left, the remaining patrolman got basic information from the four of them, names, addresses, and so on. "Was one of you the lady who called 911?"

"No, that was Jessica, Charley's wife," Claire said. "She's still in the barn."

The patrolman radioed his cohort. Soon, Jessica came out of the barn. Her face was red and blotchy, and she carried a box of tissues with her. She ran for Claire, who opened her arms wide for her. After clutching Claire for a while, Jessica pulled back.

"Oh, Claire, I can't believe it! Kyle dead. It's just too awful to think about."

Claire rubbed Jessica's back, wondering if this death of a young person was dredging up painful memories of Jessica's and Charley's daughter's death. "I know. I know. He was so young."

At that moment a large van with the logo of the El Paso County Coroner's Office on the side drove into the parking lot. A woman got out, carrying a large black case. The driver, a man, pulled a gurney out of the back of the van and followed her.

The woman came up to them and said to the patrolman, "I'm a forensic investigator from the coroner's office. Can you tell me where the victim is?"

"Victim!" Jessica wailed and grabbed a tissue from her box to dab at fresh tears.

"In the barn," Roger answered tersely and pointed.

The woman nodded, then looked at Jessica with sympathy. "I'm sorry for your loss." She turned and walked toward the barn.

Another car arrived in the parking lot, taking the last open spot. A family of four—mother, father, and two teenage boys—got out. They gawked at the police cars, fire truck, ambulance, and coroner's van.

"Who are they?" the patrolman asked.

"Oh, dear," Jessica said between sniffs. "They're the rest of the morning trail ride group."

"You'll have to cancel that ride," the patrolman said. "We don't want anyone going in that barn until we're done."

"What'll I tell them?" Jessica asked.

"Just that there's been an emergency," Claire said, "and you'll have to reschedule their ride. C'mon, Roger and I will go with you."

She looked at the patrolman for assurance and he nodded. By the time the three of them had gotten rid of the curious family, with Jessica's promise to call them later to reschedule their ride, the fire truck had left and Detective Wilson had returned.

"I'd like to talk to you first, Mrs. Hanover. Your brother tells me that you were with him when he confirmed Mr. Mendoza was dead."

He led her over to a picnic table away from the others, and the two of them sat. Claire filled him in on everything she saw after she entered the barn. After Detective Wilson had finished questioning her, she asked, "So did Gunpowder kill Kyle Mendoza?"

"Sure looks that way," he said. "But we'll have to wait on the autopsy results to be sure."

Claire shook her head. "He seemed like such a well-behaved horse when Charley introduced me to him yesterday. I can't imagine him stomping a man to death."

"If he did, that horse needs to be put down." Detective Wilson stood and slapped his notepad against his palm. "And I assume you won't be poking your nose into this case."

Claire bristled at his warning. "There's no reason to. It was an accident, a horrible accident, not a murder case where you arrested the wrong man. A man who happened to be my husband."

Wilson flinched, then seemed to realize that she was totally right and he couldn't say anything about it. "So where were you and your husband last night?"

"I thought you thought this was an accident!"

"Just being thorough."

Claire folded her arms. "We went out to eat and to a movie. I've got the credit card receipts to prove it."

He nodded and waved Roger over. "You can go while I talk to your husband."

His conversation with Roger was brief, and with the Reddings even briefer, since they hadn't gone into the barn and had no connection with the business or Kyle Mendoza. When he finished with them, he said, "You four are free to go."

"I want to stay," Claire said to Ellen, "in case I can help Jessica and Charley with anything."

Ellen nodded. "We'll get out of your hair." She turned to Jessica. "Don't worry, we'll be back. We'll reschedule our trail ride for another day."

"Oh, yes, please," Jessica replied, wringing her hands. "Once we know when we can resume them, I'll contact Claire. Thank you for being so understanding."

After the Reddings left, Detective Wilson briefly interviewed Jessica at the picnic table. Since Jessica hadn't been in the barn that morning either, Claire knew she couldn't offer much information. After a few minutes, Jessica went in the trailer and Wilson rejoined Claire and Roger and the patrolman.

Jessica came out with a sheet of paper. As she handed it to Wilson, she said, "Here's contact information for Kyle's family. I thought Charley and I were going to have to break the news to the Mendozas. It's a relief to know you'll be the one to do it, but we should still talk to them about it. I know, we both know... how devastating it is to lose a child."

She clamped her lips shut and stood looking at the ground with her eyes blinking furiously and her hands clenched around her biceps. Claire put an arm around Jessica's shoulders. They all waited silently for a moment.

Finally, Jessica sucked in a deep breath and looked up at Wilson. "When will you tell the Mendozas?"

"After we're done here. Once the coroner's office takes the body and the officer up there has finished taking photos, I'll drive over to their home." He glanced at the address. "If anyone's there, I'll tell them then. Otherwise, I'll call the father's work number."

Jessica worried the tissue in her hand. "Will you let me know once you've told them?"

"Sure thing." A noise from the barn made him look in that direction.

Everyone else did, too.

The woman and man from the coroner's office were wheeling the gurney down from the barn. A filled blue plastic body bag lay strapped onto the top of the gurney. The EMTs, Charley, and the wranglers followed silently, heads bowed as if in a funeral procession. Jorge wasn't in the group, though. Claire assumed he had stayed with Gunpowder to continue calming the horse.

No one spoke as the gurney passed Claire's group. Charley and the wranglers stopped next to them to watch the gurney continue on, and Charley put his arm around Jessica. The only sound came from a black crow's raucous caw in the distance. A man walking his golden retriever along the road stopped and reined in his dog. Both stared as the EMTs helped the coroner's team lift Kyle's body into the van.

The two patrolmen got in their cruiser, and the EMTs climbed in their ambulance. They followed the coroner's van out of the lot. Detective Wilson said his goodbyes and told Charley and Jessica he would call them after notifying the Mendozas.

"And you'll let us know what the autopsy says?" Charley asked.

"Yes, I'll tell you the final conclusion," Wilson replied. "But if you want the full report, you'll have to request it from the coroner's office." He paused. "If I was you, I'd start thinking about what to do with that horse. If it's a killer, you don't want it around tourists."

A pained look crossed Charley's face, but he nodded.

As Wilson drove off in his unmarked car, the wranglers shuffled nervously, hands in their pockets, heads down.

Charley heaved out a great sigh. "No trail rides today. Pedro and Gil, turn the horses out to pasture. Then I want you to clean Gunpowder's stall thoroughly. The cops released the scene to us.

Since there's blood on the straw, put on some of the latex gloves that are in the stable's medical kit."

The two men turned and headed for the barn.

Charley motioned for the last wrangler to join him, Jessica, Claire, and Roger. "I want to introduce you to Hank Isley. He would have been the rear guide for your trail ride, with Kyle as the lead. Hank, this is my sister, Claire Hanover, and her husband, Roger."

Hank muttered, "Nice to meet ya," as he shook their hands.

He looked to be in his early twenties. His light brown hair curled over the collar of his Western work shirt and a handlebar mustache drooped on either side of his mouth. Like all of the men, his face was tanned from working outdoors.

Charley put a hand on Hank's shoulder. "Since we've got no rides going out today, how about if you take the truck and fetch and unload this week's hay? I was going to do it, but I'll need to talk to Kyle's family instead."

A dark look passed over Hank's features, as if he disliked his chore assignment, but he just nodded and said, "Yes, sir." He turned and walked away.

Charley looked at Jessica. His eyes widened as if this was the first time he had noticed that his wife's face was tear-stained. He enveloped her in an embrace. "Sorry, honey. This has been hard on you, hasn't it?"

Jessica nodded into his chest then pulled back. "I've got to cancel the afternoon ride, then talk to Kyle's family. I can't help but remember how we felt after Faith died. I don't know how I'm going to face them."

"We'll do it together," he replied.

"This kind of thing really needs a woman's sensitive touch."

Charley stepped back and frowned. "I can be sensitive."

Claire decided to change the subject. "What can we do to help?" She took hold of Roger's hand.

Charley gave her a pained look. "Nothing right now. But come back with your friends another day. Something tells me we'll need the money."

Claire squeezed Roger's hand. *Oh, God!* When word got out that one of Charley's horses had killed someone, people would start canceling their reservations.

One by one, nails were being pounded into a coffin for Charley's business. It was dying before it had even had a chance to live—just like Kyle.

THREE:
HIPPOTHERAPY LESSON

After dropping off a wedding gift basket, Claire drove her blue BMW sedan into the Gardner's Stables parking lot Tuesday morning. She got out, hesitated, then resolutely marched toward the corral. While taking a break from constructing a couple of gift baskets the night before, Claire had called Jessica to make sure she should still come to train as a hippotherapy volunteer. Jessica had replied, "My clients still need their sessions, and I still need you, so yes, if you're willing, please come."

She spied Jessica over by the corral fence, talking quietly to a willowy young woman with a long blond ponytail. She looked to be about the age of Claire's daughter, Judy. The young woman nodded, with her head bowed. She sniffed and wiped the back of a hand across her nose. When Jessica gave her a hug and she raised her head, Claire could see the young woman's blue eyes were rimmed in red.

Claire slowed her steps, thinking to give them more time to themselves since the young woman must have known Kyle. But the girl saw her, pulled back and said something to Jessica.

Jessica turned and waved Claire over. "Claire, this is Brittany Schwartz. She's one of my hippotherapy volunteers. She does some part-time wrangling for us, too, when she's not in class at Pikes Peak Community College. I asked her to come in early to help train you. Brittany, this is my sister-in-law, Claire, who I told you about."

The two shook hands and Claire said, "I'm sorry. You must have known Kyle Mendoza."

Brittany nodded and gulped, obviously unable to speak at the moment and holding back sobs. Two tears escaped and tracked down her cheeks.

Jessica dug a tissue pack out of her front jeans pocket and handed one to her. "I figured we'd need some of these today." She turned to Claire. "I called Brittany and told her about Kyle yesterday evening, because I knew they had gone out together a few times."

Brittany blew her nose and wiped tears from her cheeks. She took a deep, hitching breath. "I can't get my head around the fact that Kyle's dead, that he won't come out of the barn any minute now with a big grin on his face. He was so careful around the horses and so good with them. I can't believe Gunpowder would hurt him, let alone kill him, even accidentally."

"This has got to be very hard for you," Claire said. "Were you his girlfriend?"

"Oh, no. We just went out a few times. We weren't exclusive or anything."

Jessica patted Brittany's arm. "It's still hard, hard for all of us. Charley and I are really going to miss him around here. He was our best trail guide and a huge help to Charley. God knows the big lug could use someone smooth around the customers. And that grin of Kyle's could lighten anyone's day."

She sighed and dropped her hand. "But, as they say, work is the best way to deal with grief, and Claire here needs to be trained. You still think you can help, Brittany?"

Brittany squared her shoulders and stuffed her sodden tissue in her jeans pocket. "Sure."

Claire noticed that both she and Jessica wore green T-shirts. The front displayed the black silhouette of a rider on horse being led by another person. The words 'Gardner's Hippotherapy' arched over the drawing.

Trying to lighten the mood, she pointed at Jessica's shirt. "So will I get one of those?"

Jessica gave a little laugh. "Yep, as soon as we get you trained."

She walked over to a gold-colored horse with a white tail and mane. The horse was saddled, and its reins were looped over the corral fence next to the gate. "This beautiful palomino is Daisy."

"I remember the name." Claire said. "She's Petey's favorite horse, right?"

"Right." A dark shadow passed over Jessica's face. "Petey's got a therapy session scheduled this afternoon, but I don't think he'll make it. Charley called the Mendozas after Detective Wilson told them about Kyle. Kyle's father, Emilio, answered and said they weren't up to talking then. I thought I'd call this afternoon to see if I could bring something over for their dinner if they don't show up."

She sighed. "We might as well get started."

She opened the gate and walked into the corral. Brittany and Claire followed. After Jessica latched the gate, she said, "Daisy is our best therapy horse because she's got the most easy-going temperament. She's the best for training our volunteers, too."

While she unhooked Daisy's reins from the fence, the horse nuzzled her ear and blew into her face. Jessica patted her neck and signaled Claire to approach. "Come and meet her."

Claire came over and rubbed the horse's neck. "Hello, Daisy."

Daisy raised her head and nickered softly.

Jessica smiled. "She's saying hello."

After coming up alongside Daisy's left flank, Brittany stood with a hand on the saddle stirrup.

"You see how Brittany's standing?" Jessica said to Claire. "That's what you'll do on the other side. Some of our clients, like the kids with cerebral palsy, can't balance themselves on the horse, so I'll sit behind them and hold them in the right position. Others, like Petey and our kids with autism, can sit by themselves on a horse, but sometimes they lose their balance and start to slide. That's what the side walkers are for, to catch them and right them."

She positioned Claire on Daisy's other side. "For a new rider, you'll walk alongside, hold their foot in the stirrup, and observe their posture. If they start to slide in your direction, you put a hand up to stop them and push slowly and firmly to right them. If they're wearing a safety belt with handles on it, Brittany should be pulling on the handle on her side. Then if the client slips the other way, you pull and she pushes."

Worried, Claire asked, "How do we know how much to push or pull?"

"You learn by feel. In the beginning, just be careful not to do too much. A gentle correction is usually enough, and if it isn't, you can always add pressure. Balance and coordination is a lot of what hippotherapy is about."

"Yeah, for the side walkers, too," Brittany quipped.

Jessica smiled. "Eventually we want our clients to make all of the corrections themselves, if they can. Think you've got it?"

"I think so." A nervous butterfly fluttered in Claire's stomach. "I have a feeling we'll soon find out."

Jessica pulled a safety harness off the corral fence and belted it on herself. "Okay, I'll be a pretend client, and you can practice on me. Sometimes, I'll try to let a foot slip out of the stirrup and you have to reposition it. And sometimes I'll slide my body to one side or the other."

She mounted Daisy and took the reins. "Normally either I or another volunteer will be walking in front, holding onto the reins to lead Daisy. Ready?"

Both Claire and Brittany said, "Ready."

Jessica clicked her tongue to get Daisy moving in a slow walk.

Surprised at first, Claire stumbled, then quickly righted herself and caught up with Daisy. She gave out an awkward laugh. "Almost took a tumble there."

"Don't worry about it," Brittany said. "I've tripped and fallen a few times, even did a face plant in a pile of manure once."

Jessica laughed. "I remember that. Cracked little Sally right up. I think she keeps hoping you'll do it again." She turned to Claire. "That's the most rewarding part of hippotherapy, seeing the smiles on the clients' faces, even hearing the kids giggle. They can feel the improvement in their bodies, and they're having fun at the same time."

As they circled the corral, Claire fell into an easy pace walking beside the horse, even started to feel a little confident. Then she noticed all of a sudden that Jessica's foot had slid out of the stirrup on her side.

"Whoops." She awkwardly pushed Jessica's foot back in.

"That's it," Jessica said. "Now keep your hand on the stirrup, and partly on my boot, so you can feel if it moves. You're looking at the ground a lot now, to get your footing. That's understandable. But after we go around the corral another time, start glancing at me out of the side of your eyes to check my balance."

"What about *my* balance?" Claire asked, as she stumbled again.

Brittany laughed. "It'll come to you. After you walk a few hundred circles in this corral, your feet will know every inch of it."

They practiced for about half an hour, with Jessica slipping sideways in the saddle or shuffling her feet. Eventually, Claire felt less nervous and thought she could actually be responsible for someone's safety on the horse.

"Let's take a break," Jessica said. "I think Daisy could use some water."

Claire realized her lips were dry and licked them. "Me, too."

After Daisy and the women had all gotten some water, Jessica said, "I need to make a couple of phone calls before we start again. I have to confirm delivery on some orders from suppliers, and I know I can't count on Charley to do it."

Irritated by yet another crack from Jessica about Charley, Claire wondered if Jessica really meant to cut down her brother like this, or if it was an unconscious means of building herself up. Maybe Jessica had some buried feelings of inadequacy or guilt after her daughter's death, and this, like the hippotherapy, was a way of compensating. And maybe that's why Charley put up with it.

"Brittany," Jessica continued, "maybe you could introduce Claire to the other horses we use for hippotherapy."

Brittany nodded and led Claire to the barn. "We didn't have a trail ride scheduled this morning, so the horses are taking a break, either in the barn or out in the pasture."

As they entered the barn, Claire heard a man shouting from within one of the stalls. "Pedro, you piece of shit! How many times do I have to tell you to clean out the brushes before you put them away?"

"He's new, still learning," said a quiet voice that Claire recognized as Jorge's.

"That's no God damn excuse!" A horse brush sailed across the aisle between the stalls and landed in a wheelbarrow full of urine and manure-soaked hay. A bitter cackle followed. "Now go clean it!"

Pedro, the young Hispanic man who ran out of the barn the day before to announce Kyle's death, stepped out of the stall behind the wheelbarrow. He held a rake that he must have been using to muck out the stall. His boots and jeans were spattered with mud and straw, and he wore an angry frown on his face.

Jorge stepped out of another stall with a hoof pick in his hand. He caught Pedro's eye and shook his head.

Pedro bit his lip and flung the rake down. He stared at the roof for a moment as if asking God to give him strength. Then he fished the brush out of the wheelbarrow and walked out of the barn past Claire and Brittany, mumbling, "*excusame por favor.*"

Brittany asked Claire, "Have you met Pedro Trujillo?"

"Not yet, not formally," Claire replied. "But that can wait. He looks upset."

"Yeah, Gil can do that to people. How about Jorge? Have you met him?"

Jorge straightened after picking up Pedro's rake. He leaned it against the stall wall and nodded at Claire. "*Señora* Hanover."

"Please call me Claire, Jorge. We'll be seeing a lot of each other since I'm volunteering with Jessica's hippotherapy charity."

He pinched the brim of his straw cowboy hat and dipped his head. "Nice to see you again, Claire."

Another man stepped out of the stall that the brush had come flying out of. Claire remembered that he was one of the men in the barn the day before. He seemed to be in his mid-thirties and had pale skin reddened by the sun. Like the other men, he wore jeans, work boots, and a tan-and-brown striped work shirt with the sleeves rolled up. He tossed his head to fling a lank of stringy dishwater blond hair out of his eyes. As he swaggered, or staggered, toward them, those watery eyes seemed to have trouble focusing on the women.

"Hey there, Brittany, you sweet young thang," he said. "Who you got with you?"

Brittany wrinkled her nose. "This is Claire Hanover, Gil, Charley's *sister*. Claire, this is Gil Kaplan, one of the wranglers who work here."

Claire realized that the emphasis on her relationship to Charley was a warning by Brittany to Gil to behave. "Nice to meet you." Claire held out her hand.

The hand that clasped hers felt roughened and dry. "Sorry about the cussing. Didn't know there was ladies present." Gil leered and arched a brow at Brittany.

The strong odor of alcohol on Gil's breath almost overpowered Claire. It was not just beer, more like whiskey, and here it was still mid-morning.

"These lousy wetbacks," Gil continued. "Take jobs away from decent, hard-working Americans, then can't even do the work. It's enough to rile up anyone."

"Pedro is not a wetback," Jorge said stiffly. "He has proper documentation. And horse sense. Otherwise, Charley would not have hired him."

Gil snorted. "Proper, my ass." He threw the brush he was holding down on the ground and headed for the barn door. "I need to take a pi—sorry, ladies." He put a hand on his chest and made a mocking bow. "I mean use the facilities."

Claire turned to watch him go and saw the outline of a flask in his back pocket. After he left the barn, she looked at Jorge. "Does Charley know Gil drinks?" Claire found it hard to believe that her brother would tolerate one of his employees drinking on the job. She found it even harder to believe that he hadn't noticed it.

Jorge straightened after retrieving the brush and began picking horse hair out of it. "I do not know, but it is not my place to tell him."

Anger at Gil boiled up inside Claire. "But here you are cleaning out Gil's brush right after he complained about Pedro not cleaning one. It may not be your place to tell Charley, but there's nothing stopping me from doing so."

"Good *vaqueros* are hard to find." Finished with pulling hair out of the brush, Jorge raised a foot and knocked the brush against the heel of his scuffed brown boots. Dust and dirt flaked out. "Gil knows horses. Just doesn't get along with people as well. He is more ornery than usual today. Something must be bothering him."

A horse whinnied at the far end of the barn, and Jorge looked back, a flicker of worry passing over his brow.

"Is that Gunpowder?" Brittany asked. "What's he doing all the way in the back of the barn?"

"I'm keeping him quiet, away from people and the other horses for a while, until Charley decides what to do with him."

"I wonder what set him off Sunday night," Brittany said. "I've never had any problem with him."

Jorge slapped the brush against his thigh. "Neither have I. Or Kyle, that I know of."

Brittany shook her head. "Kyle wasn't rough with the horses. He wouldn't have hurt Gunpowder deliberately. And Gunpowder wouldn't have hurt him deliberately either. All I can think of is that he startled Gunpowder or accidentally hit him with something while he was in the stall. But why would he have been in Gunpowder's stall?"

"I have no idea," Jorge said with a shrug. "The horses had all been fed and watered for the night before I left. And even if Kyle hurt him, Gunpowder wouldn't stomp him. Maybe a bite or a kick, that's all. He's high-strung, but he's a good horse. He's stressed now, though, won't even let me brush him. I've been talking to him, trying to calm him down."

"If anyone can do it, you can." Brittany glanced at Claire. "He's our horse-whisperer."

"That's what Charley said when he introduced us." Claire wondered if Jorge was just wasting his efforts if Gunpowder was going to have to be put down anyway. But the man obviously really cared about the horse, so she said nothing. Instead, she turned to Brittany. "So, you were going to introduce me to the other horses, right?"

Jorge tipped his hat and went back to his work. Brittany led Claire to each of the stalls and introduced the horses that were in the barn. Then she described and named the ones out in the pasture with Charley and Hank. When Pedro came back in, grim-faced and holding the dripping brush he had washed, Brittany introduced Claire to him, too.

"It's too bad you have to put up with abuse from that Gil character," Claire said.

Pedro gave a nervous glance out the barn door, as if checking for Gil's return. "*El gringo es* always *furioso*. As Jorge say, I make easy target." He sighed and headed for the tack room.

Being an easy target didn't mean he had to put up with Gil's bullying, though. Claire resolved to tell Charley, no matter what Jorge said about Gil's capability.

"Claire! Brittany!" Jessica called from the corral.

"Time to start up again," Brittany said.

When they left the barn, they passed Gil smoking a cigarette outside. He stubbed it out in an ash can placed near the port-a-potties. He strode back into the barn without a glance or word to the women. Claire thought his behavior rude, but then if he had said anything to them, it might have been even ruder.

Just as Brittany and Claire reached the corral, a green Dodge mini-van drove into the parking lot. Daisy raised her head and snorted.

"Oh, dear," Jessica said. "That's Ana Mendoza's car. I wonder why she's here now. Petey's session isn't until three." She walked toward the parking lot, with Claire and Brittany following.

Ana trudged purposefully up the path under the stable sign, tugging Petey along with her. When the wind teased her graying black shoulder-length hair, she impatiently shoved the locks out of her face, revealing dark eyes flashing with anger.

Not grief, Claire noted with surprise. *Oh dear, this is not going to go well.*

"Ana, I am so, so sorry about what happened to Kyle. Charley and I are heart-broken about it." Jessica opened her arms and moved forward to hug Ana.

Stepping away, Ana pulled Petey to her side. "We are not here for your false sympathy," she said stiffly. "We're here to pick up a jacket Petey left here Sunday and to tell you he won't be coming for therapy anymore."

Petey's lips quivered in a sad, confused frown.

Jessica's arms flopped awkwardly at her sides. "But, but why? Why stop Petey's therapy? And false? Our sympathy isn't false. We loved Kyle! We're as confused and saddened by his death as you are."

Ana pointed a wavering finger at Jessica. "It's because of your and Charley's negligence that Kyle is dead. You keep that dangerous horse here, and you exposed Kyle to him, without giving him proper training."

Claire narrowed her eyes. Those words sounded like legalese—and like they were rehearsed.

Jessica glanced at Claire and Brittany then back at Ana. "Gunpowder never acted up before—"

"See, even his name is dangerous!" Ana said. "You probably named him that because he was likely to blow up. That horse is a killer and you knew it."

"No!" Jessica's face reddened. "All of our male horses have Western gun-related names, like Sharpshooter, Rifle, and Pistol. None of them are dangerous. That's why we don't keep stallions here."

"I'm not going to argue with you." Ana let go of Petey's hand and gave him a little push. "Go get your jacket."

Rubbing her head, Jessica said, "I saw it this morning behind the port-a-potties and put it in the office. Brittany, could you go with him and get it?"

Looking immensely relieved at being able to retreat from the line of fire, Brittany held out a hand for Petey and smiled at him. After he took her hand, she led him to the trailer.

Jessica reached out toward Ana, then hesitated and let her arm drop. "Please, let's talk about this. This anger is coming out of your grief. Charley and I are grieving, too."

Ana crossed her arms. "Charley and you are responsible for Kyle's death."

"How can you say that?" Jessica's eyes teared up. "Charley and I would do anything for your family. I wanted to bring you dinner tonight."

Ana's shoulders drooped as her resolve seemed to waver.

Claire thought this might be a good time to step in. "It was an accident, Ana. Pure and simple. No one's to blame, not Charley or Jessica or even Kyle—"

She meant to add, "if he startled or hurt Gunpowder," but before she could, Ana wheeled on her.

"Kyle! Of course I'd expect you to take their side. You're Charley's sister. Kyle has no blame in this. None!" Ana stamped her foot.

Claire flushed and retreated, taking a step back. Boy, she'd put her foot in her mouth this time.

Jessica gave Claire a pursed-lip 'How could you?' glare then held out her hands to Ana. "No one is blaming Kyle. That's what Claire was saying. We don't know what happened. We may never know. Maybe we'll learn something from the autopsy."

Ana swiped a tear from her cheek. "And that's another thing. I don't want them to cut up Kyle's beautiful body, but I can't stop it." She choked up, put a fist to her mouth and bit on her knuckles.

"Oh, Ana." Jessica touched Ana's arm, but the woman turned away.

After a moment, she yelled, "Petey! We have to go!"

Petey had stepped out of the office trailer, chatting animatedly with Brittany, but he stopped when he heard his mother's voice. He looked at her then at Daisy, standing in the corral with her head raised and ears perked toward him.

"I want to say hi to Daisy," he said tentatively.

Ana let out a big sigh and started walking toward him. "You can say goodbye to Daisy. I told you. We won't be coming here anymore."

With a wail, Petey started crying. "No, no, I like Daisy. I want her."

47

He took off running for the corral, his arms opening wide. Brittany picked up the jacket he had dropped and followed.

Jessica trotted after Ana. "Why can't Petey continue his therapy, Ana? Look how this is upsetting him."

Ana wheeled on her. "Because we've talked to a lawyer, Jessica. He recommends we sue you for negligence and wrongful death. And he's contacting the city to get them to cancel your contract. My son is dead and somebody has to pay!"

As if Ana had physically punched her, Jessica staggered back, putting out an arm.

Claire caught it and held onto her sister-in-law. "Oh, God."

"The lawyer says we should have no further contact with you," Ana continued. "So I'm signing Petey up for another horse therapy program."

Petey stood sobbing at the corral, his shoulders shaking and his arms wrapped around patient Daisy's neck.

Brittany patted his shoulder, and murmured, "I'm sorry, Petey. So sorry." When Ana approached Petey and put her arm around him, Brittany gave her his jacket and withdrew.

"Come on, Petey," Ana said softly to her son. "We talked about this. We have to go. I'm going to take you to meet another horse who's just as nice as Daisy."

"Noooo," Petey moaned.

Ana gently tugged on his shoulder. "Say goodbye now. That's a good boy."

Petey sniffled and slowly released his hold on the horse. He rubbed a hand on her forehead. "Bye, Daisy, bye bye."

Ana turned him and led him toward the parking lot. Petey's steps were slow and dragging, but her hold on him was firm.

"Bye, Petey," Jessica said in a choked voice. "We'll miss you."

He turned and waved, then his mother pulled him again.

Jessica clutched Claire's arm. "Petey's the innocent in all of this, and he's being hurt the most."

Claire wasn't so sure she agreed with that, as she saw Charley and Hank approach on horseback from the pasture. If the Mendozas' lawyer managed to get the city to cancel Charley's contract to run trail rides through their land and the Mendozas went through with their lawsuit, his business would be ruined.

And so would Charley.

FOUR:
TRAIL RIDE

"THIS IS GOING TO be a blast." Ellen rubbed her hands together.

Claire nodded. "I'm looking forward to it. It's been ages since I've been on a trail ride, and, God knows, I need some fun in my life right now."

She and Ellen stood inside the corral at Gardner's Stables Wednesday morning, at one end of a row of ten riders waiting for their horses. Roger and Dave were chatting at the other end. They had rescheduled their trail ride for this morning. The day had dawned bright and clear, perfect for photos of the Garden of the Gods, with its pink and rust-colored sandstone formations slicing up through a piercingly blue sky.

Ellen ran a hand down her backside. "I just hope my butt's not too sore after it."

"That's what ibuprofen's for!" Smiling, Claire waved dust from her face, stirred up by the horses' hooves as the wranglers moved them into place. "I'm glad you and Dave could do it so soon. I think Charley's going to need as much income as we can scrape up for him."

A frown replaced Ellen's grin of anticipation. "Why? Is that young man's death affecting his business?"

"Yes, and there's more." Claire told her about Ana Mendoza's threatened lawsuit.

Ellen tsked. "Maybe Charley should talk to Dave."

"I'll suggest it." Claire knew that as a corporate lawyer, Dave had represented a lot of companies against all kinds of client lawsuits. But she worried about the expense, another drain on Charley's finances.

Hank came up to them and tipped his hat. "Ladies, ready to mount your rides?" His dandified Western snap shirt had scrolled embroidery on the collar, cuffs, and shoulders, and his oval belt buckle was huge enough to have been won in a rodeo competition.

A natural flirt, Ellen batted her eyes and put a hand on her hip. "So, who's this handsome cowpoke?" she asked Claire.

Hank winked, swept off his black felt cowboy hat and bowed, then doffed it again with a pat on the top. "Hank Isley, ma'am. At your service."

Ellen flopped her hand, letting it casually land on his shoulder. "Don't you ma'am me! There's lots of miles left in this body." She ran her hand down his bicep and gave it a gentle squeeze. "My, what muscles. I can see we'll be in capable hands."

With a sly smile, Hank smoothed his mustache. "Yes'm, my hands have handled their share of horse flesh. Especially the fillies, if you get my drift."

Claire thought the flirting had gone a little too far. "Our horses?"

Hank reluctantly took his gaze off Ellen. "Oh, yes. Right this way."

He led them into the corral. "Mrs. Hanover, since you have some riding experience, your horse is this gelding here, goes by the name of Pistol." He patted the horse's flank.

Claire rubbed the white blaze on Pistol's forehead and admired his dark brown mane and tail, white legs and red coat sprinkled with white. "What a lovely red roan coat he has. Pistol's a handsome guy."

"That he is. Just like me." Hank flashed a grin. "And he's just as frisky. He likes to break into a trot sometimes, so keep a tight rein on him. Can I give you an assist up?"

"I can manage." Claire grabbed the saddle horn and back of the saddle. She put one foot in the stirrup and stepped up, throwing her other leg over the saddle. She felt Hank's hand resting on her rump, but he removed it quickly after she glanced back at him.

Maybe he's just safety-conscious, she thought, *making sure I didn't fall backward. But then again, maybe not.*

Once she was seated, Hank turned to Ellen. "And Mrs. Redding, you'll be riding Blossom, this buckskin filly next to Pistol."

He escorted her around to Blossom's head so she could get acquainted with the tan horse with black legs, mane, and tail. He didn't ask Ellen if he could assist her. He just placed his hands on either side of her waist and boosted her up. Claire noted he took his sweet time removing his hands after Ellen was seated.

Ellen blushed. "Thank-you, Hank, and please call us Claire and Ellen. Mrs. Redding is my crotchety old mother-in-law, bless her heart."

Hank laughed, then stepped back and tipped his hat to both of them. "Okay, Claire and Ellen, let me give you a few tips." He went through how to hold the reins, the standard commands, and how to prevent the horses from trying to graze along the trail.

"Now you just holler if you need me," he finished with a lascivious wink. He moved on to some other customers, a young couple, who from the moon-eyed gazes they were giving each other, looked to be honeymooners.

Ellen leaned over toward Claire. "I bet Hank gets good tips from the ladies."

Claire smiled with Ellen, though she had found Hank's attentions to be a bit too much.

Roger waved at them from five horses down the line. "Hi, ho, ladies. How are your mounts?"

"Just peachy," Ellen shot back.

"And no flirting with the wranglers," Dave said.

"Too late," Claire replied, "Ellen's already been at it."

All four of them laughed, but Dave's seemed forced and he gave Ellen a thoughtful look.

Uh oh. Claire realized Ellen and Dave's relationship wasn't on firm ground yet.

After the ten riders were all seated on their mounts, Hank got on his. He addressed the group, introducing Brittany as the group's rear rider and explaining their two-hour circuit. They would ride down Foothills Trail to the Dakota Trail in the Garden of the Gods, go through the north end of the park, and return to the stables.

While he led the group out of the corral and under the stable sign, Jessica came out of the trailer to wave to them all. "Have a great ride!"

Her plastered-on smile couldn't hide the worry lines on her forehead and dark shadows under her eyes. Claire wondered if Jessica had gotten any sleep the night before, or if she and Charley had been up late discussing their troubles. Hopefully today, at least, nothing would go wrong.

The first hour of the ride went smoothly enough, with a taciturn Gil following them in the ATV and scooping up manure droppings until the horses left the pavement. Then he sped off erratically back toward the stable. Once in the Garden of the Gods, Hank tossed out some tidbits about the history of the park. The family of Charles Elliott Perkins gifted the park to the city of Colorado Springs in 1907, upon the urging of General William Jackson Palmer. The founder of the city and builder of the Denver and Rio Grande Railroad, Palmer had the wherewithal to donate more than 1,000 acres of his own land to become city parks.

Hank stopped the group on Palmer Trail at the Giant Footprints formation, with its huge oval pink sandstone slabs piled onto a tilted slope. He explained he would take photos of riders on their horses in front of the formation while Brittany maneuvered and held horses. While snapping photos, he kept up a running commentary about how beautiful and handsome everyone looked against the gorgeous scenery and how envious their friends back home would be.

Claire thought he was laying it on a little thick and rolled her eyes at Roger, who nodded and grinned. While they waited their turn at the back of the group, another large group of riders came up the trail from the south.

With a "Whoa," the lead wrangler halted the column and waited, leaning forward with his hands crossed over his saddle horn. He looked to be in his twenties, with short, light brown hair and a square jaw. He wore faded Wrangler jeans and a work shirt in a yellow, red, and black checked pattern.

A handsome man himself, Claire surmised he must be the charmer for his stables, Peak View Stables. They ran their trail rides from the south end of the Garden of the Gods. This group must have been on a multi-hour ride since they were so far north into the park.

Hank gave him a nervous glance. "We'll be out of your way in a minute, Vince."

He tried to hurry up the young couple he was working with, but they insisted on taking multiple poses for their honeymoon album.

As the minutes ticked by, some of the riders in Vince's column started muttering. Annoyed frowns marred their faces.

"C'mon, Hank," Vince drawled. "You're hogging the trail. We've gotta take our pictures, too."

At the sound of his voice, Brittany, who had been engrossed with running around and managing horses, turned toward him. She gave an excited little hop and wave, as if she had been waiting for the opening to speak to him. "Hi, Vince," she said in a honey-toned voice. "Nice to see you again."

Vince straightened and grinned. "Well howdy, Brittany." He kicked his horse forward until he was next to her. "Didn't expect to see you out on the trail today. No therapy sessions?"

She smiled up at him. "I have some this afternoon, but we're short-handed after Kyle, you know..." She gave a sigh. "So, I'm helping out this morning."

Vince's smile disappeared. "Yeah, sorry to hear about his death. Not a good way for any man to go. Can't say as I'm sorry my competition is gone, though." His grin returned and he tipped his hat at Brittany.

Brittany looked up at him through her lashes and swiveled her hips, but before she could reply, Hank called, "Brittany, help me move these folks away so I can take a quick shot of the Johnsons."

Brittany went to work helping him maneuver horses until the older couple in their group was positioned in front of the formations.

Looking harried, Hank glanced at Vince. "Not too much longer."

Vince stood in his saddle to look back over his shoulder at his column. The horses were blowing and shuffling their feet now, too, as annoyed with standing still as his customers.

He faced Hank. "This has got to be your last photo. We're all tired of waiting. And we should have priority. My group's bigger than yours and we were here first."

The young male honeymooner looked confused. "But we were here first."

"I meant our stable was here first," Vince said, his face darkening. "Gardner's Stables just started running trail rides in the park this season. They should show a little more *consideration* to their betters."

Claire saw that this confrontation could easily escalate, and she didn't want Charley's stable to get into any more trouble. "The four of us don't need our photos taken," she said to Hank. "We're locals and already have lots of photos of the Garden of the Gods."

Disappointment showed on Ellen's face. "But, not on horseback—"

"That's okay." Claire flashed her a 'give it up' look. "Let's just get out of these folks' way."

"Now you're talking." Vince gave her an approving nod.

Looking relieved, Hank handed the older couple their camera and quickly mounted his horse. Brittany did the same and moved to the south end of their group, while Hank moved to the north.

With a forward sweep of hand, he said, "All right, we're heading back. Turn your horses and follow me."

"Finally," the man on horseback behind Vince said.

Vince turned back to him. "Don't worry, Mr. Englewood. We won't see them again today. And when you come back next season, I'm sure this fly-by-night outfit won't be in business anymore. You stick with us, the *established* trail riding outfit in these parts, and we'll take real good care of you."

Being the second to last rider in their group, Claire heard him. She looked at Brittany, who from her furrowed brow must have heard him, too. Claire wondered how many of these confrontations with Peak View Stables Charley could manage before the relationship between the two businesses got really ugly—or was it already that bad?

———

Three hours later, Claire sat with Roger, Ellen, Dave, Jessica, and Charley on the shaded porch of the Gardner's Stables trailer. They had just finished eating a delicious surprise picnic lunch that Ellen provided. After their return from the trail ride, she had told Dave to fetch a large cooler out of the trunk of their car and invited Jessica and Charley to join them. She laid out a gourmet repast of oozing brie cheese, hard salami slices, baguettes, marinated olives and peppers, and large black grapes.

Dave had opened a magnum bottle of crisp white Riesling and poured it into clear plastic glasses. Sated and glowing from the wine and enjoying the company of friends and family, Claire felt at peace, for the moment. Charley and Jessica had skipped the wine, since they both had to return to work, but they had eaten heartily, too, and seemed equally relaxed.

Good, Claire thought, *they need a break from their worries.*

Charley leaned back, groaned and patted his stomach. "Thank you, Ellen. That was delicious."

His lazy smile disappeared, however, when a dark blue pickup truck drove into the parking lot. The logo of Peak View Stables was emblazoned on its side. When two men got out, slammed their doors, and marched up the walk, Charley rose to his feet.

"This doesn't look good," he said with a frown.

Worry furrowing her brow, Jessica stood, too.

As the two men approached, Claire realized one was Vince, the wrangler who had tangled with Hank on the trail. The other man looked much older, probably in his sixties, with receding gray hair, bowed legs, and leathery skin from a life lived outdoors.

"I've got a bone to pick with you, Charley," the older man said. "Maybe we should talk in private, away from your customers."

"These are family and friends, Tom," Charley said. He introduced them all and introduced the older man as Tom Lindall, General Manager of Peak View Stables. Tom introduced Vince as Vince Donahue.

While the introductions were being made, Ellen cleared up the picnic leavings. She closed the cooler and signaled Dave to pick it up.

"We've got to get going," she said. "I have an afternoon appointment." The two of them said their goodbyes and left.

Roger raised an eyebrow at Claire, an implicit question whether they should leave, too, but she shook her head. The two of them were witnesses to what had occurred on the trail. Their viewpoints might help, if that's why the men from Peak View Stables were there.

Charley came down off the porch to stand in front of Tom and Vince. "What can I do for you?"

Tom Lindall waved a hand at Vince. "Vince here tells me your group held them up on the trail for almost twenty minutes this morning. That caused him to return late with his riders and upset our whole day's routine. You know damn well we have so many groups going out that we have to time them like clockwork. I had to scramble to get the afternoon rides out on schedule. That kind of thing can't continue."

Charley looked at Claire and Roger. "That right?"

"I don't think it was twenty minutes," Roger said. "It was more like ten."

Hands stuffed in his pockets, Vince looked down and dug the toe of his boot in the dirt.

"And it wasn't Hank's fault," Claire said. "The honeymoon couple kept asking for more photos. Hank couldn't very well refuse without pissing them off."

"So he pissed off a whole column of my customers instead!" Tom's face grew red.

Claire put her hands on her hips. "But—"

"I'll handle this." Charley frowned at Claire then turned toward Lindall. "I'm sorry, Tom. It won't happen again. I'll talk to my wranglers, give them some advice on how to limit the photos."

"That's not enough," Tom replied. "We can't have these confrontations on the trail at all. What if some of your horses and some of mine got into an altercation, bucking off tourists and injuring them in the process?"

Charley looked confused. "The two columns were kept separate, weren't they?"

Claire and Roger nodded, and Vince, after seeing them, reluctantly joined in.

When Claire opened her mouth to say more, Roger put a hand on her arm and shook his head. She realized he was right. This was Charley's fight, and he didn't need his big sister butting in.

"This time they were," Tom said. "Who's to say it won't happen next time, while the two groups are milling around at the same spot taking photos?" He slapped his hand against his thigh. "This just isn't working. The city should never have allowed another commercial trail-riding business in the park. I'm going to call my good buddy Councilman Harvey and follow up with a written complaint."

Jessica gasped. Her wide-eyed gaze darted between Tom and Charley.

Charley put out his hands in a 'calm down' motion. "Now wait just a minute. There's no need to go that far. I'm sure we can work out a solution."

Tom pursed his lips. "You willing to stay off Palmer Trail?"

"You know that won't work for me," Charley replied. "My customers have just as much right to see all of the park formations as yours. Why don't we compare our ride schedules and routes? I'm sure we can make modifications in timing that will prevent confrontations and keep everyone safe."

"I'm not making any modifications." Tom crossed his arms and pushed out his chin. "We've been following the same routine for nigh on twenty years now. It runs like a well-oiled machine. When there aren't hold-ups like today, that is."

"Well, then, I'll see if I can make some changes," Charley said evenly. "I looked at your schedule and routes when I first planned mine, but I can make some tweaks, I'm sure. Give me a chance to make this right."

Tom uncrossed his arms and exhaled. "I guess I can give it one more go. But if this happens again, I'm going to the city."

Charley turned toward the trailer and held out a hand toward the steps. "Why don't we go inside the trailer? I've got a map with my routes on it on the wall, and a ride schedule there. We can have a drink while we talk it over. Jessica's got a pot of coffee on, and we've got sodas in the fridge."

Tom gave a begrudging harrumph and a nod. He turned to Vince. "Can you amuse yourself for a few minutes?"

Vince looked at Charley and Jessica. "Is Brittany still here?"

"She's up at the barn getting some horses ready for this afternoon's hippotherapy," Jessica said.

Vince grinned. "I'll give her a hand." He headed up for the barn while Charley and Tom went in the trailer.

"I should go inside," Jessica said. "I don't know how Charley managed to defuse that situation, and I'd better make sure they all stay on friendly terms."

Claire thought Charley had done a damn good job of keeping his cool and preventing a blow-up, but before she could say so to Jessica, Roger said, "What happens if two trail rides meet up again in the park?"

Jessica nibbled her lower lip. "I don't know. Hopefully Charley can find a way to prevent that from occurring."

"I'm sure he'll figure something out," Claire said.

But she didn't really feel that hopeful. Horses and tourists didn't follow precise schedules, and there were bound to be delays on trail rides. How could Charley keep Tom Lindall from complaining to the city, and maybe getting Charley's agreement voided?

FIVE:
A BAD FEELING

THE NEXT MORNING, CLAIRE fingered the green 'Gardner's Hippotherapy' T-shirt that lay in her lap after trying it on. "It's not only a great fit," she said to Jessica, "I love the color, too."

She was sitting on the reception sofa in the trailer at Gardner's Stables and Jessica was perched on the arm of the matching leather loveseat. Behind the reception desk across from Claire, a short hallway led to a back office with two desks. The hall also led to a storage room, a bathroom, and a small kitchenette where Jessica had made the cinnamon-laced Mexican coffee they were sipping.

"I'm glad. I thought green was good for a horse-based charity." Jessica put down her coffee cup and arranged her face in a bright smile. "So, what's our shopping itinerary?"

Jessica hadn't scheduled any hippotherapy clients that day, so Claire could finally show Jessica her favorite Colorado Springs clothing stores and boutiques for a "Ladies Day Out." Neither one of them felt particularly cheerful. But Claire thought some shopping therapy might give Jessica some much-needed relief from her troubles.

"After I deliver a couple of my 'Welcome to Colorado Springs' baskets to a realtor downtown," Claire said, "we'll start at Silent Woman. It's Ellen's favorite home decor boutique and a really cute shop. Then we'll look at the ritzy clothes at Drama. We probably won't be able to afford much, but we'll have fun window-shopping."

Jessica clapped her hands together, trying oh so hard to look excited. "I'll be exhausted after all that!"

Claire forced a smile, too. "We'll rest and eat lunch at Rico's Café in the Poor Richard's complex, with its fun bookstore and children's store. That'll fortify us for an afternoon at The Promenade Shops at the Briargate."

"What fun. We've got to remember to pick up the invitations to my fundraiser event from the engravers, too." Jessica stood and took their coffee cups to the sink. "Planning the fundraiser and getting the stable up and running was a lot harder than I thought it would be. Double-checking everything Charley did took a lot of time. I've needed this break for ages, even before Kyle's death."

"Why do you have to double-check everything Charley does?"

Jessica waved a hand. "You know men. They don't have the eye for detail we women do. Especially Charley."

"Charley was pretty thorough about homework and stuff when we were kids."

When Jessica just shrugged, Claire worried her lip. Even if Charley realized where Jessica's constant little digs came from, wouldn't they eventually chip away at his self-confidence? Claire decided to monitor his reactions to Jessica's comments more closely.

Claire stood. "I hope Charley will be able to schedule a breather soon. Working long hours seven days a week with no rest is taking a toll on him, too. Well, I guess we'd better get a move on."

They shouldered their purses and stepped outside. Two police cars sat in the parking lot, a marked cruiser and Detective Frank Wilson's gray unmarked Charger. Wilson, another man in a suit, and two officers in uniform were getting out of the vehicles.

"Uh oh," Jessica said. "I've got a bad feeling about this."

"So do I." Claire put a hand on Jessica's shoulder. "But let's see what Detective Wilson has to say first."

He approached them. "Hello, ladies. I'm afraid I have some bad news for you. The coroner ruled that Kyle Mendoza was murdered."

Jessica sucked in a breath. "Murdered!"

"Oh, God. How?" Claire asked.

"The autopsy showed that his head wound wasn't caused by the horse's hooves. It was blunt force trauma from a metal tool, one that had a much smaller diameter than a hoof, something like a hammer or crowbar." He looked at Jessica. "You got something like that on the premises?"

"We have both," Jessica replied. "And lots of other tools that could fit that description, like hay hooks, pitchforks, heavy-duty pliers and screwdrivers, you name it."

Claire furrowed her brow as she tried to absorb this new information. "So Kyle was dead before Gunpowder stomped on him?"

"Not quite," Wilson said. "The head wound was delivered first, sometime between eight and ten PM, before the other injuries. It didn't kill him right away, but it might have eventually without treatment."

Jessica's expression showed she was as stunned as Claire. "Who would do that? And why?"

Detective Wilson paused, and Claire could tell he was holding something back. "That's what I aim to find out."

He stepped onto the porch and handed a document to Jessica. "This is a search warrant for the entire premises. These men and I are going to look for anything that might be the murder weapon." He introduced his fellow detective and the two patrolmen.

"What can we do to help?" Jessica asked after the hand-shaking was over.

"Nothing," Wilson replied. "But after we finish our search, we'll need to re-interview everyone. What activities did you have planned here today?"

Jessica glanced at Claire. "Well, Claire and I were going to go shopping, but that can wait. There's no way I'm going to leave here until I know if you found something. Hank and Gil are already out on a two-hour trail ride with customers and won't be back for an hour and a half. And we've got another ride scheduled for this afternoon."

Wilson pursed his lips. "Hopefully we won't get in the way of your afternoon ride. But when the morning ride returns, I'll need to meet it."

Jessica's eyes went wide. "You're not going to tell our customers what's going on, are you?"

"No, I'll just make sure they all leave the area and that we talk to Hank and Gil before they leave the premises."

"The horses will need to be cared for first."

Wilson sighed. "I understand. Who else is on the property now?"

"Charley, Jorge, Pedro, and Brittany."

"I don't want them observing our search. Are they busy now? Can they take a break and come in here?"

"I guess so," Jessica said. "The horses have all been fed and watered. They're probably just doing chores and repairs that can wait."

"Okay, here's the plan. We'll bring everyone in here, search until the trail ride returns, then stop and do the interviews after the horses have been cared for. If we're lucky, we'll find something before the ride returns. Which is when?"

"About eleven-thirty," Jessica answered.

Wilson signaled to the same patrolman who had watched over them Monday. "Phelps, you stay with the women. One of us will bring the others here, then you'll observe them all while the rest of us search."

He turned to Jessica. "One more thing. When's your trash pickup day?"

"Tomorrow. The same company picks up our manure and soiled stable bedding, too. We store it in a dumpster behind the barn."

The other detective glanced at his loafers as if regretting his choice of footwear. Phelps smirked.

"Good," Wilson said. "What else gets removed from the property?"

Jessica thought for a moment. "The port-a-potties are emptied every two weeks, and the next time is next Wednesday."

As Jessica talked, Claire could see Officer Phelps grinning at his uniformed cohort, who was rolling his eyes. He obviously was not looking forward to the messier aspects of the search operation.

Jessica must have caught the look, too. "You know, Pedro could help you go through the manure pile, or Gil or Hank when they get back. They handle that stuff every day."

Wilson glanced back at his men, and Phelps's buddy held up a thumb. "Okay, we may use one of them when it comes to that. And for fishing in the port-a-potties. Let's get to it."

As he and the other detective and patrolman walked to the barn, Jessica let out a sigh. "Sorry about this, Claire." She took her purse off her shoulder.

Claire followed suit. "As you said, we can shop anytime. I'll make another pot of coffee. When everyone gets here, they'll probably want some." She and Officer Phelps followed Jessica inside the trailer.

Charley, Jorge, Pedro, and Brittany soon tromped up the porch steps, followed by the other detective, who opened the door and gave Phelps a quick nod before leaving. After scraping off their boots and slapping the stable dust off their jeans, Charley and the others came inside the trailer, doffing their cowboy hats as they passed the threshold.

While Claire got everyone a drink of some kind, Charley started pacing. "I can't believe someone killed Kyle!"

Brittany nodded and put a hand to her mouth, her eyes reddening.

"And I've got to pay everyone to sit around here instead of working." Charley threw up his hands in frustration and exhaled deeply. "This is getting damned expensive."

"I know," Claire said. "But what else can you do? The police have to do their work."

Charley slapped his hat against his thigh. "And cause me a basket of trouble in the process."

"The real culprit is whoever killed Kyle," Claire said. "I wonder who did it."

Everyone in the room looked at each other and shrugged or shook their heads.

Claire watched their faces carefully. "Any of you know if Kyle had any enemies? If he had any recent arguments with anyone?"

More shrugging and shaking of heads, except Pedro hesitated and wouldn't meet Claire's gaze.

She stepped toward him. "Pedro?"

"*Nada*," he said quickly, and brought a Coke can to his lips, spilling a few drops on his shirt in his haste. He glanced at Jorge.

Claire turned to the older man. "Jorge?"

Jorge's face was passive, inscrutable. "Kyle was a kind man with many *amigos*."

That really didn't answer her question. She stared at both men for a while longer but saw that she wasn't going to get anything out of them, so she turned to Brittany. "You dated him a few times. Did he mention anyone he was having a problem with?"

She shook her head. "He was always smiling, didn't seem to have a care in the world."

Jessica sat at the desk with fingers drumming on the large calendar pad in front of her. "Maybe it was a family problem, something totally unrelated to the stable."

Charley wheeled and looked at her. "I sure hope so, and I hope the police find out who did it soon. Kyle's murder, on top of the issues we're having with Peak View Stables and the neighbors, could deep-six Gardner's Stables for good."

Claire noticed that Phelps had been quietly scribbling on a notepad while standing in a corner. She nibbled on her lip. She didn't see how anything anyone had said in response to her questions could be helpful. Maybe there was some other way she could help Detective Wilson in this investigation. After all, she had done so once before, though he hadn't appreciated her 'interference,' as he called it.

Time passed slowly as they waited for the return of the searchers. At least the trailer was air-conditioned, and they weren't sitting outside in the hot sun. Brittany laid her head back on the sofa and fell asleep. When Phelps's stomach let out a loud growl, Jessica took pity on him and brought a large bag of tortilla chips out of the kitchenette. He passed the bag around and it was soon emptied.

Jorge got up and fetched a veterinarian's book about horse ailments off the bookshelf behind Jessica's reception desk. He returned to the sofa and started leafing through it and discussing it with Pedro in Spanish. Charley went into the back office to work on his computer. From the pile of invoices and receipts he was going through, Claire presumed he was catching up on bookkeeping.

Brittany woke up, glanced around with a dazed look, then checked at her watch. "Um, Jessica? I have class in two hours. Will the police be able to interview me before I have to go to it?"

Jessica looked at Phelps, who stood leaning with his back against the wall. He shrugged. "It's up to Detective Wilson."

"We'll ask him, Brittany," Jessica said.

Steps sounded on the porch outside, and the other patrolman entered. "Detective Wilson told me to fetch Pedro. We're going to have to go through the manure dumpster now."

Phelps gave a little snort, and the other patrolman shot him an angry glare.

With a look of pained resignation, Pedro rose from the sofa.

Claire felt sorry for him, but she realized he was the logical choice. Charley and Jorge outranked him, and none of the men, being the chivalrous cowboys they were, would have let Brittany handle the noxious, labor-intensive chore.

The patrolman turned to Jessica. "Detective Wilson also told me to ask you if you'd heard anything from the trail ride group."

"Hank will radio us a few minutes before they hit the paved trail in the Blair Bridge Open Space," she replied. "We should hear from him soon. We need to send Brittany out on the ATV to follow them back at that point, to scoop up any droppings."

After the patrolman nodded, Jessica added, "Could you ask Detective Wilson if he could interview Brittany after that, so she can go to her class afterward?"

"Okay." The patrolman ushered Pedro out.

A few minutes later, Phelps's shoulder radio squawked. Detective Wilson said he would talk to Brittany before she had to leave for class.

About ten minutes after that, Hank radioed that they were approaching the Foothills Trail, so Brittany headed out.

Finally Wilson opened the door to the trailer and poked his head in. "Charley Gardner, could you step outside?"

Charley walked out and Claire and Jessica followed. They stood on the porch while Charley walked with Detective Wilson and the other detective over to Pedro, who was filthy from head-to-toe. The frowning uniformed officer standing next to him had brown stains on his pants legs and arms.

A fetid stench came off the two of them. Claire's nose automatically wrinkled, but she stopped herself from waving her hand or holding her nose. The men couldn't help how they smelled, and she didn't want to embarrass them.

Pedro stood with his head bowed and his cheeks reddened. He held the handles of a wheelbarrow containing an assortment of tools, all bagged in large plastic bags.

"We're going to need to remove all of these for testing," Wilson said.

Charley put his hands on his hips and looked over the assortment. He frowned. "For how long?"

"Could be days, maybe even a week or two. And if any become evidence, we'll need to hold them until the case goes to trial." Wilson pointed to a plastic bag that Claire, from her high perch on the porch, could see contained a hammer with brown smears on its haft. "I suspect this hammer that Pedro found for us deep in the manure dumpster may be the only one we'll have to hold on to for long."

Claire raised a brow at Jessica, who put a hand to her mouth.

"Looks like I'll need to buy new tools to replace most of these anyway. I can't go that long without them." Charley slapped his hat against his thigh then slammed it on his head. "Another God-damned expense."

Wilson handed him a piece of paper. "This is a list of everything we're taking."

Charley took the list, reached up to the porch to hand it to Jessica, then turned back to Wilson. "Can poor Pedro get cleaned up and the rest of us go back to work now?"

"Afraid not," Wilson said, with an apologetic glance at the reeking wrangler. "Given the new evidence, we need to re-interview everyone. Find out who was here the night Mendoza was killed. I understand Brittany Schwartz has to leave, so we'll start with her after the trail ride gets in." He held out a set of keys to the grimy patrolman. "Put all the evidence in my trunk, then I'll need you and Phelps to observe everyone."

Grim-faced, the patrolman took the wheelbarrow from Pedro. He probably wanted to get cleaned up right away, too.

Wilson turned to the other detective. "Once Miss Schwarz gets back, you can start with her in the trailer." Then he addressed Phelps. "Ask everyone to come out here."

As Phelps went back in the trailer, Claire saw the string of horses appear from around a small rise to the west. Brittany followed on her ATV.

After that, there was a flurry of activity as the trail ride returned. Under the watchful eyes of the police, tourists dismounted. They made their thanks and passed tips to the guides, who unsaddled, brushed, watered, and fed the horses. Hank and Gil and the tourists shot curious glances at the police, but Jessica and Charley made a point of ignoring the officers. They kept up a steady patter with the tourists, so none of them had a chance to ask about the police before they found themselves gently herded into the parking lot.

Then the interviews started.

When it was finally Claire's turn for her private talk with Detective Wilson at one of the outside picnic tables, he said, "I won't keep you long. Since you weren't here Sunday night, you probably won't have much to add."

"Oh, but I do," Claire said, causing Wilson to raise an eyebrow. "Did you know that Gil Kaplan has a drinking problem and a chip on his shoulder about Mexican immigrants?"

"No, I didn't. So you think Gil reacted to Mendoza's Hispanic surname even though Mendoza was born in the Springs?"

"You know, I'd suspect Gil more if Pedro or even Jorge was the victim." She described Gil's treatment of Pedro on Tuesday. "Yes, Kyle was a U.S. citizen, but maybe he and Gil got into it, too. That man seems to have a lot of anger in him."

"I'll look into it."

"And I bet Charley didn't tell you about the run-in he had with the General Manager of Peak View Stables, thinking it had nothing to do with Kyle's death."

Wilson shook his head. "No, he didn't. Could be nothing, but tell me about it."

"Tom Lindall would love to see Charley's business just go away. And what better way is there than to set up someone to be killed by one of the horses, then spread the word that Charley's stable isn't safe?" She described both the argument on the trail and Lindall's follow-up visit.

After she finished, Wilson looked up from his notepad, where he had been scribbling during her tale. "So you think Lindall was just pretending to be mollified by Charley and willing to work out a compromise?"

Claire shrugged. "I don't know. I don't know the man. But I do know you. There was something about the autopsy findings that you didn't share with Jessica and me. What was it?"

"If I tell you, you can't share the information with anyone, not even your husband."

"I promise."

Wilson studied her, then gave a satisfied nod. "I'm only telling you because you two and your brother and his wife are neither suspects nor witnesses. Your brother's neighbors confirmed that they were at your brother's house until around eleven Sunday night.

They brought a late dinner and a cake over to celebrate the opening, then stayed to hear all about it."

Thank God Charley and Jessica had an alibi. Claire folded her arms. "So tell me."

"The clincher for the murder determination," he said, leaning forward, "was that the coroner also found abrasions on the palms of Mendoza's hands, abrasions that are consistent with being dragged. So, he concluded that someone hit Mendoza on the head, knocking him unconscious. Then he dragged Mendoza into Gunpowder's stall and goaded the horse into finishing him off, making it look like an accident."

"Oh, my. So that's why you're talking to Charley's wranglers."

"And anyone else who might have had a reason to kill Kyle Mendoza."

"That reminds me. I assume Brittany told you she was dating Kyle."

"Yes, and that they weren't serious."

"Did she tell you that there's also something going on between her and this guy named Vince Donahue who works for Lindall?"

"Nooo." Wilson poised his pen over his notepad. "But something tells me you are."

"Unfortunately I don't know much. I've just seen them flirt with each other." She told Wilson about the encounter in the Garden of the Gods Park and Vince asking to see Brittany when he and Lindall came over.

She leaned forward. "I'll be volunteering with Brittany again on Saturday for Jessica's hippotherapy nonprofit. I can ask Brittany about her relationship with Vince then."

"You stay out of this. I'll ask her myself." Wilson flipped the cover over on his spiral notebook.

"She probably won't tell you as much as she'll tell me, woman-to-woman."

Wilson sat up straighter and focused his gaze on Claire. "I know you want to be helpful, since your brother's business is affected, but I can't allow you to go around asking questions. Anything you find out would be inadmissible in court. And whoever killed Kyle Mendoza is still out there. What happens if the killer finds you snooping around?"

"I'll be careful. I'll just bring things up in casual conversation, so no one will be suspicious."

"Oh, c'mon!"

She put up her hands, palm out. "I'm not working for you, but you can't stop me, either. Look how much I've already found out. Don't you agree it's useful?"

Wilson sighed. "Maybe. I'll follow up on some of the things you've told me, but I don't want you putting yourself at risk. You're not a trained detective like I am."

Claire crossed her arms. "Oh, you already made that abundantly clear a few months ago."

A small smile quirked up one side of Wilson's lips. "I'm grateful you've told me all this. And, if you happen to find out anything else useful by keeping your eyes and ears open, I want to hear it. But don't poke your nose where it doesn't belong." He stood. "I wouldn't want to see a single hair on your pretty little head come to harm."

He walked out of the trailer leaving Claire fuming. *What a condescending thing to say!*

She had half a mind to engage in 'snooping' as he called it just to spite him. But she didn't need Wilson to give her a reason. She had enough of one. Charley's business, his future, and his self-worth were all at stake in this. And if her little brother needed help, Claire was determined to offer it, whether he wanted it or not.

SIX:
LEGAL ISSUES

CLAIRE VISITED HER MOTHER Friday morning and left feeling gloomy. Her mother was ensconced in an Alzheimer's facility in Colorado Springs and often didn't recognize Claire anymore when she visited. This morning, she had treated Claire as if she was one of the staff and kept asking what they were serving for lunch. Claire made up something, sure her mother would forget anyway by the time the meal was served.

When Claire walked into the Gardner's Stables trailer, Jessica was on the phone, talking about dozens of chocolate-covered strawberries. Claire presumed the fundraiser caterer was on the line. She waggled her fingers at Jessica and poked her head in Charley's office. He stopped his work on his computer to exchange hellos, and she gave him an update on their mother.

"I'm worried about her," she said to Charlie. "One of the aides told me she found Mom wandering the hallway late one night last week. Mom couldn't tell her what she was doing there, and the aide had to escort her back to her room."

"That doesn't sound good," Charlie said with a frown.

"Could you visit her soon and let me know what you think?"

He sighed. "I'll try. I know I should see her more often, but I get so busy here that the days keep slipping by."

Jessica hung up and called to Claire, ending the conversation. While she and Claire prepared to go out on their postponed shopping trip, Charlie went back to methodically clicking through e-mail messages between sips of coffee.

Suddenly he slammed down the cup. "God damn it!"

Jessica scooted into the back office. "What? What is it?"

Dread made Claire break out in a hot flash, and sweat beaded on her skin. She followed Jessica, flapping the front of her shirt to cool off.

Charley shoved his chair back and pointed to the computer screen. "This email is from the Director of the Colorado Springs Parks and Recreation Department. It says he's reviewing our agreement allowing me to operate commercial trail rides in the Garden of the Gods."

Jessica leaned in to read the message on the screen. "'… in light of recent events.' What does he mean by that?"

"Kyle's murder, I'm sure. It was in the *Gazette* today."

Claire had read the article before coming over. The reporter had insinuated that someone at the stable had done the deed. When she had read the byline and recognized Marvin Bradshaw's name, a reporter she and Roger had had a run-in with before, her hackles rose. She had made a mental note to contact him later and berate him for jumping to unfounded conclusions.

"Do you think Ana Mendoza's lawyer has contacted them?" Claire asked.

"Probably." Charley sank lower in his chair.

"Or could it have been Tom Lindall?"

"Maybe," Charley said. "Or both of them. I'm going to call and find out. Then give the director a piece of my mind. He can't just break the contract at the drop of a hat." He reached for the phone.

Jessica put a hand on his arm, stopping him. "Wait. You can't go charging in there like a bronc trying to throw a rodeo cowboy like you always do."

"I've got to do something!" Charley's fist pounded the desk.

"But getting into a shouting match with the Director of Parks and Rec is just going to make things worse. We need to think this through."

For once, Claire agreed with her sister-in-law. "The last thing you want to do is antagonize him, Charley."

"What is this?" His face grew red. "Are you two ganging up on me? I can't ignore the director's e-mail. If Ana's lawyer or Tom Lindall is feeding him a pack of lies, I need to make sure he knows the truth."

"Yes, we do." Jessica sat on his desk. "But we've got to be very careful how we say it, in a calm and rational way, so he believes us."

Claire had an idea. "Do you want me to contact Dave Redding? With his legal background, maybe he can look over the contract and let you know how it can be cancelled. Then he can coach you in what to say."

"What I want is for you two to stop yammering at me." Charley rose abruptly and slammed his cowboy hat on his head. "I'm going out to get some fresh air. I can't think in here." He stomped out of the trailer.

"Oh dear." Jessica slumped into the chair that Charley had just vacated. "I've got to convince him we're right."

Claire gazed thoughtfully at the door Charley had swung shut with a loud bang. "You know, I think he's got the right idea. He can blow off some steam working with the horses. Then when he does call the director, he won't be so upset."

She fished in her purse. "I've got a couple of Dave's cards in here. I'll leave one for Charley and maybe he'll contact Dave for some advice." She pulled one out and laid it on Charley's desk.

"But what if he doesn't?" Jessica asked. "And he calls and makes things worse?" She stood. "I have to go talk to him."

Claire put a firm hand on her arm. "No, Jessica. What you need to do is go shopping with me. Give Charley some space. We need to trust that he'll do the right thing."

Jessica snorted. "Charley? Do the right thing with no coaching from me? Not very likely!"

———

When Claire drove back into the parking lot for Gardner's Stables late that afternoon, Jessica's and her excited chatter about their purchases died a slow death. Detective Wilson's gray Dodge Charger sat in the parking lot.

He stood outside the corral, leaning against the fence with one foot up on a rail. In deference to the warm day, he wasn't wearing his suit coat and had rolled up the sleeves of his shirt. He was talking to Charley and Jorge, who were working with Gunpowder inside the corral. They stirred up small dust clouds with their boots while they moved around the horse.

"Uh, oh. What now?" Jessica asked as she and Claire got out of the car.

"Help me with this bear, then we'll find out."

Claire wrestled a three-foot-tall carved wooden bear carrying a Welcome sign out of the car trunk. Jessica had fallen in love with it, saying it would be a perfect greeter at the bottom of the trailer's porch steps. When she balked at the price, Claire had insisted on buying it as a gift for the new business.

While Jessica hefted her end of the bear, she said, "I still say the gift basket was enough, Claire."

"Oh, poo." Claire huffed while they lugged the bear over to the trailer. "Or Pooh Bear, as the case may be. The basket wasn't a lasting gift. This is. I'll enjoy seeing it every time I come over."

They set the bear down with a thump, then Jessica hustled toward the corral.

Claire followed a few steps behind. She wiped sweat off her brow, though it would have evaporated soon. The dry June heat had started sucking moisture out of her skin as soon as she stepped out of the car's air conditioning.

When she reached the corral, Jessica was asking Wilson, "What's going on? Why are you here?" in a loud, excited voice.

He waved a hand toward Gunpowder. "Right now, I'm watching these two work some magic on a horse."

Charley stood at Gunpowder's head, holding onto the horse's bridle. He turned at the sound of their voices. "Hi, gals. You were gone a long time. I hope you didn't break the bank."

Jessica looked at Claire, and Claire shook her head, mouthing, 'Not yet.' "Just our backs," she said to Charley and pointed at the bear.

When he saw it, he laughed. "Good idea."

A warm glow suffused Claire as she realized that was the first time she had heard Charley laugh since Kyle's death. And he looked relaxed. Doing what he loved—working with horses—had wrought this change.

Charley turned to Wilson. "So what we're doing here is getting Gunpowder used to having human hands on him again. Our farrier is coming tomorrow, and Gunpowder is due to be reshod. Jorge's gotten him to the point where we can touch his head and the front of his body, but he still shies away when we go for his hooves."

Jorge gently ran his hands up and down Gunpowder's chest while murmuring softly to the horse. He gradually extended his reach down the horse's front legs in slow circles until he was touching Gunpowder's knees. As he reached lower, Gunpowder's ears started twitching back and forth.

Claire leaned over the corral's top rail next to Wilson. "I can see Gunpowder's skin quivering under Jorge's touch."

"*Sí*, yes," Jorge answered in a calm monotone while he continued his ministrations. "That shows he is getting nervous, but he is better, much better than a couple of days ago. Aren't you, *chico*?"

Gunpowder looked at Jessica and Claire. He sniffed the air and stepped back and forth a few times before he settled down again, with Charley and Jorge both murmuring to him. Charley rubbed Gunpowder's nose, and gradually the horse's ears stopped twitching.

"He reacted a lot less to the women than to me when I came up to the corral," Wilson said.

"He didn't know you," Charley said. "That's why we had him come over and smell you and why I had you rub his head. He knows Jessica's scent really well, and he's met Claire once before. But you're right. Men seem to disturb him a lot more than women since Kyle died."

"Maybe it's because a man was the one who dragged Kyle Mendoza into his stall," Wilson offered.

Charley nodded. "Could be. Or maybe he now associates the smell of a human male, like Kyle's smell, with death. Except for those of us who've been working with him, that is. He knows our unique scents."

"It's a good thing our farrier is a woman and Gunpowder knows her well." Jorge said while he ran his hands down the full length of Gunpowder's front legs.

The horse's ears twitched a few times, but otherwise he stood still.

Jorge cradled one of Gunpowder's front hooves and slowly lifted it a few inches. "I think he will let her do his front hooves okay." He set the hoof down again. "But we will probably have to hobble him when she does his back hooves. He still won't let me touch his rear flanks or back legs."

"He'll hate being hobbled," Charley said. "Can we wait until her next visit?"

Jorge lifted Gunpowder's other front hoof and looked at the bottom. He shook his head. "He needs new shoes now. These are really worn."

"Why would he be more sensitive in the back?" Wilson asked.

"For one thing, he can't see what's going on there as well," Charley answered. "All horses are more nervous when people approach them from the rear. But Jorge and I also think Gunpowder probably kicked Kyle with his back hooves. Horses' back kicks are more powerful. Gunpowder may even have pulled some muscles there and have residual pain."

Wilson made a note on his small notepad. "Well, this is all interesting, but I'm not sure if any of it is helpful to the case. Can you take a break from this, Charley, so I can pick your brain some more?"

Charley looked at Jorge. "What do you think?"

"I can continue by myself if we tie him off." Jorge took the bridle and reins from Charley. He walked Gunpowder to the corral fence and looped the reins over the rail.

Charley came out through the gate and wiped his sleeve across his damp forehead. "Whew, I'm thirsty. How about if we have some iced tea on the porch while you ask your questions?"

"I'll fix it," Jessica said. She went inside the trailer.

Wilson followed and took a seat on the porch.

Claire headed for her car and said to Charley over her shoulder, "Could you help me bring in Jessica's bags?"

While she sorted through the shopping bags in the trunk and handed Jessica's to Charley, he lifted an eyebrow. "How much did these things cost?"

Claire crossed her fingers behind her back. "Don't worry. Not that much. We got most of them on sale. Working with the horses is your therapy, Charley. Shopping is Jessica's."

Charley nodded. "Point taken."

They settled onto benches on the porch, and Jessica brought out glasses of iced tea.

Once they were all served and Charley had downed half his glass, he looked at Detective Wilson. "So, what were those phone numbers that you wanted to check with me?"

Wilson pulled a folded sheet of paper out of his notepad, opened it up and handed it to Charley. Claire could see that the paper contained a list of phone numbers. Lots of handwritten notes were scribbled on it as well.

"We got the phone numbers off of Kyle Mendoza's cell phone and had the phone company trace them," Wilson explained to Jessica and Claire while Charley looked at the sheet. "The obvious calls are to here, his home phone, and Brittany Schwartz's cell phone. And we've identified the ones to business land lines. But we have some other cell phone numbers we're still trying to identify. Some are registered in Mexico."

Charley handed the list back to Wilson. "None of those other numbers are familiar to me."

Wilson glanced at Charley then Jessica. "Do either of you know why he'd be calling Mexico?"

Charley shook his head while Jessica looked thoughtful.

"Do you do any business in Mexico?" Wilson asked.

"No," Charley replied. "All of our suppliers are here in the U.S., and I've never bought a horse from Mexico."

Jessica leaned forward. "Does the Mendoza family have any relatives in Mexico?"

"I already asked his mother that," Wilson said. "And she said no, no close ones. No one that they still keep in touch with. She and her husband didn't recognize any of the numbers either."

He paused and looked at Charley. "Some of Kyle Mendoza's calls were to Pedro Trujillo's cell phone. Do you know why he'd be calling Pedro?"

"Kyle recommended Pedro to me," Charley said. "When I asked him what he knew about Pedro's work experience, Kyle said he hadn't worked with Pedro personally, but that a stable manager he had worked with before had vouched for him. Maybe after Kyle and Pedro started working together, they developed a friendship."

"Was the stable in Mexico?"

"I don't know, but I assumed it was in the U.S. I never asked Kyle for the contact information for the other stable manager. I needed wranglers right away, so I hired Pedro on a trial basis. When I saw what a hard worker he was and how good he was with horses, I didn't need to follow-up on the reference."

"Is Pedro here?"

"This is his day off," Charley said. "My wranglers all work six days a week. Each one gets a different weekday off, except Brittany, who's part-time."

Wilson pulled out his cell phone and dialed a number from the sheet of paper. He waited for a few moments, then broke the connection and pocketed his phone. "Pedro's not answering."

"If you want, I'll ask him tomorrow about that other stable, see if it was in Mexico and get the number from him if it was."

"I'll take care of it. I'll stop by his place later." Wilson tapped the end of his pen on his open notepad. "Is Pedro documented?"

Charley straightened, his back ramrod stiff. "Of course. I know the law. I don't hire illegal immigrants. Just like all my employees, Pedro showed me his social security card and driver's license when he filled out his paperwork."

"His English doesn't seem that good," Wilson responded, doubt lacing his voice.

"It's not what you think," Charley said. "I ran into that a lot with my wranglers when my stable was in Durango, and I do here, too. A lot of them come from the San Luis Valley. It's a rural farming area. They grow up around horses and learn how to handle them while they're still kids. Many of the families who live there speak Spanish in the home, even though they're U.S. citizens. That's their heritage."

"I don't understand," Jessica said to Wilson. "Why don't you just call the Mexico numbers and see who answers?"

"If Kyle Mendoza was into anything illegal that got him killed," he replied, "and these contacts are drug dealers or smugglers, they aren't about to identify themselves to us on the phone. And, by calling, we'll let them know we have the numbers. They'd throw away their cell phone SIM cards and get new ones. I'd rather see if any of Kyle's associates know what the phone numbers are for."

Jessica settled back against the porch railing. "I guess that makes sense."

Wilson refolded the phone number list and tucked it in his notepad. "And I guess my work is done here today. Thanks for clearing up those other two numbers, Charley." He nodded to them all and walked away to his car.

"What other two numbers?" Claire asked Charley.

"A feed supplier and hardware store," Charley answered. "Detective Wilson had started asking me about phone numbers when Jorge came out of the barn with Gunpowder and asked for my help. Wilson had the business names, but he wanted to know why

Kyle called them. Remember when we were first setting up and kept sending Kyle out to fetch things for us?" he asked Jessica. "I guess he called a couple of times to get directions."

"Speaking of getting directions," Jessica said. "Did you call Claire's lawyer friend before you blew your top at the park director?"

Ouch. Claire winced internally. She wouldn't have worded the question that bluntly.

Charley frowned. "Yes, I called Dave Redding. He told me to send him a copy of the e-mail and the contract. He said he'd look at them over the weekend. We'll talk about what to do on Monday, but I'm not sure how much I want him to do for us. He sure ain't cheap."

He finished off his glass of iced tea and put it on the tray. "And speaking of spending money, how much money did you spend today?"

Ouch again. Claire glanced from Charley to Jessica and wondered if their marriage was really on the rocks or if they were just taking out their stress over Kyle's murder on each other.

"Don't worry," Jessica said. "I know money's tight right now. Claire found us some great bargains." She placed the empty glasses back on the tray and stood with it. "I'm going to look over tomorrow's trail ride bookings and make sure we're all set before we head home. Claire, can I get you anything?"

"No, thanks. I need to get home and fix dinner for Roger. Today was fun, though."

Jessica grinned. "It sure was. Thanks again for making me take the break. I really needed it." As she went inside the trailer, she started humming to herself.

Charley watched her go in then turned to Claire. "Jessica really does seem a lot more relaxed. I guess I should thank you even if our bank account took a hit."

"Now we just need to get you to take a break," Claire said with some relief. It seemed like Charley and Jessica were just stressed out, not having serious marital problems.

Charley exhaled. "Maybe after the cops figure out who killed Kyle. In the meantime, I've got my hands full, with constant searches and questioning interrupting our work."

He rose to follow Jessica into the trailer, but Claire put a hand on his arm. "Speaking of which…you gave Detective Wilson a good story about your workers, but do you hire illegals?"

"Of course not! Not deliberately. Do you think I'm an idiot?"

"No, just concerned about saving money. You could pay illegals a lot less."

"You must not think much of me as a businessman, Claire, if you think I'd stoop to that." Charley jammed his hands on his hips and frowned.

Claire could tell he was hurt by the implication. "I'm sorry. I do think a lot of you, Charley, I really do. Wilson's questions just concerned me. How careful can you be, really, about checking that all your workers are legal?"

Charley threw up a hand. "That's the problem. With the mess of immigration laws we have now, employers are stuck between a rock and a hard place. We can be fined if ICE finds out we hired illegal immigrants, even unknowingly, and—"

"Ice?"

"Immigration and Customs Enforcement," Charley explained. "But employers can't legally ask to see a green card from someone like Pedro who doesn't speak English well, if he shows what seems to be a valid social security card and driver's license. That's all you need on the I-9 form."

"Can you require all your employees to be U.S. citizens?"

Charley shook his head. "No, that's discrimination, because the people who are permanent residents and have green cards can't be denied work just because they weren't born here."

"And they don't have to show you those green cards to work for you."

"Right, because legally, to get a social security card, they either have to prove citizenship or show their green card."

"So you're covered!"

"It's not that simple. Social security cards are easy to forge and to buy, and the government's E-verify system for checking I-9's is notoriously bad at finding identity fraud. If your employee turns out to have a fake card, you're still liable. And ICE can fine you up to two thousand dollars per illegal employee."

Claire rubbed her forehead. The complexity of the issue was giving her a headache. "You have got to be kidding me."

"Unfortunately, I'm not." Charley raised his hands and shrugged his shoulders in a helpless gesture. "Because a lot of illegals work in stables in the U.S., I consulted an immigration lawyer about this in Durango."

"What did he say?"

"He told me to make copies of my employees' social security cards and driver's licenses when I hire them to prove that I checked them. And he told me that if ICE ever wants to check my records, I have the right to ask for three days to get them in order. But I can't ask new hires any questions about citizenship status, where they or their parents were born, or to see a birth certificate, passport, or green card."

"Do you know if Pedro and Jorge are legal?"

"No, I really don't," Charley said. "And I don't know if Brittany and Gil are either, or if Kyle was. All I know is that they all showed me social security cards and driver's licenses. And I have copies. That's why Wilson's questions were making me nervous."

"And if one of your wranglers isn't legal," Claire added, "questions about citizenship and green cards would make him nervous, too."

"Damn right." Charley slapped his hat against his thigh.

"Nervous enough to kill whoever was asking?"

Charley peered up at the barn. "I don't know. But why would Kyle be asking?"

SEVEN:
DIGGING FOR CLUES

Claire was walking beside Daisy in the corral the next morning, with Brittany on the other side of the horse and a small, sprightly boy with autism who was about nine years old in the saddle. A strong wind sluiced down Pike's Peak in the west, flinging the dust stirred up by Daisy's hooves into Claire's hair, eyes, and ears. She pulled the bandana tied around her neck up higher over her nose and mouth and glanced at Brittany, who had done the same thing. They both wore sunglasses, as did Jessica, walking in front of Daisy, but they weren't much protection from the swirling wind. Claire wondered if she was squinting as much as Brittany was.

"This wind bites, doesn't it?" Brittany said over Daisy's shoulder, her voice muffled by the bandana.

Claire nodded then glanced at Donny, the boy in the saddle.

A huge grin split his face as he bounced in the saddle and said, "Go, go, go," to Daisy. The wind and dust didn't seem to bother him at all.

He held Daisy's reins in one hand and a large plastic ring in the other. The task that Jessica had given him was to pick up rings hanging from both ends of a tall T-shaped pole planted in the dirt near one end of the corral. Then he had to slide the rings onto three tall straight poles sticking up from the ground near the other end of the corral as Daisy walked past them. Each pole already had one colored ring on it, red, blue or yellow, and Donny had to slide the colored rings he picked up onto the matching pole. The activity of guiding the horse and positioning the rings was designed to make him focus on interrelated work tasks while still having a good time.

He was doing more of the latter than the former, though, as the reins lay ineffectively against Daisy's neck.

"Donny, hey, Donny," Jessica called to get his attention. "Pull the reins to the right to turn Daisy around the pole. That's it. Now bring her close enough so you can reach the next one. Good!"

Donny leaned too far over to Claire's side to lasso the pole with his ring, and Claire steadied him with a hand at his waist. She could feel Brittany tugging gently on his safety belt on the other side.

"Sit up straight," Jessica said, "and try to stay in the center of the saddle." As Donny followed her directions, she said, "Good job. Now turn Daisy back to the T to get the next ring."

She kept up a steady monologue of directions and positive reinforcement as Donny went through his paces. The patter constantly redirected his attention from the distracting sensations he was experiencing back to his job.

Finally he finished and Claire joined Brittany and Jessica in clapping and cheering Donny's success. By then, his session's time was up, so they helped him dismount and returned him to his waiting mother. While Jessica talked to the mother about her son's progress, Claire and Brittany walked Daisy back to the barn.

After they got inside and slipped the bandanas off their faces, Claire figured it was a good time to talk to Brittany about her love life.

"Even with the dust, that was fun," she said. "I had a good time on the trail ride Wednesday, too. Until we had that run-in with Peak View Stables at Giant Footprints, that is."

"I think Hank handled it as well as he could." Brittany held Daisy's stall gate open so Claire could lead the horse in.

"Yeah, and I don't blame their trail guide. He had his hands full with antsy clients and horses. Couldn't help but notice how handsome he is." Claire smiled at Brittany. "And I think you noticed, too."

A blush stole up her neck. "We've dated some."

"I figured as much, given his comment about his competition being gone after Kyle died. Have you known him long?"

Brittany stepped to Daisy's head and started unfastening her bridle. "We took an animal husbandry class together at Pikes Peak Community College last fall."

Claire tugged on Daisy's saddle strap to loosen it. "Was Vince jealous of Kyle?"

"I didn't meet Kyle until we both started working here. For a while, they didn't know about each other. Then when Kyle and I were at the movies a few weeks ago, I saw Vince in line with a group of wranglers from Peak View. I ducked behind a wall, but he must have seen me, because he brought it up the next time we saw each other."

"I bet he was steamed."

Brittany shrugged and slid Daisy's bridle over her ears. "I guess so, but since we'd just started dating and weren't exclusive or anything, he couldn't do much about it. He asked me to stop seeing other guys then, but I said I wasn't ready."

"Good idea. It takes a while to get to know a guy well, and you're young and have lots of time." Claire had unfastened the saddle strap and grunted while trying to lift the saddle.

"I'll get that." Brittany came around to slide the saddle off of Daisy's back. She hung it on the gate rail then turned to Claire. "You know, it's nice to be able to talk to you about this. My mom would get all negative and tell me I shouldn't have dated either of them."

That made Claire wince a little inside. If her daughter, Judy, had been in the same situation a few years ago, she might have acted the same way. No need to tell Brittany that, though. "It sounds to me like you've been pretty mature about the situation."

"Yeah, I didn't want there to be any secrets, so I told Kyle about Vince, too. Figured I didn't want to make him mad either."

Claire slid the saddle blanket off Daisy's back, shook the dust out, then hung it on the side of the stall. "And how did Kyle take it?"

Brittany smiled shyly. "Pretty much the same way. Asked me to stop seeing Vince."

Laying a hand on her hip, Claire gave Brittany a teasing wink. "Lucky you, having two guys fight over you."

"It's not like I'm a flirt or anything," Brittany said defensively.

Claire waved her hand. "I'm just kidding. What attracted you to each of them?"

"Well, along with being a wrangler, Vince is practicing to compete in rodeos. He hunts for elk every fall, and he took me fishing a couple of weeks ago. I like how confident he is, especially in the wild."

"Sounds like a real hunk." Claire picked up a brush and began brushing Daisy with it.

Brittany nodded and began brushing Daisy's other side. "And Kyle was a lot of fun, cracking jokes and being real friendly with everyone. I loved hanging with him. I liked how he always could make me laugh." She bit her lip. "I miss him."

"I'm sure lots of people do. He seemed very nice. Still, it's probably a good thing Vince and Kyle didn't work together. Speaking of which, I hadn't realized that Kyle got Pedro his job here. Did you know that?"

Brittany's hand stilled, then she vigorously started brushing Daisy again. "Yes."

Claire peered at Brittany. "You say that like you're not happy about it."

"Oh, I'm happy Pedro got the job. He's nice, and I like working with him—unlike Gil."

"So what's wrong?"

With a sigh, Brittany said, "It doesn't matter any more what I say about Kyle, but I don't want to get Pedro in trouble. That's why I didn't say anything to the police."

Claire stopped brushing. "Kyle was murdered, Brittany. If you know anything that might help the police find out who did it, you should tell them."

Dropping her hands to her sides, Brittany pursed her lips and dug the toe of her boot into the straw lining the stall floor.

Claire tried another tack. "If Pedro is involved in something that got Kyle killed, he could be in danger, too."

Brittany's head jerked up, and she automatically began brushing Daisy again. "Oh, no, it's nothing like that. The man Kyle worked for liked him and his results. He never would have hurt him—or Pedro."

Claire resumed brushing her side of the horse, too. "Maybe you should tell me exactly what's going on, who Kyle worked for and what he was doing. Then I can help you figure out what to tell the police."

"But I can't. You're Charley's sister. You'll tell him, then he'll fire Pedro."

"I think I already have a pretty good idea what you're talking about," Claire said. "Pedro is an illegal immigrant, isn't he?"

"Shit. I shouldn't have said anything." Brittany squinted her eyes shut as if she was in pain.

"Yes, Charley's my brother, Brittany, and if I find out anything that threatens him or his business, I've got to tell him."

"And if Charley knows Pedro's illegal, he has to fire him." Brittany's voice took on a worried whine. "If he doesn't, then he's in trouble."

Claire thought for a moment. "Okay, here's what I can do. Charley knows that if ICE asks to see his records, he can request three days to get them in order. And he will. I won't tell him about Pedro until or unless that happens. So spill."

Brittany looked around the barn. Claire did, too, but she knew they weren't within earshot of anyone else. Jorge and the farrier were in the back treatment area working on a horse. Gil and Hank were out on a trail ride, Charley was in the trailer, and Jessica was still outside with Donny and his mother.

"No one can hear us." Claire put down her brush, picked up a mane comb and started combing Daisy's mane.

While doing the same, Brittany exhaled. "Okay, here's the thing. Kyle wasn't bringing in illegal immigrants, but he was helping them once they got here. There's this guy in town named Oscar Vargas who brings in people from Mexico and gets them fake ID's. Kyle found jobs for those who can work with horses."

"And I suppose this guy Vargas paid Kyle for every job he found."

"Yes, but Kyle didn't do it for the money. He said he did it to help people who are really poor and can't find work in Mexico."

"Like Pedro."

Brittany nodded. "Like Pedro. And Pedro has to give part of every paycheck to Vargas until he's paid off the fee to get him in the U.S. So, Vargas has no reason to hurt him. He knows Pedro will keep quiet, and he wouldn't want to stop his payments."

"And Vargas was happy with Kyle's work?"

"Sure. Just a couple days before he was … killed, Kyle told me he'd recommended two people for jobs at a stable in Monument, and they were hired. So Vargas was going to give him a bonus. Kyle said he'd use the money to take me to Cheyenne Frontier Days next month."

Claire thought for a moment. "So far, I don't see a motive for murder here. But where there's a secret, especially one this big, there's the possibility of that secret getting out, and of someone getting mad as a result. Maybe Vargas thought Kyle had ratted on him to the police."

"Kyle wouldn't have done that," Brittany said. "He swore me to secrecy before he told me. And he only told me because I asked where he got the money for a trip to Wyoming. I knew the money came from somewhere fishy. Now I wish I hadn't pushed him to tell me!"

"And because of your promise to Kyle, and to protect Pedro, you haven't said anything to the police."

Brittany nodded, her eyes wide. "If I do, then I'll be the rat, and Vargas might come after me." She gave a little shudder and rubbed her arms.

Claire came around Daisy and put an arm around Brittany's shoulders. "Have you ever met this guy?"

"No."

"Does he know who you are? That you were seeing Kyle?"

"I don't know."

"How about this for a plan? I'll tell Detective Wilson what you told me about Kyle arranging for the two people to get jobs in Monument, but I won't say anything about Pedro. If he asks me where I got the information, I'll say I can't tell him. I'll also ask him not to let anyone know where he heard it. Then no one will make a connection to you and you'll be safe."

"I guess that would be okay."

"Good. Now, Daisy here has been awfully patient with us. Let's finish up."

The two of them finished grooming Daisy, who had stood chewing on oats while they talked, enjoying the lengthy brushing. Then they stepped out of her stall, carrying their gear.

While they were putting things away, Jorge came out of Gunpowder's stall. He led the horse back to where the farrier was waiting after finishing her work on the other horse. He looked at Daisy, then at Gunpowder as if he had an idea.

"Brittany, could you bring Daisy to the treatment area?" he asked. "Gunpowder likes her, and she might help calm him down while *Señora* Dietz works on him. I don't want him to kick her."

"Sure," Brittany said.

"Could you use another set of hands?" Claire asked.

"*Sí*, probably." He waved for the two of them to follow him.

They went back and got Daisy. Once they reached the treatment area, Jorge introduced them to Louise Dietz, the farrier. She was a tall woman, almost six feet, Claire guessed. She looked to be in her thirties with short-cropped reddish-brown hair and well-defined biceps. She wore a teal T-shirt, jeans, work boots, and a pair of well-worn, stained leather chaps. She smelled of leather, too, and steel and horseflesh. But her aroma wasn't unpleasant, just earthy, as the woman herself seemed to be.

Louise held up her filthy hands. "I'd offer to shake, but you don't want to touch these, even if you've been working around horses." She had no compulsion about reaching up to rub Gunpowder's nose while Jorge tied him off, though. "So, big fella, I hear you've had a traumatic week."

"That's why I brought these two and Daisy to help," Jorge said. "Daisy's company should help keep him calm, and I have some carrots in my pocket, too."

Brittany positioned Daisy so she was nose-to-nose with Gunpowder and tied her up. The two horses nuzzled each other.

"Gunpowder should let you work on his front hooves just fine," Jorge said to Louise, "but he's still twitchy around the back end.

Once you are ready to do those shoes, I'll have Brittany and Claire help hold him still. I don't want him to hurt you."

"And I don't want to hurt him, either." Louise moved her knee-high tool cart on wheels near Gunpowder. "If he moves too much while I'm nailing the shoe on, I could quick him."

"What's that mean?" Claire asked.

"Driving the nail into the sensitive part of the hoof," Louise said. "Same as if you cut your toenail in the pink part instead of the white, then tried walking on your tippy toes."

"Ouch."

"That's what the horses say—in their own way." The farrier rubbed her hands together. "Let's get started. Hopefully, Gunpowder will be soothed by the familiar rhythm of his pedicure, and we won't have any problems."

Louise ran her hands down Gunpowder's chest and front left leg, checking for any sensitivity or twitching. Seemingly satisfied with his response, she moved her tools within reach. She stood with her back to Gunpowder's head and gently lifted his hoof. She snugged his lower leg between her thighs and above her bent knees so she had access to the bottom of the hoof.

"I've never seen a horse shoed before," Claire said. "Do you mind explaining the process?"

"Not at all." Louise picked up a tool. "These are pincers, to remove the old shoe." After some tugging to loosen the nails, she removed the worn-down horseshoe, then picked up another tool. "Now I'm going to trim the bottom of his hoof with this pick. When horses wear shoes, their hooves don't wear down like they do in the wild, so we need to trim them."

As she worked, she said, "Nice and clean and healthy, Jorge, as usual." She looked at Claire. "Jorge here takes good care of Charley's horses."

Jorge smiled at the compliment, but he continued watching Gunpowder and rhythmically stroking him.

After cleaning the hoof, Louise picked up another tool. "After I trim the hoof wall with these nippers, I'll file it down so it will be ready for a new shoe." She made quick work of that, then pulled a steel horseshoe out of a sack and held it up to Gunpowder's hoof. "Almost perfect."

Louise went over to an anvil and banged on the horseshoe. She sized it up against Gunpowder's hoof and banged on it again. She stuck a half dozen nails in her mouth and nestled Gunpowder's hoof between her thighs. After hammering in the nails, she turned around so she had access to the top of the hoof.

Then she picked up her file. "I'll just file these nails off so they're smooth, and we're done."

She went through the same motions on Gunpowder's other front hoof with no problems. But when she ran her hands down his back flank and approached his left knee, his ears went back, and he stepped away.

She stopped and looked at Jorge. "Yep, still kinda twitchy there."

Jorge nodded. "Brittany and Claire, could you stand on either side of Gunpowder's head? You need to keep him still up there while I hold him back here." He handed Brittany his baggie of mini carrots.

While they were getting into position, Louise pulled out a short metal stand with a hoof-shaped sling on the top. "This is a hoof jack," she explained to Claire. "I find some horses like resting their hoof on it better than just having it between my thighs, especially the rear hooves where they can't see what's going on. It doesn't move like I do."

Jorge pushed Gunpowder's right rear up against the wooden wall of the treatment area. He positioned himself to lean against the horse with one hand on Gunpowder's back and the other against his left flank. Gunpowder's ears went flat, and he turned his head to eye Jorge.

"Brittany," Jorge said, "give him one of those carrots."

Brittany clicked her tongue to get Gunpowder's attention. She held a mini carrot on her palm under his mouth. He gobbled it up greedily. His ears went forward as he sniffed around for more.

"Try now," Jorge said to Louise.

She ran her hands down Gunpowder's left leg again. The horse twitched and shuffled. But when he tried to move and couldn't, he seemed confused.

"Another carrot," Jorge said. He murmured soothing words to Gunpowder and steadied the horse with his hands.

The second carrot, Daisy's presence, and the soothing hands and words of the familiar people around him finally settled Gunpowder. Louise was able to slowly lift his left leg and lay it on the hoof jack. She still had his leg between her thighs and her shoulders up against his thigh to help hold him in place.

"This one's not as clean." She flicked some mud clods off the bottom of his hoof with her pick.

"He hasn't let us get to it," Jorge replied. "I've been working on getting him calmed down first."

Louise started pulling on the old horseshoe with her pincers. "Hmm, something's stuck on this nail." She grabbed her pick and scratched at the top of the nail until something came free.

"What is it?" Claire asked.

Louise peered at it. "Looks like a little piece of cloth. Must have gotten snagged on the nail."

Claire made sure Brittany had a good hold on Gunpowder's head, then she let go and came closer. "What color is it?"

"It's covered with mud, so it's hard to tell." The farrier raised an eyebrow at her. "Why the heck does the color matter?"

"Just humor me." Claire took a pair of pliers off of Louise's tool cart. "May I?"

"Be my guest."

Claire gently pulled the scrap of cloth off the hoof pick. She took the pick from Louise. Using the pick and pliers, Claire smoothed the cloth out on a flat surface on the tool cart and scraped some mud off.

She and Louise peered at it.

"I see yellow and red," Louise said.

"And maybe black," Claire said, "if this isn't just a mud-stain. Looks like a checked pattern."

"Probably from a shirt," Louise said.

Gunpowder shook his head and strained to look back. Brittany struggled to hold his head in place without Claire. She frowned at Claire. "Why is that scrap more important than helping me with Gunpowder?"

Claire stood and looked at Jorge. "Kyle was wearing a blue-checked shirt when he was killed, right?"

He nodded.

"So this isn't from him."

Brittany inhaled sharply.

"This could be evidence." Claire looked at the mud clods Louise had flicked onto the stable floor. "And those could be, too. We need to call Detective Wilson."

EIGHT:
AN ENVIOUS RIVAL

CLAIRE GOT OUT OF Jessica's beat-up, but trusty, eight-year-old blue Honda CR-V. She reached into the back seat and grabbed a stack of rubber-banded trifold fliers about her sister-in-law's hippotherapy nonprofit. She handed the stack to Jessica, who was pulling large brochures out of her side of the back seat. Claire took out another stack of fliers for herself. She stood up too quickly and felt a flush of heat all over her body.

It was mid-morning on Monday and the bright June sun was already baking the asphalt of the parking lot. But that wasn't what caused her to flush. She flapped her golf-shirt to create a breeze on her damp chest.

"Whew, hot flash," she said to Jessica.

"Don't you just hate those?" Jessica asked with a laugh. "Want some water?"

"No, it'll be over soon." Claire shouldered her purse. "We ready?"

"I guess so." Jessica pushed her key fob to lock the car, then started toward the door of the Colorado Springs Childhood Services Center. "I really appreciate you helping me pass out these fliers. Don't you have work to do for your own company?"

"Just two deliveries today, and I'll take care of them after we're done. Roger left on a business trip yesterday, so I kept myself busy last night constructing three gift baskets. That was much better than sitting around moping because I was lonely."

Jessica turned toward Claire. "What's Roger doing?"

"Another independent financial audit, this time for a manufactured housing company in South Dakota."

"Seems like he's doing more and more of those. Could it turn into full-time work?"

"He does about one or two a month. He really doesn't want to do more than that. It's enough work to keep him stimulated, as he calls it. After losing his high-stress CFO job in February, he decided he'd ease into retirement."

"Well, since you're on your own, do you want to have dinner with Charley and me tonight?"

"No, don't worry about me. I'm fine. I've got the fixings for a lovely strawberry spinach salad in the fridge. I'll have that and a glass of white wine, then snuggle up with a good murder mystery. But thanks for asking."

Jessica put a hand on the center's glass-fronted door. "Well, okay, if you're sure, but the invitation is open for any night he's gone and you want some company."

"I appreciate it."

They entered a waiting room furnished with banks of plastic chairs hooked together. In one corner stood a child-sized table with crayons and coloring books. A crate of brightly colored plastic toys sat next to it. Two kids rolled cars on the floor next to the crate, making revving noises with wet lips, while a third colored. Their moms chatted a couple of seats away, and a few other people were scattered around the room.

A young woman sitting behind the reception desk looked up when Jessica and Claire approached.

"Hello," Jessica said. "I'm Jessica Gardner. I'd like to speak to the director for a moment, please."

"Do you have an appointment?" the receptionist asked. "She's very busy."

"No, but Mrs. Franklin knows I planned to stop by this morning. We talked on the phone a few days ago."

The receptionist nodded and looked at the wall clock. "She'll be done with a client in ten minutes. I'll let her know you're here. Would you like to take a seat?"

"Sure."

Claire sat next to a woman who was leaning over to dab some drool off the chin of a girl in her early teens sitting in a wheelchair. She had what looked to be cerebral palsy from her stiff, contracted limbs and the uncontrolled loll of her head.

Jessica sat next to Claire and leaned forward to smile at the woman. "Hello, my name is Jessica and this is my sister-in-law, Claire."

"Hi, I'm Tina, and my daughter's name is Lily."

Claire nodded and smiled at them both, and Jessica said, "Hello, Lily."

Tina studied the fliers in Claire's hands. "What's hippotherapy?"

"It's the use of horses in various kinds of therapy, such as physical or occupational," Jessica answered. "I'm a licensed occupational therapist, and I run a hippotherapy nonprofit. We're here to leave some of these fliers at the center."

"May I have one?" Tina asked.

"I guess so. Hopefully Mrs. Franklin won't mind." Jessica handed her one. "Your daughter has spastic cerebral palsy, right?"

"Yes, from birth," the mother replied with a sigh. "And it just seems to slowly get worse."

"Hippotheraphy can help with muscle control and flexibility," Jessica said. "Such as Lily's scissored legs here. I've had CP clients start a session with their knees pulled up almost to their chest and end it with them hanging loose on either side of the horse." She smiled at Lily. "Would you like to try riding a horse, Lily?"

Lily's mouth opened into a grimaced approximation of a smile, and she jerked her head forward in a nod.

Tina looked at the brochure in her hand then at Jessica. "But how safe is it? How would Lily stay on a horse?"

"Oh, I would sit in the saddle right behind Lily and hold her in place, help her guide the horse with her hands. So, it's perfectly safe. Why don't you take that brochure with you to her next doctor's appointment and ask her doctor about it?"

"Okay, I'll do that."

Claire noticed that Lily's gaze followed her mother's actions as Tina stuffed the flier in her purse. Lily was definitely interested and hopefully could convey that to her mother.

At that point, the receptionist said, "Mrs. Gardner, the director is coming out now to talk to you."

"Nice to meet you both," Claire said to Tina and Lily as she stood with Jessica.

Jessica gently took Lily's hand. "I hope to see you soon, Lily."

A short round woman bustled out of the door behind the receptionist. Claire would have said the woman looked like Tweedledee or his brother Tweedledum if she were a man. The woman looked around. "Jessica Gardner?"

"That's me." Jessica held out her hand. "Nice to meet you in person, Mrs. Franklin."

"Oh, call me Amy, please." The woman shook her hand.

After introducing Claire, Jessica said to Amy, "As we discussed on the phone, I'd like to display my brochures in your waiting room. I even have this display case to put them in." She held up a clear plastic container sized to hold about fifty of the trifold fliers and dropped some fliers into it.

Amy nodded. "That's fine with me."

"And this is a free invitation to our fundraiser event this coming Saturday. We'll have drinks and desserts at the Marriott, and a silent auction. My sister-in-law here is even donating one of her spectacular gift baskets to the auction."

"Actually two," Claire said, eliciting a look of pleased surprise from Jessica. "One with a horseback riding theme for the riders who come, and one with a family game night theme for the non-riders."

Amy looked up from the invitation. "Sounds like fun. Can I bring my husband?"

"Sure! And, I'd like to make one more request," Jessica continued. "If it's okay with you, I'd like to give all of the service providers who work for you this more detailed packet. It explains the benefits of hippotherapy for different types of childhood disabilities. And I'd like to give you some more of the fliers for them to keep in their offices. That way, if the providers see a particular client that they think would benefit from hippotherapy, they could hand them one of our fliers."

Amy pursed her lips. "I'll have to think about that. While we like to let our clients know about all of the available services in the area, I don't like to recommend any particular one over another."

"There's only one other hippotherapy nonprofit in the area that I know of," Jessica said, "and I'm sure the need is greater than the two of us can handle. I would have no problem with you recommending both. The other one is run by Nancy Schwartz." She turned to Claire. "Brittany's mother."

Claire raised her eyebrows in surprise. She was about to ask why Brittany was volunteering for Jessica rather than her own mother when a woman walked in the glass doors. Of medium height, she was middle-aged with gray-white streaks in her blond hair.

The woman's mouth narrowed into a thin line when she saw Jessica. "So you beat me here."

After a moment's hesitation, Jessica said brightly, "Hello, Nancy," then turned to Amy Franklin. "This is the woman I mentioned, Nancy Schwartz, who runs the other hippotherapy nonprofit in the area."

Speak of the devil. Claire wondered at the timing of Nancy's visit. Had she somehow found out about Jessica's planned visit and decided to time hers accordingly?

While Nancy and Amy shook hands and exchanged how-dos, Claire noted the resemblance between Nancy's features and her daughter Brittany's, although Nancy carried about twenty-five more pounds on her frame.

Nancy handed Amy a stack of business cards. "As I promised yesterday, here are some more cards for my nonprofit. I hope Jessica hasn't been saying unkind things about me," she said with an unnatural laugh.

"Of course not," Amy replied. "In fact, her planned visit is why I called you to ask for more cards. I thought I should have information about both of your nonprofits available to our clients."

Nancy eyed the fliers and packets in Jessica's hands. She pulled one of Jessica's fliers out of the plastic holder. "I didn't bring fancy paperwork like she did, but I have fliers, too."

The way she said it made Claire doubt that she really did, and that she had planned to just leave the business cards. But Claire was sure Nancy would print up some fliers right away—after studying Jessica's, that is.

A look of annoyance passed over Jessica's face, but she quickly masked it with a brilliant smile that she focused on Amy. "So, problem solved. Your providers could pass out both fliers to clients they think would benefit from hippotherapy."

"I guess that would be fair," Amy said.

"How many information packets would you like?"

"Six should do it."

When Jessica passed the packets to Amy, Nancy eyed them, like she wished she could take one of those, too. "How sweet of you to promote hippotherapy for both of us, Jessica," she said with a voice that dripped honey. "Especially since you have so much to deal with right now. I heard about the Mendozas' lawsuit." She tsked.

113

"What lawsuit?" Amy asked.

Nancy turned to Amy. "A man was killed by a horse at her stable, and his family is suing them."

Amy's eyes widened. "Oh, my."

"That man was not killed by a horse," Claire said quickly. "He was murdered by a person."

"Oh my," After echoing Amy, Nancy cocked an eyebrow at her, then peered at Jessica. "Aren't you scared that you may have a killer working for you?"

"Now wait just a God damn minute," Jessica said hotly. "There's no proof that any of our staff killed Kyle. And none of this has anything to do with the quality and safety of the hippotherapy we provide."

"Then why did the Mendozas pull their other son out of your program?" Nancy shot back.

"It was an emotional response," Jessica said, "as was the lawsuit. I'm sure they'll drop the suit and be back once they find out what really happened."

Claire sure hoped so. But in the meantime, Amy had stiffened and backed away. She looked nervously at the people in her waiting room, who were watching the scene in the lobby with fascination.

Thrusting the packets at Jessica, Amy said, "I'm going to have to ask you all to leave. Now. You're upsetting my clients and I refuse to get in the middle of this."

Jessica's shoulders sagged. "But—"

Amy held up her hands, palms out. "You can both set up an appointment with me in two weeks and make your pitches. I'll decide what I'm going to do then. And I don't want either of you putting fliers in our waiting room until after I say you can." She turned on her heel and beat a hasty retreat.

"Well, Nancy," Jessica said bitterly, "you just lost a referral source for both of us."

"Not for me," Nancy replied with a triumphant smile. "I'll be back in two weeks. We'll see if you're still in business by then." She, too, turned on her heel and sailed out of the glass entrance doors.

"What is with that woman?" Claire asked, hands on her hips.

"She's upset about me moving here and competing with her, though I keep telling her there are plenty of potential clients for the two of us," Jessica replied with a sigh. "And Brittany volunteering to work with me just made it worse. Some of the bitterness between those two has rubbed off on me, I guess. You know, typical mother-daughter stuff."

"Oh, I know." Claire looked back toward the waiting room and saw Tina slipping Jessica's flier out of her purse and dropping it into a trash can. She looped her arm in Jessica's and pulled her toward the door so she wouldn't see. "Let's get out of here."

This damn murder was tainting not only Charley's trail-riding business, but also Jessica's nonprofit. The sooner the killer was discovered and put in jail, the better. Claire decided that a visit to Detective Wilson was called for. But in the meantime...

Claire opened the center's front door. "C'mon, sis, I'll treat you to an iced caramel latte while we figure out your next move."

———

After completing her basket deliveries, Claire drove to see Detective Wilson. Knowing she would need to soften him up first, she rehearsed her opening while following a policeman into the detectives' pen at the Gold Hill police station in downtown Colorado Springs. She glanced around to see if she recognized any of the people she had embarrassed herself in front of during her last visit.

A few detectives sat at some of the dozen desks in the large room but none raised their heads to look at her. They were busy typing on computer keyboards, reading case files or talking on telephones. Claire breathed a sigh of relief, then wrinkled her nose. Someone had recently burned a bag of microwave popcorn and the acrid odor lingered in the large room.

When she reached Detective Wilson's desk, he rose and shook her hand, though he didn't smile.

"Thanks for agreeing to meet with me," Claire said as she sat in his visitor's chair. "Kyle's murder is really hurting both Charley's business and Jessica's hippotherapy nonprofit. I know you're working hard on the case and doing everything you can, but I found out a few things that I thought might be helpful." When Wilson opened his mouth to speak, she held out a hand. "And no, I didn't endanger myself by snooping around."

He shot her a skeptical look then opened his notebook. "Okay, shoot."

"First is information about the Schwartzes, Brittany and her mother, Nancy. While volunteering with Brittany, I brought up her relationship with Vince Donahue." She told Wilson about his jealous reaction to Brittany dating Kyle, ending with, "That sounds like a legitimate motive for murder to me."

Wilson gave a shrug. "Could be. Depends on how enamored he was with Miss Schwartz and if he's got a violent personality. And in addition to motive, we need means and opportunity."

"So are you going to interview him to find that out?"

He scowled at her. "Are you trying to tell me how to do my job?"

Claire realized she had pushed too hard and backpedaled. "Sorry. I got carried away and shouldn't have said that. But there's something else you need to know. Jessica and I had a run-in with Brittany's mother this morning."

She told Wilson about the confrontation. "Do you think Nancy Schwartz could be jealous enough of Jessica's competing nonprofit, and that her daughter was working for Jessica, that she killed Kyle Mendoza to give Jessica's work a bad name?"

"That's pretty far-fetched." Wilson tapped his pen on the page he had filled with scribbled notes. "I'd suspect her more if she had something against Mendoza personally, some reason she didn't want him seeing her daughter, for instance. Anything else?"

Claire had to trust that he would interview Nancy Schwartz, too. She shifted in her seat. This next bit would be tricky. "On Friday, you asked Charley about the phone numbers from Mexico in Kyle's cell phone. I found out something about those, but I promised not to tell you who gave me the information." She told him about Oscar Vargas and his smuggling gang and Kyle arranging for jobs for two illegal immigrants at the Monument stable.

Wilson leaned back in his chair and stared at her. "And you won't tell me your source. You know, even though you're telling me this, I've got to suspect that since Mendoza worked for your brother, he's involved somehow."

"No, I know for a fact that he isn't," Claire said firmly. "After you left Friday, I asked Charley if he hired illegals. He was upset I asked. He knows the law and checks the documentation of all his hires. He'd never knowingly hire an illegal immigrant."

"And I know for a fact that you're his sister," Wilson shot back. "And you probably would try to protect him if he's doing something illegal."

Claire crossed her arms. "That's not what's going on here. Why would I tell you this if Charley was involved in any way? In fact, I don't want Charley to know I'm telling you this."

Wilson peered at her then exhaled. "Doesn't matter anyway. I'll have to notify ICE about this Oscar Vargas. They'll start an investigation, and I'm sure they'll include Gardner's Stables, since Kyle Mendoza worked there. Better tell Charley to get his paperwork in order."

"There's no need to." Claire uncrossed her arms and leaned forward. "It's already in order." But contrary to her show of bravado, she still planned to warn Charley.

"These Mexican smugglers can be ruthless," Wilson added. "Especially if their own necks are in danger. Of all the things you've told me today, this is the most useful. If Mendoza crossed Vargas in some way, then I can see Vargas killing him or arranging for him to be killed, then covering it up by making it look like an accident."

"What about the hammer that came out of the manure dumpster? Did you get any fingerprints off of it?"

Wilson shook his head. "Too bad, too. I'd love to be able to match one to Vargas or someone in his gang. Maybe ICE has something on him or can come up with something, so we can bring him in for questioning."

"That scrap of cloth the farrier found on Gunpowder's hoof might belong to someone in Vargas's gang," Claire said hopefully, "It could point to Kyle's killer, especially if there's any DNA on it."

"It's still in the queue for testing."

"Did you match it to anyone's clothing at the stable?"

"Nope, or at least not anything that's in anyone's closet. Of course, it could have nothing to do with Mendoza's murder. It could have been picked up off the ground some other time."

"Given Jorge's diligence in cleaning the horses' hooves, I kind of doubt that."

The two of them settled into an uneasy silence until Claire asked, "Who do you think did it?"

Wilson gave her an enigmatic smile while closing his notebook. "Why would I tell you?"

"Because I'm telling you things!" Claire said indignantly. "I'm trying to be helpful."

"And I appreciate that," he said. "But this is a police investigation, and we don't share everything with civilians. I will tell you that I try to keep an open mind until the facts and evidence point me in some definite direction."

"It doesn't sound like you're very close to arresting someone, and every day this case drags on is another nail in the coffin for Charley's business." Claire's mind raced. What else could she find out that would help Wilson solve the case?

"I know you," he said forcefully, breaking her out of her reverie. "You're already making plans to do more snooping on your own. Well, don't. Especially around Oscar Vargas. I don't want another murder case on my hands."

"I understand." Claire rose from her chair and said goodbye.

As she walked to her car, she made a decision. She would have to leave finding out about Vargas's immigrant smuggling operation to ICE. But with Roger out of town, nothing was preventing her from spending as much time as possible at Charley's stable.

NINE:
SECRETS

"SCREW THIS! WHO TIED this anyway?" Gil's shout came from a stall somewhere in the middle of the barn right after Claire had walked inside.

At the sound of the angry words, Claire paused in her search for the special saddle Jorge had fashioned for Jessica's next hippotherapy client. Jessica had told her it was hanging in the back tack room, but Claire didn't want to get into the middle of one of Gil's tirades.

He stepped out of the stall, reddened eyes blazing and hands on his hips. Claire instinctively ducked behind the nearest stall wall, though she could still peek above it.

"Pedro!" Gil hollered.

The young Mexican came out of a stall in the rear of the barn.

When Gil saw him, he waved Pedro over. "Did you cinch this saddle on Rifle this morning?"

Pedro looked in the stall. "No. Hank do it."

Claire had seen Hank and Charley leave moments before on the afternoon trail ride. Both the small number of clients, with only six riders on the trip, and the deep furrows in Charley's forehead had worried her.

"That dickhead," Gil shouted. "How's he expect anyone to undo a knot this tight?"

"I do it." Pedro moved inside the stall and began working on the black horse's saddle.

Gil looked around, then stepped out of Pedro's line of sight. He took a hasty swig from a flask he pulled out of his hip pocket. It took two tries for him to return the flask to his pocket. Claire suspected that his booze-impaired fumble fingers, instead of the tightness of the knot, was the cause of Gil's problem with the saddle cinch.

Sure enough, Pedro emerged from the stall soon after Gil had wiped his lips with his sleeve. Pedro hefted the saddle in his arms as if showing it off. "Knot no *problemo por* me," he said with a grin.

"No *problemo*, no *problemo*," Gil mimicked. "Speak English, you wetback. And don't be taking that cocky attitude with me. I know where you came from. With one word from me, ICE will toss your ass on a bus right back there." He shoved Pedro hard on the shoulder.

The push sent Pedro stumbling backward down the aisle until he tripped. He landed on his butt in a pile of manure- and urine-soaked straw that one of them must have just mucked out of a stall.

Gil guffawed. "Right where you belong."

Pedro's face reddened and his shoulders tensed. The young man had obviously reached his limit, and he wasn't going to take any more abuse without a fight. He flung the saddle aside, scrabbled to his feet, and charged at Gil with his head lowered like a raging bull.

His head hit Gil's stomach, expelling Gil's air with a loud "Oof."

The two of them went sprawling. Gil landed flat on his back with Pedro on top.

Pedro started swinging furious body blows at Gil's midsection.

Gil rolled back and forth. He elbowed Pedro in the face then slammed a knee into his groin.

Pedro fell off Gil, moaning and holding his crotch.

Gil back-crabbed away, then stood. He stuffed his hand into his front pants pocket. He drew out a long buck knife and flipped it open.

Pedro's eyes popped wide.

Claire gasped.

Focused on his prey, Gil didn't seem to hear Claire. An evil grin split his sour face. He stepped toward Pedro. "I'm gonna cut you, you roach."

"Stop!" Pedro held out a palm. "I no fight you no more."

Gil straightened. He jiggled the knife in his hand. "You need to show some respect for your betters, boy."

Just as Claire was debating whether showing herself would stop the fight or escalate it, Jorge walked in the barn. Leading a sandy-colored mare by the bridle, he passed Claire without seeing her. He stopped and took in the tableau before him. "What the hell is going on here?"

Gil folded his knife and slipped it back into his pants pocket. "Just teaching this wetback some manners."

Greatly relieved, Claire thanked God that Gil still had some respect for Charley's second in command.

"Back off," Jorge said. "He's not a wetback."

"The hell he ain't," Gil said. "I know about Vargas's operation, and Kyle's hand in it. I have half a mind to go to ICE and shut the whole fucking thing down. Send Pedro and all his friends packing across the border."

Pedro struggled to his feet. He picked up the saddle he had dropped. "I clean this and unsaddle Rifle." He backed away a few steps and hesitated, as if waiting to see if Gil was mollified.

His groveling broke Claire's heart.

"God damn right you will," Gil pointed a shaky finger at Pedro then harrumphed at Jorge. "I need a smoke." He stumbled past Jorge and out of the barn.

Jorge stepped toward Pedro. "Unsaddling Rifle was Gil's chore. You don't need to do it for him."

"*Sí*, I do," Pedro said. "I need this job. *Mi mamá y hermanas* cannot live without *el dinero* I send them."

"I should tell Charley about Gil," Jorge said. "He doesn't do half the work he's supposed to around here because he's too drunk. Charley should fire him."

"No! Then Gil will tell him what he knows and Charley will fire me."

Jorge exhaled and looked down, shaking his head. "This can't continue."

Claire agreed.

When Jorge and Pedro moved together toward the back of the barn, she took the opportunity to slip out the door, checking for Gil first. He wasn't in sight. She stood outside the barn for a few moments, sucking in deep breaths to calm herself, then walked back in.

"Jorge," she yelled in a cheerful tone. "Jessica sent me for that special saddle you made—the one with a large round grip for two hands on the front instead of a saddle horn. Do you know where it is?"

———

Throughout the afternoon hippotherapy session, Claire debated whether or not she should tell Charley about the confrontation she had witnessed. She knew he would be touchy about her interfering in the running of his business. But Charley really needed to know that Gil had a drinking problem. And if he already knew that, he needed to know that the drinking problem was causing other problems. Regardless of Gil's capability with horses, he was dangerous.

On the other hand, she knew that if Charley found out Pedro was illegal, he would have no choice but to fire him. And as Pedro said, he was supporting his mother and sisters with his earnings. Claire didn't want to be responsible for taking food money away from a whole family, no matter where they lived.

The conundrum kept her mind so occupied that she almost let one little girl slide out of the saddle toward the end of the day. A quick tug on the girl's harness by Brittany saved the girl from taking a spill.

Brittany peered at Claire as they put Blossom, who was almost as gentle as Daisy, back in her stall. "You okay, Claire? You seem spaced out."

"Sorry, Brittany, if I've been inattentive. I am worried about something, but it doesn't concern you."

Brittany exhaled. "That's good. I was afraid you had some kind of issue with me."

Claire waved her horse brush in the air. "Oh, it's nothing like that. We make a great team, don't you think?"

Brittany smiled and nodded as she brushed down Blossom's other side. "Yeah, sure. And can I ask you a favor? Jessica told me you live in Coyote Hills, and our house is in Fox Glen, pretty close to there. Do you mind giving me a ride home? My mom's got the car, and she's tied up in a meeting."

"I don't mind." Claire gave Blossom a pat. "But I need to talk to Charley first. If you finish up Blossom here while I do, then you won't have to wait for me."

Brittany gave her a thumbs-up. "It's a deal."

Claire walked over to the trailer and stuck her head in the back office, where Charley was studying some paperwork. "Can we talk?"

He looked up. "You checking up on me? Your friend Dave contacted the Director of Parks and Rec and told them we expect them to abide by the contract."

"No, I'm not checking up on you," Claire said, wondering at Charley's touchiness. "But I'm glad Dave could help."

"Yeah, he's willing to help, to the tune of a few hundred dollars so far. So far!" Charley tossed the papers on his cluttered desk. "Unfortunately, he told me there are a couple of clauses in the contract that give the city wiggle room if they want to default. And if it comes to that, I'll be paying him a lot more to straighten out the mess."

"At least now they know you have legal representation, so they'll move more cautiously." Claire glanced at a stack of papers on the other chair in the office. The top one had a big red notice, Past Due, on the top. "But I needed to talk to you about something else. Mind if I sit?"

As she moved toward the chair, Charley lunged forward. He grabbed the papers off the chair and slid them under a *Western Horseman* magazine on his desk. He waved a hand toward the empty chair.

"Is it about Mom?" Charley asked. "I stopped in to see her yesterday. You're right. The fog is definitely closing in. She forgot again that I'd moved here from Durango. And when I mentioned Jessica, she got this blank look on her face like she'd never heard the name before."

Claire sat and scooted the chair closer to Charley. "It might be time to move Mom, though I know she won't like it. Any kind of change really upsets her now. But no, that's not why I'm here."

She reached out and closed the door behind her, because Jessica was talking in the reception room to a couple who had just come off the last trail ride of the day. "I overheard a conversation, actually a fight, between two of your employees today, and I thought you should know about it."

Charley shifted in his chair and opened his mouth to speak.

She held up a hand. "Not that I want to interfere with your business or anything. I'll leave it up to you to decide what to do with what I tell you."

She described the fight between Gil and Pedro. She included Gil's drinking, Jorge's statement about Gil not doing his work, and hiss name-calling of Pedro. But she left out his statement about Vargas's and Kyle's smuggling operation.

She felt guilty holding that back, but she wanted to protect Pedro and his family. The potential harm to Charley was just a fine, but that to Pedro and his family was destitution. Besides, she figured that if ICE asked to see Charley's records, he would tell her. Then she could tell Charley about Pedro. Hopefully it would never come to that, but if it did, Charley could get rid of Pedro before ICE did their inspection. Since Pedro would no longer be a current employee, Charley wouldn't have to pay the fine.

But what if Gil spills the beans when he's fired? Or what if he thinks Pedro told on him and goes after Pedro?

"I don't want Gil blaming any of his co-workers for ratting on him," Claire said. "So be sure to tell him that it was me who told you about his drinking."

Charley stood and looked out the small office window at the barn, drumming his fingers on his thigh as he thought.

Finally he turned to Claire. "Thanks for telling me. I knew Gil drank, but I thought he had it under control. And I'd sensed some tension between Gil and almost everyone else except Hank, but I didn't know the cause. I guess I will have to fire him."

He plopped back down in his chair. "We're short-handed as it is without Kyle, which is why I'm so far behind on this blasted paperwork. I've had to go out on more trail rides myself. Frankly, I enjoy them a lot more than pushing a pen around." He gave Claire a wry smile.

She returned the smile. "You're a natural horseman, Charley. I saw how much you were enjoying working with Jorge on Gunpowder. Have you advertised for Kyle's position?" Claire wondered if he was trying to make do with fewer employees to save on expenses.

Charley nodded. "But no takers yet. Thank God for Hank. He stepped right into Kyle's lead trail guide position and has the tourists eating out of his hands, especially the women. But I'll still have two wrangler positions to fill."

"You could wait to fire Gil."

"Nope, not after what you told me. I don't want him on the property, especially around the customers."

Claire stood. "I'm sorry to be adding to your troubles."

Jessica opened the door while Claire was still speaking. "What troubles?"

"I'm going to have to fire Gil," Charley answered. "Claire saw him drinking and picking a fight with one of the other wranglers."

Jessica looked from Charley to Claire and back again. "How come she's so much more perceptive than you?"

Oh, God!

Charley's neck reddened. "I've been a little busy lately, if you haven't noticed." When Jessica opened her mouth again, he held up a hand. "I'll take care of it. Pronto."

He ushered Claire out of his office and onto the porch, where Brittany stood waiting for her.

Claire put a hand on his arm. "Good luck, Charley."

He nodded and pushed his cowboy hat down on his head. With a grim face, he strode off for the barn.

Brittany gave Claire a quizzical look.

"Don't ask," Claire said. "You know, I've got a hankering for a nice thick chocolate shake. There's a Diary Queen on the way to your house, if I'm not mistaken. Want to join me?"

"Sure, but make mine vanilla."

The two of them got in Claire's car. While Claire drove to the DQ, she and Brittany chatted about their clients that day. Claire figured she would try to find out more about Brittany's strained relationship with her mother.

"Does your mother often drive you to and from the stable?"

"We have two cars," Brittany said. "A nice one for Mom, but the other one's a clunker and I have to share it with my brother. So, yeah, she has to drop me off or pick me up a lot."

Claire maneuvered into the drive-through lane. She ordered their shakes then turned to Brittany. "Did your mother pick you up after the grand opening was over?"

Brittany looked down at her hands in her lap. "You mean the night Kyle was killed? Why do you want to know that?"

Claire couldn't very well tell Brittany that she was wondering if Nancy Schwartz may have had reason—and an opportunity—to kill Kyle. "Maybe your mother saw something that evening. Something she may not even realize is important."

Brittany thought for a moment. "Could be. After I got in the car, Mom said she had to use the restroom. She got out and went in one of the port-a-potties while I waited."

And the port-a-potties were hidden from view of the parking lot. Claire inched the car forward in the drive-through line. "Was she gone long?"

With a shrug, Brittany said, "I wasn't paying much attention. I was listening to my iPod. She may have gone to the barn looking for Jorge, but I know he'd already left."

"Why would she be looking for Jorge?"

Brittany grinned at Claire. "They're seeing each other. Mom and Dad got divorced when I was twelve. She met Jorge the first

130

week I started working here when she came to pick me up, and I guess they hit it off. They both love horses. That's kind of what drove Dad off, I think. He wants nothing to do with horses."

Now that's interesting. Claire inched her car forward again, then she had a thought. "I'm surprised your Mom used the port-a-potty rather than the bathroom in the trailer."

"Charley and Jessica had already left and locked it up."

Claire frowned. This didn't seem like Charley and Jessica. "They should have stuck around until you left."

"They were going to, but I could see how pooped they were. And Gil and Kyle were still there, so it wasn't like I was all alone. I told them to go ahead, since Mom would be coming soon anyway."

Claire had reached the server window. She handed Brittany her shake and took a sip of her own. *Ugh, strawberry.* She hated fruity shakes.

She handed it back to the server. "I asked for chocolate and this is strawberry."

While the server went to fix the order, Brittany reached for her purse. Claire stayed her hand. "This is on me."

"Thanks." Brittany took a slurp of her shake. "Mine's right."

"Good." *Now, where were we?* "Okay, so you explained why your mom didn't go in the trailer."

"Mom wouldn't have gone in there anyway. She tries to avoid seeing Charley and Jessica when she picks me up and drops me off." Brittany looked askance at Claire. "She and Jessica don't really get along."

"I know your mother runs a hippotherapy nonprofit, too," Claire said. "Jessica tells me that there are plenty of clients for both charities, but your mom doesn't seem to share that point of view."

131

Brittany sighed. "It's a part of her control complex. Anything she has a hand in, she has to own one hundred percent." She cracked a smile at Claire. "She must not have learned the lesson about sharing in kindergarten."

The server returned with another shake, and Claire took a sample sip. It was chocolate heaven, just what she needed after a stressful day. She paid for the shakes and drove off.

"I hope your mom doesn't have the same control attitude about you. What did she think of you dating Kyle?"

Brittany rolled her eyes. "It's like she hates everyone I date. She doesn't like Vince, either. She keeps saying I could do better, that I should look for some guy who can set me up in style. But I'm not looking to get married. I just want to have some fun."

"I agree. You're too young to be settling down." Claire thought the same thing about her own daughter, who was close to Brittany's age, but Judy had fallen head-over-heels in love and planned to marry her sweetheart in a year.

"And if I point out to Mom that she's dating Jorge, she just blows up, says that's not the same thing. I guess she's already been 'set up in style' by my Dad." Brittany sneered while she made quote marks in the air with her fingers. "I wish I could move out, but I'm stuck at home until I graduate and get a real job. I hate Mom trying to control everything about my life."

"Is that why you volunteer for Jessica's nonprofit instead of hers?" Claire turned into the entrance to Brittany's neighborhood.

"Yeah. I like helping people and being around horses, but I knew I couldn't stand working for my mom."

Claire tried to envision what it would be like to have Judy working for her. Nope, it wouldn't work. They would be butting heads in a day.

"You know," she said to Brittany, "I don't think there are very many young women who would work well with their mothers. I think you've got to make that break first, stand on your own two feet to get some distance, then maybe it would work."

"I wish my mom was as smart as you." Brittany pointed to the next street on the left. "Turn there."

Claire laughed. "I'm not that smart. I've had my share of fights with my own daughter. I finally figured out that I had to let her make her own mistakes, though."

Soon after she turned onto Brittany's street, a brown Buick passed them going the other way.

"Honk your horn!" Brittany yelled. "That's my mom." She started rolling down her window.

Claire laid on the horn, and Nancy Schwartz stopped her car.

"Mom," Brittany yelled out her window and waved her arm.

Nancy Schwartz backed up until she was opposite Claire's stopped car. She pushed the button to roll down the passenger side window.

"I thought you were at a meeting so I got a ride home," Brittany said to her.

She peered at Brittany and Claire with an annoyed expression on her face. "I finished early, and I figured I'd pick you up. Why didn't you call me?"

"I'm sorry." Brittany gave a feeble shrug. "We stopped to get shakes and got to talking."

"And you ruined your dinner, too."

Brittany gave her mother a look of disgust. "It's just a shake."

Nancy exhaled. "What am I going to do with you?" She shook her head and started backing up into her driveway.

"Nothing," Brittany mumbled. "Absolutely nothing."

Brittany quietly thanked Claire for the ride and got out of the car. She strode up to her house, giving her mother's car a wide berth. She pushed through the front door into the house, letting the door slam behind her with a loud bang.

As Claire drove away, she thought, *wow, the woman really is controlling if she's monitoring the eating habits of her grown daughter.* How far would someone like that go to discredit a business rival—or to get rid of an unsuitable suitor for her daughter?

TEN:
DEATH RETURNS

CLAIRE DROVE TO CHARLEY's stable on Wednesday morning. She hadn't planned to be there again. In fact she thought she should give Charley some space, given how touchy he was about her "interference" in his business. But she needed to pick up some items from Jessica to put in the horseback riding theme basket she was constructing for the silent auction on Saturday. She wished she had remembered to get them Tuesday, but the trouble with Gil had pushed all other thoughts out of her mind.

While stopped at a traffic light, Claire watched dark clouds boiling over the ramparts of the Front Range. An uncommon morning thunderstorm was in the works. She hoped to be back home before the clouds dropped their load, and possibly hail.

Flashing red and blue lights tinted the gray sky. Puzzled, Claire looked for the source once she started moving again. After cresting a rise, she could see Gardner's Stables. The flashing lights came from a police car and an ambulance sitting in the parking lot. Her stomach lurched as a sick sense of déjà vu hit her.

A policeman at the entrance to the parking lot stopped her from turning in.

She rolled down her window. "What's going on?"

"This is a crime scene, ma'am. We're not letting anyone into the area."

"What crime? Is everyone okay?"

"Sorry, I can't say."

"Look, I'm the sister of the owner. I need to know if they're okay. If I park on the road, can I walk around the crime scene tape to get to the business office?"

"Yes, ma'am. But stay away from the crime scene."

Claire parked and hurried over uneven ground covered with weeds and prickly yucca, making a wide circuit around the parking lot. She had to focus on her path, but checking on Charley and Jessica was foremost in her mind. Once she reached the trailer, she was relieved to see them standing on the porch, watching the activity in the lot. Charley had his arm around Jessica's shoulders in a protective gesture. Jessica's shoulders were hunched as if she were chilled.

"What's going on?" Claire climbed up the porch steps and stood next to them. She craned her neck to see the police working in the lot. Two patrol officers were systematically searching the pavement, and a third was taking photos. A police technician was on her knees next to a parked car, collecting evidence off the asphalt surface and bagging it. Detective Wilson stood nearby, studying the scene and writing in his notebook.

"It's horrible." Jessica clutched an empty coffee mug like it was going to spontaneously combust. "When Charley and I drove in this morning, Gil's car was in the lot. He's never here early. He just seemed to be sitting in the car with the windows open. So, Charley went over to talk to him. But ..." She teared up and put a hand to her mouth.

"He's dead," Charley said flatly. "Shot through the head."

Claire sucked in a breath.

"When I came around the driver's side," he continued, "I could see blood all over his head and on the car door. I refused to let Jessica get anywhere near the car."

Jessica shuddered. "I'm glad. I don't think I could handle it. Did you see him when you came up?"

"No," Claire said. "The ambulance blocked my view, thank God." The ambulance's two EMTs were also silently watching the scene while one stowed equipment back into the rear of their vehicle.

"You have experience, at least," Jessica said. "You've seen someone shot before. I'll probably have nightmares, even though I didn't get close." She put a hand to her stomach.

"It's not something you ever get used to." Claire's own gut clenched at the memories.

Charley looked up at the leaden sky. "Damn, I feel so guilty."

"Guilty!" Flabbergasted, Claire turned to him. "Why do you feel guilty?"

He focused his heavy gaze on Claire. "Because I fired him last night. There was a note on the passenger seat, though I couldn't read it. He had a gun in his right hand. It looks like he shot himself."

"Oh, Charley, I'm so sorry. And it was because of what I told you that you fired him." A shudder ran through Claire. She chafed her arms. "Gil sure didn't seem like someone who would commit suicide."

Frankly, it seemed more likely that he would have shot Charley. With that thought, Claire enveloped Charley in a fierce hug.

"Whoa," he said. "That was a surprise attack."

Claire released him and swallowed hard. "I'm just glad you're okay, that he didn't go after you."

"Oh my." Jessica pinned a wide-eyed gaze on Charley. "I didn't even think of that."

Claire looked over at Detective Wilson. He returned her gaze, as if he had been watching them for a while, then gave her a brief wave, almost a salute.

After she returned the greeting, he shouted, "Stick around," before going back to work.

She looked at Charley. "Has he talked to you?"

"Yes, he interviewed each of us when he arrived, but he said he'd want to talk to us again after he studied the crime scene."

The coroner's vehicle drove into the parking lot, and Detective Wilson walked over to talk to the forensic investigator. She was the same woman who had come for Kyle's body. Claire watched in silence with Jessica and Charley. After the EMTs talked to the forensic investigator, they left in their empty ambulance.

Detective Wilson talked to an officer next. Charley told Claire the man was the first one to respond to their 911 call. After that, Wilson talked to the photographer and forensic technician then walked carefully around the car while taking notes. The forensic investigator examined Gil's body. They all worked mostly in silence, except for short exchanges with each other that Claire couldn't hear.

Finally Jessica looked at her watch and sighed. "It's almost nine thirty. I need to reschedule my meeting with the hotel event director. Guess I'd better cancel the ten-thirty ride, too. We don't want customers seeing this."

Charley gave a solemn nod. "Tell them it's because of the weather, that it looks like it's going to pour."

"Good idea." Jessica went inside.

Wilson put on latex gloves, opened the passenger door of Gil's car, and lifted a piece of paper off the passenger seat. He sealed it in a plastic bag, then straightened and read it. When he finished, he glanced up at the trailer and studied the note again. He gave the bag to the forensic technician, talked again to the forensic investigator and trudged up the path to the trailer.

"Was that a suicide note?" Charley asked as Wilson neared.

Wilson put a foot on the first step and nodded at Claire before returning his gaze to Charley. "Before I answer that question I'd like to ask a few more of my own, and I'll be recording your answers." He took out a small tape recorder and pressed the record button. "Tell me again when the last time was that you saw Gil Kaplan."

"Yesterday, just before we closed up for the day. That's when I fired him, and probably caused him to do this. He left in a huff shortly after six, and I left soon after that."

"Why'd you fire him?"

"Claire told me about a fight he'd gotten into with another staff member."

Wilson cocked his head at Claire, and she explained what she had overheard in the barn. Then Charley described his own conversation with Jorge after that. Jorge had reluctantly confirmed that he had seen Gil drinking and picking on Pedro.

When Charley got to his conversation with Gil, Wilson asked him to try to remember the exchange word-for-word, or as closely as possible. While they talked, Wilson moved up to the porch and the three of them settled into chairs. As Charley finished up, Claire went inside to fetch coffee mugs and a pot and poured a round for them all.

Wilson took a sip of coffee and gave a nod of thanks to Claire. "Did anyone stay after closing last night, who might have seen Kaplan return?"

"No," Charley said. "I was the last to leave. So, he … did it last night?"

"The forensic investigator gave me a rough estimate that he's been dead for six to ten hours."

Charley nodded. "Did he blame me in the note?"

"I think you'll be surprised by what the note said," Wilson said. "Kaplan wasn't suicidal because you fired him, but because he blamed himself for Kyle Mendoza's death."

Claire sat bolt-upright, sloshing coffee on her jeans. "What? So he was the one who hit Kyle in the head with a hammer and threw it in the manure dumpster?"

Wilson nodded. "So the note says."

"Christ!" Charley shook his head and leaned forward. "Did he say why?"

"He said Mendoza had threatened to tell you about his drinking and slacking off. The two of them got into an argument, and it got physical."

"Given what I saw between Pedro and him," Claire said, "I could easily see that happening. But why would Gil commit suicide?"

"The note said he couldn't live with being not only a drunk and a slacker but also a murderer." Wilson glanced at the bloodied car then at Charley. "Does that fit with his personality?"

Charley shrugged. "Offhand, I'd say no, but the man wasn't very forthcoming with me."

Gil committing suicide was also hard for Claire to imagine, but … "Maybe Gil's outward anger was covering up an inward self-loathing."

Tapping his pen on his notepad, Wilson said, "That's possible."

Charley took off his hat and scratched his head. "Then after Kyle was killed, Claire told me about Gil a few days later, and I fired him. Come to think of it, he was pretty quiet through it all, didn't say much. I thought he'd blow his top."

It sounded like Gil hadn't said anything about Pedro to Charley, which relieved Claire. "So Gil dragged Kyle into Gunpowder's stall after he hit him?"

"That's one thing that doesn't make sense." Wilson paused and rubbed his chin. "In the note, Gil said he left Kyle lying in the aisle between the stalls."

"So we're to assume Kyle regained consciousness but was still groggy?" Claire asked. "Then he stumbled into Gunpowder's stall, spooking the horse?"

Before Wilson could respond, rain splattered on the ground and the porch roof above them. The people working the crime scene stopped to retrieve slickers from their vehicles. A gust of wind frothed up dust from the yard and sent the new trees whipping against their restraints.

Claire shielded her eyes from the wind-borne grit and turned her back to the gale. Something nagged at her brain, then she remembered the coroner's results. "But what about the evidence of dragging on Kyle's palms?"

Wilson peered at Charley. "Do you have a phone in the barn?"

"Yeah, in the tack room," Charley said. "Nowhere near Gunpowder's stall. Do you think Kyle woke up confused and tried to drag himself to a phone, scuffing up his hands that way? Maybe he was so disoriented he mistook Gunpowder's stall for the tack room."

"I'll have to talk to the coroner," Wilson said. "See if that's a reasonable scenario for the abrasions on Mendoza's palms."

He stood, turned off his recorder and pocketed it. "If that's so, and ballistics matches the bullet that the forensic investigator thinks is still in Kaplan's head to his gun, then he's given us a gift. The gift of both solving the Mendoza murder case and getting rid of the killer. A nice package all tied up with a pretty bow." He smiled wryly at Claire. "Much like one of your gift baskets."

"Getting back to some semblance of normality here would be great, but our reputation's going to get worse before it gets better once word of another death gets out." Charley set down his coffee mug and rubbed his face. Lines of worry and fatigue etched his brow. "I still feel guilty for firing Gil."

Wilson put a hand on his shoulder. "I may have helped nail the lid on his coffin, too. Given that Kaplan was the last person to see Mendoza, I was pushing him—hard. I'd asked him to come in today for another interview. Hell, that's probably what made him decide to do himself in."

A flash lit up the Western sky, followed almost immediately by a loud boom. All three of them flinched.

"With that final note, I'll head out." Wilson walked off the porch into the rain.

As Claire watched him go, she fervently hoped that the ballistics test and the coroner backed up Wilson's conclusions. If not, they would have not just one, but two unsolved murders on their hands—and on Charley's property.

———

An hour later, Claire looked out the trailer window. The heavy rain that had swept off the mountains had slowed to a drizzle. After stowing Gil's body in the coroner's van, Detective Wilson and most of the investigative team had left soon after the deluge started. One patrol officer remained, stationed in the parking lot to watch over Gil's car until a city tow truck came to take the car to the police impound lot.

Wilson had said the tow trucks usually respond quickly to crime scenes, but there had been a multi-car crash on Powers Boulevard involving city vehicles. Charley had promised to keep his employees and customers away from the parking lot and the drooping police tape staked around it while they waited. The officer had just come in the office for a restroom break and asked Charley to watch Gil's car while he did. The way the man was mincing his steps told Claire he had waited as long as humanly possible before taking a break.

She stood and picked up her purse and a plastic sack. It held Jessica's contributions to the horseback riding gift basket, including a certificate for a buy-one-get-one trail ride. Charley had originally planned to donate a free trail ride for two, but with the negative effect of the recent events on his business, he had asked Jessica to change it. This was yet another reason for Claire to worry about her little brother—who nowadays stood five inches taller than she.

She waved goodbye to Jessica, who was on the phone, and stepped out onto the porch, where Charley stood watching Gil's car. "Looks like I can head home now."

Charley looking up at the gray clouds. "Depressing day, huh? I can't see how things could get any worse."

Just then a faded red Honda pulled into the lot. Something about the vehicle seemed familiar to Claire. While she stared at it, a short middle-aged man with wispy brown hair got out. He walked over to the police tape surrounding Gil's car.

"Marvin Bradshaw!" Claire spit out the name and trotted down the porch steps.

Charley followed her. "Who?"

"A reporter from the *Gazette*," Claire shot over her shoulder.

Bradshaw raised the police tape and stepped under it.

"Hey," Charley yelled. "Get away from that!"

Startled, Bradshaw jerked, dropping a small camera onto the wet asphalt. "Shit!"

He bent down. His fingers scrabbled to pick up the camera while he kept glancing at Claire and Charley's approach. He was able to pocket the camera and slip back outside the police tape before the two of them arrived.

Claire was huffing from exertion and indignation. "I've got a bone to pick with you," she said to Bradshaw, swiping a drop of rain off the end of her nose.

Recognition dawned in his widening eyes. "What are you doing here?"

"No," Charley said. "What are *you* doing here?"

Bradshaw dug a card out of the pocket of his rain jacket and handed it to Charley. "I'm a reporter from the *Gazette*. I know who she is." He jerked his thumb at Claire. "But who are you?"

"Charley Gardner," Charley answered. "Her brother and the owner of this property."

"How do you do?" Bradshaw held out a hand. When Charley didn't shake it, he let his arm drop. "So, what happened here?"

"Don't say a word, Charley." Claire advanced on the reporter, fists clenched. "You've already insinuated that someone here at the stable killed Kyle Mendoza, costing Charley who knows how much business. Why in the world should he talk to you if you keep jumping to unfounded conclusions? Conclusions that hurt his reputation and livelihood!"

Bradshaw stepped back and held up his palms. "Look, I tried to talk to someone here before I published that story, but the woman who answers the phone kept saying, 'No comment.'"

Claire and Charley looked at each other and said simultaneously, "Jessica."

"You ended up cooperating with me before on that other case, Mrs. Hanover. As I said that time, if I can get both sides of the story, I can publish a more accurate article."

"Both sides! Who have you been talking to?" Claire had a sneaking suspicion.

"A Nancy Schwartz and her lovely daughter Brittany."

Claire rolled her eyes at Charley. "Who knows what kind of garbage that jealous woman told him." She sighed. "I think you'd better talk to him."

Bradshaw grinned. "Thanks, Mrs. Hanover. I really appreciate it."

Charley furrowed his brows. "Maybe we should ask Detective Wilson before we talk to this guy."

"Ah, now that I know who's caught the case," Bradshaw said, "I can get a lot of what I need directly from him."

"But first we need to know what Nancy Schwartz told you," Claire said. "And we need to make sure you don't print her lies and wind up being sued for libel." She glared at Bradshaw.

"Yes, I would advise that." He rocked back on his heels. "Wholeheartedly."

Charley looked to the heavens, and drizzle ran off the brim of his Stetson. He blew out a breath and focused his gaze on Bradshaw. "I suppose you should come inside."

So much for finishing that basket today. "If you want, I'll stay while you talk to him."

"Please." Charley turned toward the trailer.

Bradshaw fell in step beside him. "Now, tell me, who was murdered this time?"

Claire grabbed him by the elbow. "You have got this story so wrong!"

———

That evening, Claire walked into the local fire station's public meeting room, following Charley and Jessica. Trepidation slowed her steps. While they had been talking to Bradshaw, Charley answered a call from the board president of the homeowner's association for the neighborhood nearest the stable. The board had organized an emergency meeting after receiving numerous calls from members with complaints and questions about the stable after the news of Gil's death hit the TV and radio stations. The president invited Charley and Jessica to come and answer questions—and presumably defend themselves.

Wanting at least one friendly face in the room, Charley had asked Claire to come, too. Since Roger was away on his business trip until Friday, she accepted readily. She took a seat on one of the folding chairs set up in rows before a cafeteria-sized table where the board would sit. Jessica and Charley walked up to the table to talk to the board president.

While they conferred, Claire studied the others who had come, about forty overall. A few were glancing at Charley and Jessica with curiosity, but others' looks were full of hostility—or fear. Then the little old man who had complained to Charley at the opening event walked in. His jaw moved as if he was grinding his teeth, and his hands were clenched tightly.

Uh oh, trouble. Claire glanced up front, and Jessica gave her a thumbs-up sign. Claire returned it but knew her thumb was lying. This meeting would not go well.

Standing behind the table, the board president banged a gavel on the top. He asked everyone to take their seats. Chairs squeaked as bodies settled into them. Charley and Jessica sat in front next to the board members' table.

The president held up a hand for quiet. "Thank you for coming on such short notice. The board has received several phone calls from residents about the death at Gardner's Stables this morning. Rather than let rumors propagate through the neighborhood, we asked Charley and Jessica Gardner here to answer those questions themselves."

He nodded to the two of them. "We appreciate you taking time out of your busy schedule to talk to us."

He turned back to the audience. "I'll start with what we know. I just got off the phone with the police department. The victim this morning was Gil Kaplan, a wrangler who worked for Charley Gardner and lived alone. They won't know for sure what the cause of death was until after they process the evidence they collected and conduct an autopsy. But Mr. Gardner here, who found the victim, told me that suicide is suspected."

A man held up his hand. "Any connection between this suicide and the murder of the Mendoza guy?"

The president looked at Charley.

Jessica made as if to speak, but Charley shook his head. He stood and wiped his hands on his thighs before speaking. "There's some indication that Gil Kaplan may have been the one who killed Kyle Mendoza. We suspect he committed suicide out of guilt, but we won't know for sure for a few days."

The little old man who had confronted Charley at the opening celebration stood. "What if it's not that at all? What if both of these men were murdered? Maybe something dangerous is going on at Gardner's Stables, something that could spill out in our neighborhood and harm us. For all we know, you could be dealing drugs there."

The room erupted into murmurs, some angry and some scornful of the man's inflammatory words. *Thank goodness some of these people have some sense,* Claire thought. Many heads were nodding in agreement with the old man, though.

Charley held up a hand. "You folks are welcome to come to the stable and check us out. You won't find any drugs on the property, except medications for taking care of sick horses. The police have thoroughly searched the grounds, too, and they haven't found drugs or anything else illegal."

"As for danger," he added. "I don't see any. If it's true that Gil murdered Kyle, then both cases will be closed, and the killer is no longer with us. You shouldn't need to worry about the safety of your families any more than you usually do."

The old man screwed up his mouth as if he had tasted something bad and was ready to spit it out. "Only about the safety of our dogs, and our kids, and ourselves when we take a walk in the open space, for fear some out-of-control horse will stomp on us. Isn't that how that Mendoza guy was killed?"

More rustling and talk came from the audience until Charley held up his hand again. "The police have evidence that Kyle Mendoza was hit on the head with a tool. That's probably what killed him, not the horse."

Charley was exaggerating a little, but the truth wasn't far off. Claire looked around. This time the audience seemed quieter, a little more respectful.

"Regardless," the old man said, "we didn't have any of these issues until your stable muscled its way into our neighborhood. It's smelly, dangerous, and you're not good neighbors."

Charley reddened, and Claire could tell he was working hard to hold back his anger. "That's not true. Jessica and I have made a concerted effort to be good neighbors. We've contacted all the HOAs in the area, given coupons to all of you for discounted rides. We invited you to our opening and to stop by anytime."

Jessica stood and took Charley's arm. It was a show of support, but Claire knew it was also a hint for Charley to calm down. "We clean up after our horses on the paved trails," she added. "And we keep our stable clean. As for the smell, we keep it down by storing our manure in a dumpster with a lid. It's hauled away every week."

Charley turned to the board president. "We've bent over backward to be good neighbors, but if there's anything else you think we should be doing, we'll listen."

The old man bristled, "But that—"

"That's enough, Norm," the board president said. "We're not here to rehash old arguments that have already been resolved. We're just here to answer questions about the deaths that have occurred at the stable. Please take your seat."

About time! Claire felt like applauding.

The president paused and stared down the old guy until, huffing with indignation, he sat. A tall, muscular man sitting behind Norm gave him a pat on the shoulder and a thumbs-up, then settled back with his arms crossed. His belligerent frown showed he had already made up his mind that Charley's stable was bad news.

When Charley and Jessica retook their seats, Claire wished she could give her brother a pat on the shoulder, too. She glanced around. Many people still looked either worried or angry.

The president surveyed the rest of the audience. "Now, does anyone else have a question or concern?"

After that, the questioning was more polite. Claire tuned out the give and take while she mulled over the heated exchange with the old man. The horse barn wasn't ever locked. That was so if a wildfire threatened the stable, anyone could get the horses out.

Could Norm, or someone else in the neighborhood who resented the stable's presence just as much, have gone into the stable after Gil walloped Kyle, maybe to cause some mischief? Could he have come across Kyle Mendoza's unconscious body? Then dragged Kyle into Gunpowder's stall, hoping the horse would batter Kyle and the stable would be discredited? But Claire couldn't see Norm standing up to Gunpowder.

His large friend, though, she could.

ELEVEN:
APOLOGIES AND WOUNDS

"I STILL CAN'T BELIEVE Gil killed himself," Brittany said to Claire the next afternoon.

They were walking on either side of Daisy while keeping an eye on the balance of the plump teenage girl with Down syndrome in the saddle. She was following directions from Jessica, who was walking about ten feet in front of the horse and studying the girl's moves.

"We probably shouldn't talk about this in front of Robin." Claire glanced up at Robin.

Thankfully, Robin seemed to be focused on steering the placid horse without messing up her fingernails rather than on Brittany's words. Someone had painted Robin's nails expertly with baby blue polish that matched her eye shadow. And her cologne was a pleasant lilac scent that lightened the corral's earthy aromas of straw, horseflesh, and sun-baked dirt.

Claire returned her attention to Brittany. "I do need to tell you something, though. Charley and I had to spend a lot of time with that *Gazette* reporter Marvin Bradshaw yesterday. We had to clear up all the misconceptions he got from talking to you and your mother." She peered at Brittany over Daisy's rump.

Brittany bit her lip and gave Claire a remorseful look. "I'm sorry. I didn't want to talk to him in the first place, but Mom dragged me into it."

"Believe me, I know how mothers can be. Remember I'm one myself." Claire rolled her eyes to lighten the mood. "But I'm sure you don't want Charley's business or Jessica's charity to be hurt, either."

"Oh, no, not at all!" Brittany's eyes widened, then she frowned. "I won't talk to that reporter ever again. But I can't keep Mom from talking to him."

"I understand." But Claire wondered if there was some way she could put a clamp on Nancy's rumor-mongering.

A delighted laugh from Robin turned Claire's thoughts to happier things. It was a beautiful sunny afternoon, and she was helping this girl gain self-confidence along with physical coordination and balance.

"That's great, Robin," Jessica said with enthusiasm. "Now see if you can make Daisy do the whole figure eight without my help. Use the reins to turn her."

Claire looked up at Robin. She was in her late teens, but her Down syndrome features and her smile of pure glee made her look younger. She stuck a tongue out between her teeth and focused on pulling Daisy's reins to the left so the horse would turn around the tall pole stuck in the ground. As the horse made the turn, Robin leaned into it—a little too far. Claire pushed against Robin's side and Brittany pulled Robin's harness from the other side.

"Way to go, Robin, that was a very good turn," Jessica said. "But remember to sit up straight in the saddle even when you're turning."

Robin immediately adjusted her posture, earning a "Great job!" from Claire, who let go for a moment and gave the young woman a thumbs-up.

Claire realized the words could just as well apply to herself. This was good work she was doing. She may not have been very helpful so far to her brother in dealing with his problems, but she could help Robin by making a positive difference in her life.

As they neared the end of Robin's session, a car drove into the parking lot. Ana and Petey Mendoza got out. Petey was hopping with excitement and looked like he wanted to sprint toward the corral. But Ana held him back until Claire and Brittany had finished assisting Robin with her dismount.

Jessica walked with Robin to where her father waited at one of the picnic tables and waved to Ana and Petey. "I'll be with you in a minute."

When Brittany finished tying Daisy to the corral fence, Petey went immediately to the horse. He cooed at Daisy and rubbed her forehead. Daisy nuzzled the boy's head as if she, too, had missed seeing him.

Claire arched a brow at Brittany and glanced at Ana with curiosity, but didn't say anything. She figured Jessica should be the first one to talk to Ana.

While Jessica gave Robin's father a report on her session, Robin returned to the corral and stood next to Petey, petting Daisy's neck.

The two young people stole glances at each other, and Robin smiled shyly.

Ana stepped forward after Jessica finished her report, her hands clenched in front of her. Claire joined them, too. Acting as if nothing was wrong, Jessica introduced them both to Robin's father. During the pleasantries, Claire noted how nervous Ana appeared. Rightly so, given how mad she had been the last time they had seen her.

Jessica smiled over at the two young people vying for petting space on Daisy's neck and forehead. "Petey and Robin, since you both like Daisy so much, you should say hi to each other," she said loudly so they could hear her. "You have something in common."

Petey ducked his head and peeked up through his lashes at Robin. "Hi," he said shyly.

"Hi," Robin said back.

When they both seemed to be at a loss for what to say next, Brittany stepped in with two mini carrots. "Why don't you both give Daisy a treat? Robin, do you want to go first?"

After watching Brittany make another attempt to get Robin and Petey interacting with each other, Robin's father said, "I like seeing Robin make friends with someone like herself. Mind if I go over there and help them along?" He looked at Ana.

"That would be very nice," Ana said with a smile. "Thank you."

After he left, she took a deep breath and turned to Jessica. "I heard about Gil Kaplan's death when a reporter from the *Gazette* called me for a statement. Mr. Bradshaw made it sound like Gil committed suicide because he felt guilty about killing Kyle. Is that true?"

"That's what Detective Wilson thinks happened," Jessica said. "Gil left a suicide note that said he hit Kyle in the head while they were arguing."

Ana looked pained. "What were they arguing about?"

"Kyle was going to tell Charley about Gil's drinking and slacking off work," Jessica explained. "Charley already knew Gil drank sometimes, but he thought Gil had it under control. And as far as we knew, Gil never fought with anyone at work until the day before yesterday when Claire saw him get into a scuffle with Pedro. Charley fired Gil that afternoon, which may have contributed to his suicide. Charley's really upset about it."

Claire jumped to Charley's defense. "Gil didn't say that in his note, and Detective Wilson said he was pressuring Gil since he was the last one to be with Kyle. Wilson thought that might have been what drove Gil over the edge."

"Regardless," Jessica looked from Claire to Ana, "the police think Gil killed Kyle, not Gunpowder. Gunpowder was just a clumsy ruse used by Gil to try to cover up what he'd done."

Ana exhaled and gave a quick nod. She swallowed and unclasped her hands. "Emilio and I owe you and Charley a huge apology. I'm so sorry we jumped to conclusions and blamed the horse—and you—for Kyle's death. Can you forgive us?"

"Of course." Jessica gave Ana a hug then drew back with her arms still around the woman. "You were grieving, and it looked like Gunpowder did it at first."

Ana wiped a tear from her cheek. "We were angry, so angry that our son was taken from us at such a young age. You and Charley were the closest targets."

"I know," Jessica said softly, dropping her hands and stepping back.

"But we should've known better. We know you both, how safe you are with the children," Ana turned and swept a hand toward Petey and Robin. "We should've known you wouldn't keep a dangerous horse at the stable. I'll call our lawyer and tell him we want to withdraw the lawsuit."

Claire clapped her hands together and brought them to her chin. *Hallelujah!*

"Thank you, Ana." Jessica hugged the woman again. "Thank you so much. Charley will be so relieved. The lawsuit has hung over him like a thundercloud."

Ana's face crumpled in distress. "Again, I am so sorry for the trouble we caused you both. I apologize for my hurtful words last week."

"Apology accepted, and we certainly understand," Jessica replied.

Claire had a thought. "You've already done so much, and I hate to ask another favor, but will you also have your lawyer contact the city? Tell them you no longer want Charley's contract cancelled?"

"Oh, yes." Ana turned to Jessica. "And may Petey start his sessions again? He has missed Daisy almost as much as Kyle." She swallowed again and took a moment to compose herself. "And now we have no one to take care of Petey when Emilio and I are gone. We had counted on Kyle to do that since our daughter has cut us out of her life."

Jessica's eyes widened in surprise. "I didn't realize you had a daughter, too."

Ana nodded. "Sophie was born in between Kyle and Petey. She was only two when Petey came into our lives and took up so much of my time. She got lost in the shuffle, probably felt unloved. She got into trouble as a teenager." Ana sighed. "I blame myself for not seeing that she resented Petey and all the attention he was getting. She moved to California and now has no contact with us."

"None at all?" Claire asked.

"Kyle tried to call her a few times, talk her into returning to the family. But the last time, she yelled at him, said that between Petey being the baby and him being the star of the family, no one paid any attention to her. So why should she pay any attention to us now?"

"Oh dear." Claire could see some parallels between Sophie's words and Charley's about Claire getting all the attention from their parents.

"Does Sophie know about Kyle's death?" Jessica asked.

"I left a message on her answering machine. But she hasn't called back."

Jessica put a hand on Ana's shoulder. "Do you think she'll come to Kyle's memorial service?"

Ana shrugged. "I told her when it will be in the message, but I don't know if she'll come."

"Maybe this will be the push she needs to reunite with her family," Claire said hopefully.

"We can hope, but I doubt it." Ana looked at Petey with sad eyes. "We can't bring his big brother or sister back to Petey, but I hope we can bring Daisy back into his life."

"Of course we can," Jessica said. "And maybe even right now. Claire, can you stay for another session?"

"I'd love to," Claire replied. And then she was going to have a talk with her brother.

———

After Petey's session, Claire and Brittany took Daisy back to the barn. While they were caring for the horse, Claire overheard Charley and Jorge talking in the treatment area. They had Gunpowder tied up in there and were standing off to the side and studying the horse. Gunpowder kept shuffling his feet and swinging his head, as if he couldn't keep still.

"He was doing so well," Charley said. "What do you think caused this backslide?"

"Don't know," Jorge said. "I noticed he was getting more sensitive to anyone touching his rear end a couple of days ago."

"Look at his ears, how they're laid back. And his swishing tail. He's angry about something."

"Or something is bothering him, like maybe he's in pain." Jorge paused then snapped his fingers. "Maybe this has nothing to do with Kyle. Maybe he has a sore somewhere we can't see—like under his tail."

"You could be right. But there's no way he'll let either of us examine him there without being tied up. We'll have to get help." Charley stepped out into the aisle and yelled, "Hank!"

When he got no response, he said, "Where's he gone off to?"

"He never seems to be around when I need help with Gunpowder," Jorge said. "Maybe he's afraid of him now."

Charley slapped his thigh. "That's just plain dumb." He spied Brittany and Claire and waved at them. "You two about done with Daisy? Could you lend us a hand?"

"Sure," Brittany answered.

Claire followed her into the treatment area, where Jorge positioned them on either side of Gunpowder's head with a ready supply of carrots. While they cooed to the horse, fed him and petted him, Charley and Jorge made quick work of tying off his back legs so Gunpowder couldn't kick them.

Jorge gently lifted Gunpowder's tail.

The horse's eyes rolled back. He pushed his weight off his front legs, as if preparing to buck. But his back legs yanked at the ties, which held, and they went nowhere. He floundered and struggled to regain his footing. Brittany held his bridle tightly to keep his head level.

Once Gunpowder had regained his footing, Claire held out a carrot on her palm under his nose. But the horse wanted nothing to do with it. Instead he let out a loud squeal of protest.

"Whoa boy, whoa there." Charley ran his hands along Gunpowder's shivering flank while Jorge stood motionless, Gunpowder's tail half-raised in his hand. When the horse had quieted, Charley nodded to Jorge. "Try again."

Jorge slowly lifted the tail higher while Brittany and Charley kept up a steady stream of calming words and Claire rubbed Gunpowder's neck. The horse shifted nervously, but he seemed to realize he could go nowhere. He gave a loud snort and stopped pulling against the restraints. He made do with expressing his displeasure by stomping his front feet and blowing and snorting.

"Watch your feet," Brittany warned.

Claire stepped back, but stayed within arm's length of Gunpowder so she could continue to soothe him.

Jorge ducked his head then let out a low whistle. "Get a flashlight, Charley, and look at this."

Charley grabbed a flashlight off the built-in shelves along the back wall of the treatment area. He shone it on the area of Gunpowder's rump under his tail and leaned down next to Jorge.

Jorge pointed. "See these three wounds?"

"Yeah, and they're infected," Charley said. "I'm surprised we didn't smell it before."

"From the amount of pus and the scabbing," Jorge said, "I'd say these wounds are over a week old."

"Looks like punctures. And they're in an almost straight vertical line." Charley stood and stared at Jorge. "What caused this?"

Jorge measured the gap between the wounds with his thumb and forefinger then stood with them held that width apart. He studied the gap for a moment. Then he let go of Gunpowder's tail with his other hand and walked to where the mucking tools were stored. He lifted a three-pronged hay fork and held it up to his thumb and forefinger.

The widths matched.

"Some *bastardo* poked him with one of these," Jorge said. "And under the tail, where it wouldn't show. That's why Gunpowder is so touchy."

"Shit. I'll call the vet to come treat him," Charley said. "We'll probably need to dose him with antibiotics, too."

"While we are waiting for the vet, I can try to clean the wounds," Jorge said, "as long as you three are here to calm him. We need to get that pus out of there."

Claire had been thinking during this exchange. "I think you should wait on that, Jorge. And you've got another call to make, Charley."

"To who?"

"Detective Wilson. He's going to want pictures of Gunpowder's wounds for his case file. If they're over a week old like Jorge said, then Gil must have lied in his suicide note. He must have dragged Kyle into Gunpowder's stall and poked him with the hay fork to get him to stomp on Kyle."

Brittany gasped.

Jorge nodded. "That makes sense. I couldn't figure out why Gunpowder would stomp on Kyle, even if Kyle dragged himself into his stall. But if Gunpowder was being poked with the fork and feeling pain, all he would think about is trying to get away from the person torturing him."

"Poor guy." Charley massaged Gunpowder's flank. "We'll get you fixed up soon." He went off to make the phone calls while the others kept the horse calm.

When Charley returned, he said, "Detective Wilson said you could clean the wounds, Jorge. He said you're probably as good a judge as a horse vet of how old the wounds are. But he said not to bandage them before he takes photos. He needs to know the depth and width of the punctures. And we're in luck with the vet. He's on another call at a private stable near here and said he'll stop by once he's done there."

Claire, Charley, and Brittany spent the next twenty minutes keeping Gunpowder calm while Jorge cleaned and flushed the wounds with antiseptic soap and warm water. Detective Wilson and the vet arrived at about the same time. After Wilson took photos and measurements and wrote down Jorge's and the vet's statements about the approximate age of the wounds, the vet went to work.

He gave Gunpowder a shot of painkiller followed by one containing antibiotics. Then he sewed up and bandaged the wounds. By the time he finished and Charley led Gunpowder back to his stall, the horse was a shivering wreck.

The vet shook his head while packaging his supplies. "Those wounds were deep, and I'm sure very painful. No wonder Gunpowder was giving you problems." He handed Jorge a bottle of huge pills. "Give him one of these antibiotics twice a day."

While the vet briefed Jorge on continued care for Gunpowder, Detective Wilson signaled to Charley and Claire. "Can we talk privately?"

They passed Hank on the way out of the barn. He was returning from the back pasture. In answer to Charley's question, he said he had taken two of the horses out there so he could clean their stalls. Then he went to work mucking out their stalls, which were well away from Gunpowder's. Claire noticed his worried glances at Gunpowder's stall and the vet.

Once outside and away from everyone else, Wilson turned to Claire and Charley. "Contrary to what I thought yesterday, this case cannot be wrapped up in a tidy package. I'm back to looking for a killer. The coroner said the abrasions on Mendoza's palms couldn't have been self-induced, and now we have these wounds from the hay fork."

"Could Gil have been lying in his suicide note?" Claire asked. "Maybe he didn't want to admit that he dragged Kyle into the stall and poked Gunpowder to get him to stomp on him."

"I might've thought that except for one more very interesting piece of evidence. The bullet in Mr. Kaplan's head didn't come from his gun. In fact, it came from a rifle."

"What?" Charley shouted at the same time that Claire said, "Oh, God!"

Then Claire had another thought. "Was the suicide note fake, then?"

"We confirmed that it's Gil Kaplan's handwriting," Wilson said. "But he could've been forced to write it by someone holding a rifle to his head. Or, he really was considering suicide, but before he could carry out his plan, someone else took care of it for him."

"Who?" Claire and Charley asked simultaneously.

"My current theory is that it's the same person who killed Kyle Mendoza. He could've hit Mendoza on the head, then dragged him into Gunpowder's stall and prodded the horse into stomping on him. Or, he just finished off Mendoza after Kaplan left him lying on the barn floor."

"And he killed Gil because Gil saw him kill Kyle?" Claire shook her head in confusion. "No, wait. If that was the case, Gil wouldn't have blamed himself for Kyle's death. So, he must've been forced to write the note."

"A more important question is why wouldn't he have told the police what he saw?" Charley added.

"Could be that Kaplan didn't see who killed Mendoza, that the first part went down just the way he said in the note," Wilson said. "Could be the killer just thought Kaplan saw him finish off Mendoza and eliminated a potential witness."

"And forced Gil to write a suicide note first?" Claire asked.

Wilson shrugged. "Maybe, maybe not. Maybe Kaplan really was going to kill himself. Regardless, the case is still wide open. Someone killed Mendoza, using Gunpowder as the murder weapon. Then that same person probably shot Kaplan. I need to find out who."

"Then I need to tell you about Nancy Schwartz," Claire said. "Brittany told me that her mother went up to use one of the port-a-potties before she took her home that night. Nancy could've gone into the barn, too." She looked at Charley. "By then you and Jessica were gone, and Brittany didn't have a good view of the property from her mother's car."

"Nancy?" Charley said disbelievingly. "You can't suspect her. What reason would she have to kill Kyle?"

"Two actually," Claire replied with a glance at Wilson. "To discredit your stable and more specifically, Jessica's hippotherapy nonprofit, which she views as competing with her own. Also, she didn't approve of Brittany dating Kyle. She told Brittany she could do better. And I should know, when a mama bear is out to protect her cub, the claws come out." Claire turned to Wilson. "I talked to Brittany about it when I drove her home last night."

Wilson nodded. "When I interviewed Brittany Schwartz, she said she left before Kaplan."

Claire shrugged and said, "Maybe Gil hit Kyle before Brittany left. If she was working somewhere other than the barn, she may not have seen or heard anything."

"She was," Wilson said. "She was cleaning the port-a-potties."

"Then when Nancy came to pick up Brittany, she could have gone into the barn for some reason when she went to use the port-a-potties. If she saw Kyle lying there unconscious, she may have seized on the opportunity to drag him into Gunpowder's stall. She's used to being around horses, so Gunpowder wouldn't scare her."

Wilson scribbled in his notepad. "I'll look at the timing again. The coroner put time of death as a couple of hours later than that, but I'll see what he thinks his margin of error could be. Then I'll talk to Nancy Schwartz."

"Oh, c'mon." Charley put his hands on his hips. "Nancy not wanting her daughter to date Kyle doesn't sound like reason enough to kill him either."

"Would you have thought Gil could knock Kyle unconscious and leave him for dead?" Claire asked. "Who knows what twisted thinking goes on in some people's heads!"

"Cripes," Charley said. "What about the rest of us? Will whoever killed Gil decide to shoot someone else, too? Are we safe?"

Wilson pocketed his notepad. "I wish I could say yes."

TWELVE:
DRINKS AND DEDUCTIONS

CLAIRE PICKED UP ROGER at the airport late Friday afternoon. While driving him to the Phantom Canyon Brewing Company in downtown Colorado Springs, she filled him in on what had happened at Charley's stable since they had last talked on the phone.

"I'm really worried about Charley and Jessica's safety," she said. "We don't know who killed Kyle or Gil Kaplan or why. Since they've targeted two people at the stable, who's to say they won't go after someone else there?"

Roger nodded. "Has Charley done anything to increase security?"

Stopped at a red light, Claire glanced at Roger. "If the killer's one of the staff, or related to one of them, how do you secure against that?"

"At the least, I'd make sure the locks are secure at home, and I'd be sleeping with a gun under the bed."

"Really?" That surprised Claire. Yes, Roger knew how to shoot a rifle and had gone elk hunting, but he had never felt the need to have a weapon nearby at home. In fact, he kept his hunting rifle in a locked case.

Roger reached over and patted her thigh. "To protect you, I'd do anything. I'm sure Charley feels the same way about Jessica."

"Thanks, honey." *How's Charley responding to the threat?*

Chewing on her lip, Claire turned into the parking lot opposite the historic building that housed the brew pub and its upstairs billiards hall and banquet room. They got out of the car and headed for the brewery.

Phantom Canyon was a favorite of theirs among Colorado Springs' growing selection of brew pubs. The building was originally the office of the Chicago, Rock Island and Pacific Railroad, and then the Cheyenne Hotel. Claire loved its solid brick exterior that exuded steadfastness and warmth. Its downtown location made it a perfect place for a pre- or post-theater meal, and Claire and Roger had dined there often.

Glad to have Roger back with her, Claire looped her arm in his and settled into a familiar pace beside him. "You sure you don't mind coming here directly from the airport? You're not too tired?"

"No, and I'm looking forward to having a couple of beers, since you're the designated driver." He smiled at her. "I picked up a few discrepancies in the audit. I did some digging, then I had bad news to deliver to the CEO. After that final, testy meeting today, I'm looking forward to some pleasant company."

"Good. With all the turmoil at the stable, I thought Charley and Jessica needed some pleasant company, too. That's why I set this up."

Claire paused while Roger opened the heavy wooden door to Phantom Canyon. She walked in and scanned the crowded and noisy interior for Charley and Jessica. She spotted them at a round table for four near the front window.

"There they are!" She tugged on Roger's arm.

Jessica was waving at them, but Charley sat with his hands cupped around his beer, staring into the glass. *Uh oh.*

Once they were seated and had ordered Zebulon's Peated Porter for Roger and a home-brewed root beer for Claire, she put a hand on Charley's arm. "What's up?"

After heaving a great sigh, he took a gulp of beer. "A city attorney contacted me this afternoon. They're going to move forward on canceling my contract."

Claire sucked in a breath. "Did you tell them that Ana was dropping her suit?"

Charley shot her a dark look. "Of course. But he said they'd also gotten a complaint from Peak View Stables. And he'd heard we had an employee drinking on the job."

Brow furrowed, Roger asked, "How in the world did he find that out?"

So much for pleasant company. Claire took a sip of her root beer and wished it was something stronger.

"When I asked the attorney who told him," Charley replied with a scowl, "he wouldn't say. But since he mentioned it in the same breath with the Peak View Stables complaint, I'm wondering if Tom Lindall was the one."

"How would Tom Lindall know about Gil's drinking?" Claire asked.

With a shrug, Charley said, "Who the hell knows? There aren't that many wranglers in town, and they're a tight community. The attorney said that with customers being put at risk by drunken staff, and with the two deaths that have occurred on the property, they had grounds enough to cancel the contract, even without Ana Mendoza's lawsuit."

Jessica pursed her lips as if she had tasted something sour, and Claire didn't think it was her Queen's Blonde Ale. "I don't think you yelling at him helped any," Jessica said.

"That prick. I told him I'm not responsible for the deaths and the staff problem had been taken care of."

"He should have reacted positively to that," Claire said hopefully.

"He just made a crack about the unsavoriness of the stable's reputation." Charley took another gulp of beer and slammed the glass back down on the table. "I asked him how I was supposed to stop a murderer when I didn't even know who it was. Sure, it could be someone who works at the stable, but as Detective Wilson said, it could be someone else in Kyle Mendoza's life. How in the world could I or the stable be at fault?"

"What did he say then?" Roger asked.

"He spouted some garbage about the city needing to protect the safety of their patrons, about me being responsible for what happens on the premises. That's when I blew my top." Charley leaned back in his chair and ran his hand through his hair. "The asshole hung up on me before I could tell him where to stick it."

"Oh, dear." Claire took a sip of root beer while she tried to figure out what to say and how to help Charley get through this.

Jessica rubbed Charley's shoulder. "I tried to get Charley to call back and apologize, but he refused."

"Probably wouldn't have done any good," Roger said.

"There!" Charley threw up a hand. "Finally, someone on my side."

"We're all on your side, Charley," Claire said. "What about Dave Redding? Did you contact him? Maybe he can find a way to stop the city from doing this."

"Yeah, I called him after Jessica stopped yelling at me." Charley glared at her.

Avoiding his gaze, she looked into her beer.

"Then *he* lit into me for not letting him handle the conversation," Charley continued. "Said he'll call the city attorney on Monday and try to do some damage control, find out what clause they're basing the cancellation on. Then he said he'd figure out if we can fight it and how. He had the nerve to tell me not to talk to the city attorney anymore and to let him handle it."

Frankly, Claire agreed with Dave, but she wasn't going to say that to Charley, who was looking beat-down enough. "Good, good. So there's still hope. I'm sure Dave will find a way to stop them."

"He's not going to help me if I can't pay him." Charley downed the rest of his beer and signaled for another one. "I don't even know if I can afford the new wrangler I hired yesterday morning. If she even shows up. I hired her before Wilson told us we have a serial killer roaming the grounds."

"Serial killer's a little extreme—"

"That's the way it's going to seem to this new wrangler, Claire." He gave her a baleful look. "I thought the case was closed because Gil had committed suicide, so I didn't bother to tell her what happened. But now, I've got to warn her tomorrow that someone killed two people on the grounds, and we don't know who. I wouldn't be surprised if she quits right then and there."

"Well, then you won't have the extra expense." Roger plastered on a false grin, obviously trying to lighten the mood.

Charley slumped, resting an elbow on the table and his head in that hand. "Trying to do the work of the two missing staff along with my own work is killing me, though. I don't know. Maybe I should just chuck it all in, admit I'm no businessman. I haven't been able to turn a profit in two years. This move was supposed to change things, and I'm only deeper in debt."

"None of this is your fault, Charley." Claire stared at Jessica and jerked her chin at Charley to prompt her to encourage him.

Jessica sat up straighter. "Claire's right. You've got great horse sense, Charley, and running a stable is what you were meant to do. All the things that have gone wrong lately—the two deaths, the run-in with Peak View Stables, the city getting spooked—would have stymied even the best businessman. Even someone who'd gotten a business degree and learned the ropes before plunging into owning his own business, who'd started small and built up gradually."

Claire stared at Jessica in horror. *Could the woman have said anything worse?*

"Like Claire did, huh?" Charley said through gritted teeth. "Got her college degree, made her parents proud, then married someone with the funds to bankroll her business."

Roger set his beer down hard and made a move to jump into the conversation, probably to defend her.

But Claire gripped his arm and shook her head. "Charley, there's no way you can say my art degree prepared me to own my own

172

business. I started out knowing nothing, just like you, and just like a lot of other small business owners. And my business is miniscule compared to yours. You're the successful businessman in our family, and I'm sure Dad would be proud of you if he were still alive. And Mom, too, if she was still lucid."

Claire winced internally at this tactless reference to their mother. Claire had visited her again at the Alzheimer's facility that morning. This time her mother hadn't been in a mood to talk at all. When Claire tried to engage her in conversation, she just rolled over in bed, turning her back to Claire.

"Jessica, wouldn't you say my business is nothing compared to Charley's?" Claire widened her eyes and nodded her head toward Charley's, which was sinking lower into his hand.

Jessica finally seemed to catch on. She swept her hand in a pooh-poohing motion. "Oh, yes, she doesn't have any employees to worry about, or animals..."

Claire relaxed a bit. *Good, she's on the right track.*

"And, you know, how hard can it be to cram a bunch of stuff into a basket and tie it up with a pretty bow?" Jessica seemed to warm to the subject of belittling Claire's work. "It doesn't take any special artistic talent."

Oh yes it does.

"There are amateurs who make gift baskets all the time that look just as pretty."

But there's no theme or color scheme or attention to the interests of the recipient. Claire was beginning to feel prickly. She plastered on a fake bright smile.

"And it doesn't take any special training, like my occupational therapy degree for the hippotherapy I do." Jessica beamed, as if sure she had set things right. "So you see, Claire's business is nothing special, Charley."

Charley raised his head and glared at his wife. "Her business is too something special, Jessica. She's an artist."

"Thank you," Claire said quietly.

Jessica looked stricken, as if wondering what she had done wrong.

Roger stepped into the silence. "Well, there's nothing we can do about any of this tonight except try to forget it. We're here to have a good time, right?" He stood and picked up his beer. "Come on, Charley, I challenge you to a game of pool upstairs. Let's escape from the women for a while."

Good move. Claire smiled at Roger.

When Charley hesitated, Roger said, "Loser buys the winner a beer, and I can tell you that I play a lousy game of pool." He grinned and pointed with his chin toward the stairs.

Finally Charley rose. "Okay. Lead the way." He followed Roger up the stairs.

Once the men were out of earshot, Claire turned on Jessica. "You do know, don't you, that you managed to insult both Charley and me to the core in the space of a few minutes?"

Jessica's eyes widened. "But you wanted me to agree with you when you said your business was nothing compared to Charley's."

"I meant small, not talentless," Claire said. "And the whole point was to build up Charley's self-confidence, not tear down mine."

"I'm sorry. I screwed it all up, didn't I?" Jessica's shoulders slumped.

Claire scooted her chair closer to Jessica. "I really don't care what you say about me. It's Charley I'm worried about. His self-worth is shredded. And instead of making him feel better, you're constantly cutting him down."

Jessica drew back, eyes wide with shock. "What?"

"You're always nit-picking at him, telling him he's doing things wrong. You say he doesn't have a woman's touch, and his decisions aren't well thought-out. Even if all that's true, you don't need to keep shoving it in his face."

"Oh, hell."

Jessica's stricken expression made Claire say, "Do you even realize what you're doing?"

A tear trickled down Jessica's cheek. "No, but now that you've pointed it out, I can see it. Damn, I've been so selfish."

"Selfish how?"

"You may think Charley lacks self-confidence, but he's downright cocky compared to me."

Now it was Claire's turn to be shocked. "But you're so good at what you do!"

Jessica stopped in mid-motion of wiping away the tear. She looked at Claire as if to check if she was serious then finished the action. "Thank you. But I'd throw it all away if I could have Faith back, if I'd been able to prevent her death."

"There's no way you could have prevented it, Jessica."

"I could've fought the insurance company harder, and faster, when they turned her down for a bone marrow transplant. I could've pushed the hospital to look for a match even though we hadn't figured out how to pay for it yet."

Claire put an arm around Jessica. "The transplants are still not proven to work, even this many years later. You may just have prolonged her agony—and yours and Charley's. I think you both did everything you could have done."

Jessica tucked her hands in her lap and looked down at them. "Just like with Faith, I get so discouraged sometimes with my clients. I love the kids, and the disabled adults, too. And I want so much for them. But sometimes I feel like I'm spinning my wheels, that the therapy isn't helping them, not permanently. That all I'm giving them is a fun horse ride."

"It is helping them, Jessica. It is. Even in the short time I've been volunteering with you, I can see benefits. You can't solve all their problems or take their disabilities away, but you're certainly making their lives easier—and happier."

Jessica nodded. "I hope you're right about that." She sighed. "But I know you're right about what I've been doing to Charley. While I've been trying to build myself up, I've been subconsciously cutting him down." She looked at Claire. "I'll try to do better. Really."

Claire smiled. "That's all I'm asking. And I think it'll improve your relationship with each other, too."

"God, I hope so. I'm afraid these murders are going to tear us apart."

———

"Why do I always end up lugging these bloody things?" Roger tottered under the weight of Claire's huge horseback riding themed gift basket.

It was Saturday night, and they were making their way from the parking lot to the ballroom of the Colorado Springs Marriott hotel. It was the night of the fundraiser for Jessica's hippotherapy nonprofit. Claire had already given Jessica her family game night themed basket, but she had been working until the last minute on this one.

She held open the glass lobby door of the Marriott for Roger. As he went through, she peered at his face behind the fly whisk and two-piece lunge whip sticking out of either side of the basket. *Is he kidding?* She hoped so.

His sardonic smile said yes, so she adopted a teasing tone in response. "Because you're such a strong, handsome lunk, that's why." And he *was* handsome in his dark blue suit and crisp white shirt.

"And you're such a beautiful babe in that hot number that we couldn't risk mussing a hair on your head," Roger shot back.

She looked down at her slinky topaz gown, the hem of which brushed her calves. *Not bad.* She had worn two-inch heels to make her legs look longer, but she was feeling very unsteady on them. "I'd kiss you for that, but the basket's in the way."

Instead, Claire slipped a hand under the back of his suit coat and gave his rump a stealthy squeeze. She wanted him to know that she appreciated having him back in town and back in their bed. And, she wanted him to know that there might be a repeat performance of the welcome home they'd had Friday night after returning from Phantom Canyon. Absence did indeed make the heart grow fonder.

Roger winked at her. He had gotten the message.

Following the strains of the high school jazz trio that Jessica had asked to play for tip money, Claire preceded him into the ballroom. She found the spot on the silent auction table that was reserved for the gift basket. With a whoosh of relief, Roger set it down and stepped back. Claire adjusted the position and made sure the list of contents could be read by anyone wandering by. A squeal of delight from behind her made her turn.

A woman stepped in beside her. "Oh, I'm bidding on that!" She picked up a pen and wrote her name on the bid sheet with a flourish.

A warm glow infused Claire. She put a stack of her business cards next to the basket and gave the woman one. "Thank you, and if you ever need a gift basket, please call me."

"I will, definitely. This one is beautiful." The woman slipped the card into her purse and moved down the table to scan the rest of the auction items.

Roger linked his arm in Claire's and led her toward the bartender's station. "We're off to a good start."

Claire looked around the ballroom and made a quick mental count of the attendees. Not quite the hundred that Jessica had hoped for—at least not yet. Claire crossed her fingers and prayed for a successful outcome for this drinks, desserts, dancing, and silent auction event. In between therapy sessions, phone calls and paperwork for the stable business, and interruptions due to the murder investigations, Jessica had been working on the fundraiser non-stop. Hopefully if the event succeeded, it would shore up her confidence and she could share some of that with Charley.

After getting his beer, Roger went off in search of desserts, but Claire decided she had better stay as far from that table as possible. She sipped her white wine and looked for Jessica and Charley. She spotted them talking to a distinguished-looking older couple that Claire recognized from the society column in the *Gazette*— frequent charity event attendees. The woman's huge diamond engagement ring and matching earrings were a brilliant beacon to all that they had money, and lots of it.

Claire held back, not wanting to interrupt if Jessica was soliciting funds from the couple. After they said their goodbyes and moved off to the silent auction table, she sidled up to Jessica and whispered, "Are they going to donate?"

Jessica held up two crossed fingers. "They have a grandson with autism. I invited them to bring him out sometime next week for a free trial session. If that goes well, maybe I can talk them into donating." She looked Claire up and down. "You look lovely!"

Claire blushed, stopped herself from saying, "Oh, this old thing!" and gave a small curtsy instead. "Thank you, and so do you. That wine color goes very well with your hair."

Jessica smiled and smoothed her hand down the front of her floor-length gown. She linked her arm in Charley's. "And how about this handsome stud. Doesn't he look dashing in his tux?"

Charley tugged at his collar. "I don't know how I let you talk me into wearing this. I don't see anyone else here in a tux."

"As Jessica's escort, you're the most important man here," Claire said. "So you should—and do—look the best."

Jessica patted his arm. "And that's why I'm hanging on to you. I've already caught a couple of women eyeing you. I want to make it clear that *you're* not on the auction block. It's not often a good provider comes in such a handsome package."

Charley rolled his eyes, but his smile showed he enjoyed the praise, even though it was lathered on a little clumsily and thick.

Claire gave Jessica a knowing look. Then she asked the question that had been nagging her. "Did you sell enough tickets?"

"Just barely," Jessica said. "They've covered the cost of the food, bartender, and room, thank God."

"And I'm glad we were able to give two tickets to each of our staff," Charley added. "They've worked hard these last few days with us being so short-handed. They deserve the reward."

Jessica nodded. "I'm counting on the silent auction to bring in lots of money for the nonprofit, though. Thanks again for donating the two gift baskets."

Claire waved her hand. "I was happy to help."

Another couple came up to talk to the hosts, so Claire slipped away. She spotted Jorge Alvarez standing at the bar, looking spruced up in a leather-shouldered sport coat and bolo tie. When he left with two glasses of red wine, her gaze tracked him to Nancy Schwartz. Nancy took a sip of her wine, then snuggled close to Jorge and gave him a discreet peck. He responded by leaning over as if whispering in her ear, but nipped it instead.

Well, those two are certainly lovey-dovey.

Roger appeared at her elbow with a small plate piled high with gooey desserts. His gaze followed hers. "Charley's horse whisperer sure cleans up well. Who's he with?"

"That's Nancy Schwartz, Brittany's mom."

He frowned. "Isn't she the one who bad-mouthed Jessica's nonprofit?"

Claire nodded. "I'm surprised she had the nerve to show up here, though I suppose Jorge invited her."

"They do look like they've got the hots for each other. Speaking of hot, you should try this chocolate-stuffed jalapeno pepper. I know you like dark chocolate, and its kick isn't that bad." He held the plate out to her.

Claire inhaled the intoxicating scent of the chocolate, and her resolve to avoid the desserts weakened. She picked up the pepper and took a bite. A moan escaped her lips as the soft, rich chocolate coated her tongue. But as she chewed, the fire from the jalapeno took over and bloomed in her mouth. Some seeds must have been left near the stem. She coughed and tried to finish it quickly, so she could swallow it. But that just released more fire. And heat crept up her neck, the start of a hot flash. Tears filled her eyes.

"Crap, I'm sorry, honey. I guess you got a hot one." Looking worried, Roger held out a napkin.

Claire grabbed the napkin, spit the pepper into it and balled the mess up. She took a gulp of her wine and fanned her sweaty chest. "I need to go outside and cool off. That pepper started a major hot flash."

Roger ushered her out of the ballroom. He led her across the lobby to the glass doors opening to the outdoors. Once out on the sidewalk, Claire took a couple of big breaths of the evening air. The cool, dry breeze evaporated the dampness on her skin. Finally she felt her flush receding.

Roger swallowed the bite of blonde brownie he was chewing and studied her. "You okay?"

"I'll live, but no more chocolate jalapenos for me."

"Sorry about that." He held out his plate. "You want something else?"

She waved him off. "No, I should have stuck to my resolution to stay away from the desserts." She looked up at the clear night sky and could barely make out the wispy trail of the Milky Way. "Don't the stars look beautiful tonight?"

"Sure." Roger didn't sound impressed.

Then Claire heard the familiar giggle of a young woman nearby, followed by the deep-throated laugh of a man. She turned toward the sound. Brittany was walking up from the parking lot with her arm in Vince Donahue's. Her head was turned toward him and away from Claire. Her spiked heels clicked on the pavement, and her short metallic skirt swirled around her slim hips. Oh to have slim hips again, Claire mused as she watched them go inside.

Roger drank the last of his beer and waggled the empty glass. "Ready to go back in? I could use another."

"Sure."

They followed Brittany and Vince at some distance through the doors. Before Claire could catch up to them to say hello to Brittany, the young couple paused to talk to Tom Lindall and Hank Isley in the hallway.

Claire put a hand on Roger's arm. "Stop for a moment. Say something to me."

"What?" Looking confused, he glanced at the group ahead then back at her. "Is that the manager of Peak View Stables?"

Claire watched Tom drape a companionable arm over Hank's shoulder while the men all laughed at something. "Yes, and it looks like he knows Hank Isley pretty well, too."

"Maybe Hank used to work for him."

"I'll have to ask Charley."

Vince, Brittany, and Tom turned to walk into the ballroom together. But Hank hung back, as if trying to distance himself from them.

Claire turned Roger so they were both facing away from Hank. Roger gave her a questioning look, and she glanced over her shoulder. Hank slowly sauntered into the ballroom.

"Remember Charley mentioning that Tom Lindall seemed to know about Gil's drinking problem?" Claire said to Roger.

After Roger nodded, she said, "I don't think Brittany would have told him. I wonder if Hank is Lindall's spy."

THIRTEEN:
IMMIGRATION PROBLEMS

"SHE TOOK IT WELL, thank God, and didn't walk off the job." Jessica took a sip from her water bottle.

"I'm surprised." Claire was standing outside the corral at Gardner's Stables with Jessica after a hippotherapy session Monday afternoon. She had asked Jessica what the new wrangler's reaction was to Kyle's and Gil's unsolved murders.

"Kat's a tough broad. She mentioned she'd fought her way out of a couple of tight spots in the past. I got the impression one was an attempted rape." Jessica frowned. "Kat told me she has a concealed carry permit and could defend herself if anyone threatened her. I'm not sure I like one of our wranglers carrying a loaded weapon."

"What's Charley think?"

"He doesn't know yet. He's been back in his office all morning, on the phone. I thought it would be better for me to be the one to talk to Kat."

Jessica looked out toward the western horizon, where a trail ride had just departed. Hank was leading the group, and Brittany and Kat were both bringing up the rear, so Brittany could train the new wrangler.

"I don't know if there's much you can do about it, if she has a permit," Claire said. "And maybe it's a good idea to have a weapon on the premises. I'm glad she decided to stay on. You definitely need the help. But on to another topic. I've been itching to ask you, how much money did the silent auction bring in Saturday?"

"Even more than I hoped for." Jessica smiled, and her whole attitude brightened as she talked excitedly about what she planned to do with the money. Soon, however, the frown reappeared. "Damn, there's that detective again."

Claire turned and watched Wilson's car drive into the parking lot. Another unmarked car followed Wilson's into the lot, and two men got out. Like Wilson, they weren't in uniform, but from their bearing, they looked like cops. They wore khaki pants, dark polo shirts and athletic shoes. One was middle-aged with black-rimmed glasses, and the other was tall and well-muscled and looked to be in his late twenties. The older one talked to Wilson while they walked up from the lot. The younger one scanned the grounds of the stable as if sizing up the operation—or looking for something.

"Whatever they want, I'm sure Charley will need to be involved." Jessica headed toward the trailer where Charley was making phone calls. Claire followed. They ended up reaching the porch at the same time as Wilson and his two cohorts.

"Hello, Mrs. Gardner, Mrs. Hanover." Wilson waved a hand toward the middle-aged man. "This is Sam Unger with Immigration and Customs Enforcement. He has some questions for you and Mr. Gardner."

"I'll get Charley," Jessica replied.

While Jessica went inside, Claire invited the men to sit on the benches on the porch. Her heart thudded, but she tried to hide her nervousness while she sat with them. The younger ICE guy took a seat where he could have an unobstructed view of the whole stable yard.

Charley followed Jessica out of the trailer and joined them. He looked worried. "So, what's up?"

Wilson introduced Sam Unger to him. "Remember those phone numbers from Mexico in Kyle Mendoza's cell phone? We have reason to believe he was involved in an illegal immigrant smuggling operation."

Claire tensed, but Wilson didn't reveal his source. Nor did he look at her. Unger did, though, so he knew.

"As part of that investigation," Wilson continued, "these men need to examine your employment records."

Oh dear, Claire thought. *That starts the clock on Pedro losing his job.*

Charley frowned. "And if I don't have every T crossed and every I dotted in my paperwork, I'm in trouble. Is this really necessary?"

"I'm afraid so," Unger said.

"In a murder investigation," Wilson added, "we need to explore every possible lead."

"Shit." Charley put his hands on his hips. "Do you have a warrant?"

Unger handed over a piece of paper.

Charley studied it. "I know I can request three days to get my records in order."

Now it was Unger's turn to frown. "Yes, you have that right, though I'm disappointed that you aren't being more cooperative. I was hoping to move forward in my investigation today." He paused and quirked a brow at Charley. "You don't have anything to hide, do you?"

"No, I don't, but I know my rights, and I'm not going to change my mind."

"We'll be back on Thursday, then. Were you aware of Kyle Mendoza's activities?"

"Hell no," Charley said. "If I'd found out, he wouldn't have been working here anymore. First I heard anything was when Detective Wilson here told me about the Mexico phone numbers."

Wilson glanced at Claire. "Yes, and your employee Pedro Trujillo told me that he knows nothing about them, even though he knew Mendoza."

Unger lounged back in his chair, as if perfectly relaxed, but Claire could sense that behind his sunglasses he was peering intently at her brother. "You know," he said with a languid drawl, "I find it very difficult to believe that neither Mendoza's close friend nor his employer knew anything about his illegal activities."

Charley crossed his arms. "Well, I didn't."

"But your sister did." Unger glanced at Claire.

"What?" Charley and Jessica said in unison and stared at Claire.

Claire slid deeper into her seat. "Someone told me in confidence about Kyle's involvement in an immigrant smuggling ring, and I passed that information on to Detective Wilson."

Charley looked incredulous. "And you didn't tell me?"

"I'm sorry, Charley. I had to promise I wouldn't."

"I think I have a right to know about anything illegal going on at my business," Charlie said with a scowl.

"Nothing illegal was going on here. In fact, Kyle wasn't really doing anything illegal either. He wasn't involved in any actual smuggling. He was just recommending people for jobs." Even to Claire, her back-pedaling seemed lame.

Charley bunched a hand into a fist, then crossed his arms as if to prevent himself from hitting something. "I can't believe this! Aren't I more important to you than whoever you made this promise to?" His voice rose with each word.

Jessica glared at Claire. "It must have been someone here at the stable."

Rubbing his chin, Charley thought for a moment. "You know, I never asked Pedro about those phone numbers. Since he and Kyle were friends, he probably does know something."

He glanced at Claire, as if for confirmation that Pedro was her source, but she remained still and silent. Then he looked at Wilson. "I know he didn't talk to you, probably because he's suspicious of cops. But he might talk to me. If you all wait here, I'll go up to the barn and ask him about those numbers."

No, don't!

Unger's smile was predatory, hungry. "Good idea. I'll go with you."

He began rising from his chair, but Charley stopped him with a hand on his shoulder. "The barn's not part of the public area of my business. You can't go there without a warrant or invitation, and

I'm not inviting you. As I said, Pedro's probably suspicious of cops, so if you want your information, I need to go alone."

Unger glanced at Wilson, who nodded, then sank back into his chair.

Claire's mind raced while Charley stood and walked down the porch steps. Charley was unknowingly putting Pedro at risk. "I'll go with you. Pedro likes me." She hustled down the stairs and walked toward the barn at a fast clip so no one would have time to stop her.

Charley caught up with her. "Why are you coming along? Was Pedro your source?"

Claire glanced back at the group sitting on the porch and judged that they were out of earshot. "No, he wasn't, but I've got to tell you something else about him before you put him in danger. And you can't show any reaction to what I'm saying in front of the cops."

Charley stopped and stared at her.

Claire grabbed his arm and pulled him toward the barn. "Keep walking."

"What's going on?"

"Pedro was one of Kyle's clients. He's an illegal immigrant."

Charley's face reddened. "Damn it! Why the hell didn't you tell me before?"

"I didn't tell you until now because I knew you'd ask for three days if ICE came to see your records. I thought you could figure out what to do about Pedro in that amount of time." She clutched Charley's arm. "He's supporting his mother and sisters with what he makes here. I wanted to give him a chance to earn as much money as possible before you had to fire him."

Stopping in the open entrance to the barn, Charley turned to her. "We could have avoided all of this if you told me. I'm going to have to let Pedro go now. If he's still an employee when ICE comes back, I'll be fined. And they'll arrest him and deport him."

Claire rubbed her throbbing head. "I was trying to do the right thing, but I just seemed to make things worse. Again, I'm really sorry."

Charley exhaled loudly. "At least with three days' notice, maybe Pedro can make some kind of plans. I hate to do that to him, but I don't have any choice now that ICE is here."

At that moment, Pedro came out of a nearby stall pushing a wheelbarrow full of soiled hay. He stared in shock at Charley, then dropped the handles. The wheelbarrow tipped over, spilling its contents.

"ICE," he hissed, his eyes wide in alarm. He bolted out of the barn.

"Wait," Charley yelled. "Don't go. You're safe here!"

He started to go after Pedro, but he lost ground fast. Pedro's legs were pumping wildly, propelling him around the fenced-in pasture. He headed toward the hill at the back of Charley's property that separated it from the Blair Bridge Open Space.

Charley stopped and his shoulders slumped as if he realized trying to stop Pedro was hopeless. He trudged back to Claire. "Damn." He tore his cowboy hat off his head and slapped it against his thigh.

Claire put a hand on his shoulder. "There's no way you could have caught up to him."

"ICE didn't have a warrant to search my private buildings for people." Charley's voice was strained with regret. "Only one for my records. I could have protected Pedro for a while. But if ICE catches him now, they can deport him immediately."

Probably having realized the same thing, the young ICE officer had taken off running after Pedro. He passed them and headed for the hill. His athletic shoes and loose clothing had an obvious purpose now.

Pedro scrambled up the rise, his panic evident in his uncontrolled movements.

Claire and Charley watched the desperate chase in tense silence. Jorge came out of the barn and stood with them, concern etched in the weathered lines of his face.

The ICE officer slowly gained on Pedro. He methodically worked his way up the hill while Pedro clawed and slipped on the loose scree.

Unger swaggered up to Charley, a smug smile on his face. "We have a patrol car stationed on the other side of that hill, Mr. Gardner. We'll get him. Since he's running, he must be illegal."

"You've got to believe me that I didn't know," Charley replied.

"Doesn't matter," Unger said. "You'll be fined. And if you've got any other illegal immigrants on the property, you'll be fined for them, too."

Unger followed his cohort. His stride was confident and unhurried, as if realizing the young ICE officer wouldn't need his help.

Charley threw his hat on the ground. "Shit!"

Jessica and Detective Wilson came up, and Jessica bent down to pick up Charley's hat. Jorge listened intently while Charley explained the situation to Jessica.

The two young men crested the hill and disappeared from view. After a few tense minutes, they both returned. The ICE officer was pushing Pedro ahead of him. Pedro's hands were handcuffed behind him and his head was lowered in defeat. Sam Unger met them about halfway down the hill. He took one of Pedro's arms and the three of them picked their way slowly back down.

"Do you know where Pedro lives?" Charley asked Jorge.

Jorge nodded.

"Once they get back, I want you to get Pedro's key and pack up his stuff for him. You'll still be on the clock for the time you spend there." He turned to Wilson. "Do you know how soon they'll bus him back over the border?"

To Wilson's credit, his expression was sympathetic. "They send a bus most mornings. It leaves from Denver and stops here for any local deportees before heading down to Mexico. But I'm going to request a deportation hold on him. I may need to question Pedro some more before these murder cases are closed. Hopefully my request will be approved."

"Just in case it isn't," Charley said, "I'll make sure I get his stuff and back pay to him before tomorrow morning."

"Can't we do anything else for poor Pedro?" Jessica asked. "Can we sponsor him for a green card?"

"I'm afraid not," Wilson said. "If someone enters the country illegally, they have to go back to their home country. Then they have to wait ten years before petitioning to enter legally."

Jessica's mouth dropped open. "Ten years! What kind of stupid law is that?"

Wilson shrugged. "We cops don't make the laws. We just enforce them."

"I hate to think of the impact this will have on his family." Claire turned to Charley. "Is there any way we can help him find work in Mexico?"

"What about your former boss in Oaxaca?" Charley asked Jorge.

"I will call him," Jorge said quietly.

"And I'll give Pedro a good reference. You know, with his English skills, he might do well working at a stable in one of the tourist areas in Mexico. Ask your former boss if he's got any contacts, and we'll follow up with them." Charley rubbed his hands together, energized now that he had a plan for helping Pedro.

By then, the ICE officials had arrived with Pedro in tow. He looked heartbroken, his eyes reddened but defiant, a scratch leaking blood down his dusty cheek.

Jessica hugged him. "Oh Pedro, I'm so sorry this happened."

"*Sí*." The word came out choked. Pedro clamped his lips shut, as if afraid he would break down if he said anything else.

The young ICE officer tugged on his arm, directing him toward the parking lot, but Charley stepped toward them. "May I have a moment, please?"

The officer glanced at Unger, who nodded.

Charley briefed Pedro on their plan. He confirmed with Unger that he could bring Pedro's things to the jail while he was on immigration hold. Unger assured him the money and clothes would be held in a safe place and given to Pedro before he boarded the bus.

Jorge took Pedro's apartment key, got directions on what to pack for him, and clamped a hand on Pedro's shoulder. A long moment of silence passed between them before Jorge squeezed and released Pedro's shoulder and turned away.

Unger watched all this with his arms crossed. He stepped up to Pedro. "You know, I can make this easier for you, recommend to the judge that he give you thirty days for voluntary departure if you give me some information on Oscar Vargas."

Pedro drew back, his eyes wide. "I no can do that."

"Why the hell not?"

"He shoot me. Just like Hector."

Wilson perked up. "Hector Garcia, the illegal immigrant whose body we found two weeks ago dumped in Monument Creek?"

Pedro hesitated, then nodded.

"How do you know Oscar Vargas shot Hector Garcia?"

Pedro shrugged. "Everyone know."

"Hot damn," Wilson said. "This is the first good lead we've had in that case."

Claire had a sudden memory flash. "There's something I didn't tell Charley about the fight between Gil and Pedro that might help here," she said to Wilson. "Remember I told you that Gil said he knew about Vargas's operation, and Kyle's hand in it, and he threatened to tell ICE?"

"It sure would have saved us a lot of trouble if he had," Sam Unger said sarcastically.

Wilson nodded. "Vargas may have killed both of them, especially if he found out that Kaplan threatened to go to ICE. And now we know he's killed before." He turned to Pedro. "Did you tell Vargas about Kaplan's threat?"

"No, sir."

"You sure?" Wilson waited while Pedro nodded then turned to Unger. "This is helpful information for me, at least. It could lead to closing three murder cases, the two here and Hector Garcia's." He turned to Pedro. "Where can we find Oscar Vargas?"

"*No sé.* He find me when I need pay him."

"Pay him?" Jessica asked.

Claire explained the smuggling fee to her while Wilson continued to pressure Pedro. Finally he asked, "Do you have a phone number for him?"

Pedro shook his head. "He have mine."

Unger shot Pedro a skeptical look. "We'll need your cell phone, then, so we can back trace the calls. Where's he hang out?"

"*No sé.*"

"Don't tell us you don't know. I think you're just afraid to say," Unger spat back. "Look, this Vargas can't get you in Mexico."

Pedro shrank back. "*Sí*, he can."

The cops stood there with arms crossed. They were at an impasse.

Wilson sighed. "Take him. We've got enough to work with now to find Oscar Vargas on our own. If not, Pedro and I will have another talk."

Claire chewed on her lip. Hopefully they would find Vargas before he found Pedro—or anyone else at the stable he might think would rat on him.

———

Late that afternoon, Claire was back in the reception area of the Gardner's Stables trailer office. She had gone home to fetch an old duffel bag and brought it to the trailer. When Jorge returned with Pedro's belongings stuffed into a well-worn backpack and a large black trash bag, Claire repacked the clothes into the duffel. Jessica added some nonperishable snacks and a couple of bottles of water.

Charley returned from the bank with cash for Pedro's back pay. He put the envelope in the outside pocket of the backpack.

"Should we hide the money?" Claire asked.

"No," Charley said. "When I turn this stuff over to ICE, I'll have them count the money and give me a receipt. That's the best way to make sure it isn't stolen. They're going to search all his stuff anyway."

"Do you think Pedro will just turn around and try to cross the border again?" Jessica asked.

"Most illegal immigrants do. I hope Pedro won't, given our plan. I hope he'll wait to find out if Jorge and I can find him a legal stable job in Mexico." Charley stood with hands on his hips, surveying Pedro's meager pile of possessions. "Well, I guess I'd better take these over to the jail."

He shouldered the backpack and picked up the duffel by the handles. Before he could leave, the trailer door opened and Jorge and Nancy Schwartz stepped in.

"We have to talk to you." Jorge's expression was solemn, his hat clenched in his hand. "It's important."

"Sure." Charley put down Pedro's gear and swept a hand toward the sofa. "Have a seat."

While Charley settled into a chair across from them, Claire and Jessica shared a puzzled glance. *Why was Nancy here?*

Nancy sat primly on the end of the sofa with her hands clasped in her lap. She looked at Jessica. "First, I owe you an apology for saying those nasty things about your stable at the Childhood Services Center. I called the director and explained to her that the Mendozas have dropped their suit. I told her that what I said was done out of jealousy, not based on any facts. And if you're willing, I'd like us to go back there together when the two weeks is up."

"Apology accepted," Jessica said. "But why the sudden change of heart?"

Nancy looked at Jorge, who covered her hands with one of his. "Jorge told me how much you two have helped him, how kind you are. He helped me realize that you weren't my competition and that we could work together." She paused and took a deep breath. "And we're all going to have to work together to solve a bigger problem."

Charley's brow furrowed. "What problem?"

"My problem." Jorge shifted in his seat and took a deep breath. "This is very hard for me to say. After the ICE man said he would fine you for Pedro and for any other illegal immigrants you employ, I realized I could not stay quiet any longer. You see, I legally entered the United States on a temporary work visa. But that expired many years ago, and since your friend was still anxious to have me work for him, I just stayed. I got a fake social security card and used that to get a New Mexico driver's license. Your friend thought I had gotten my green card. So, I am an illegal immigrant, too."

Charley closed his eyes and let his head fall back against the chair back. "Damn it all to hell."

Claire and Jessica exchanged stricken looks.

"This is where I come in." Nancy's tongue flicked across her lips. "I would like to offer Jorge a job at my stable, so he'll no longer be on your books when ICE comes."

"Even though you know that's illegal?" Claire asked.

"For someone I love, I'm willing to take that chance. Then after things settle down, maybe he can come back here to work." Nancy smiled at Jorge. "Or maybe he'll like working at my stable and will stay."

He frowned. "We did not talk about that."

Charley opened his eyes, sat up and shook his head. "I'm already down two staff again, with Pedro gone. Another of my wranglers is still green, having just started today. I need Jorge here. I'd rather contact an immigration lawyer in town and see what we can do. I think the laws are different if you entered the country legally than if you crossed the border illegally like Pedro did."

"But that's risky for Jorge," Nancy said.

"We've got three days," Charley replied. "Give me that time, at least, to see if we can solve this."

Jorge looked at Nancy for acceptance.

She sighed. "I guess so."

Charley's sad gaze fell on Jorge. "I don't want to lose you, Jorge. You've been a damn fine employee and a good friend. I rely on you for a lot."

Jorge looked pained. "It hurts me to cause you so much trouble, especially on top of your other problems."

"And I just thought of another thing," Charley said, with widening eyes. "I've been paying social security for both you and Pedro, and neither one of you will ever see any of that money."

Jorge nodded. "The pay we get after taxes is still much more than we would get in Mexico—if we could find the work. But I have heard that ICE carefully researches the numbers when they search a business's records, and that will tell them I am not legal."

Charley exhaled. "And they don't give employers a way to reliably check the numbers other than with E-verify, which misses a lot of cases of identity fraud. Of course, if I'd found out your identity documents weren't legal, I wouldn't have hired you—and benefited from your expertise."

"I am very, very sorry." Jorge's face screwed up as if he were in pain. "If the lawyer cannot help, I will leave before ICE returns, so you will not have to pay the fine for me."

Rubbing his forehead, Charley grimaced. "I don't know how this stable can function without you."

"This sucks." Jessica said. "It's not fair, not to you, not to us. You're just trying to earn a living, and we're just trying to run a business."

Everyone was quiet.

First Kyle, then Gil, then Pedro, and now Jorge, Claire thought. Charley's stable was being decimated not only by loss of business from news of the murders, but also by the loss of most of his employees. Only Hank Isley, part-time Brittany, and the new hire remained. Thinking back on the murders reminded Claire that Nancy hadn't been completely ruled out as a suspect. Maybe she could push some of Nancy's buttons and see what came out.

"Nancy?" she asked. "I see you and Jorge are dating, but you disapproved of Brittany dating Kyle Mendoza. Isn't that a little unfair?"

Nancy frowned. "We're completely different. I've already raised my family, and I'm supporting myself since Brittany's father and I divorced. I don't need anyone to support me."

"Neither does Brittany," Claire said. "She seems like a capable young woman who can support herself."

Nancy snorted. "As a wrangler?" She glanced at Jorge. "No offense, but I want more for Brittany, much more."

"So you wanted to get Kyle out of her life."

"Yes, and that damn Vince Donahue, too."

Nancy was getting emotional. Claire decided it was time to move in for the kill. "Brittany told me that when you came to pick her up on the night Kyle was killed you went up to the port-a-potty. She couldn't see you from the car, so you could have gone in the barn then, too."

"Why? Jorge's car was gone, so I knew he wasn't there."

"But Kyle was there. Maybe you wanted to get him out of Brittany's life, as you said."

Nancy shot to her feet. "You can't be serious. You're trying to pin his murder on me?"

Claire gave a theatrical shrug. "If the shoe fits."

"Claire!" Jessica came around from behind her desk. "I don't know where this idea came from, but Charley and I don't agree with Claire, Nancy. Not at all."

Damn. There went all of the momentum out of Claire's accusation. Her heart sank.

Nancy advanced on Claire, her face red and her hands balled into fists. "I'm not a killer. I may not have liked Kyle, but I wouldn't have killed him. No way."

Claire held up her hands. "Okay, I'm sorry."

Nancy wheeled on Jorge. "Come on. We're getting out of here."

Jorge rose and the two left, Nancy literally huffing as they walked out onto the porch.

Charley followed and shook Jorge's hand, holding on to it for a long moment before releasing it. Claire inched past him to watch Jorge and Nancy march toward the parking lot. Nancy's stiff back could reflect true indignation, or she was an awfully good actress.

Charley yelled after them. "We'll make this work, Jorge!"

Jorge nodded then put an arm around Nancy. He bent his head toward her, saying something that was obviously meant to calm her.

Charley turned on Claire. "Why the hell did you say those things to Nancy?"

A movement in the stable yard caught her eye. Hank Isley was trotting toward the barn, from the direction of the back of the trailer. She poked her head back in the trailer and saw that both the front and back windows were wide open, to let in the breeze.

She looked back at Charley. "A more important question is, did Hank Isley just overhear our whole conversation?"

FOURTEEN:
AN INFORMER

CLAIRE'S MIND WAS WORKING faster than her fingers Tuesday morning. Sitting at the large oak table in her basement workroom, she was constructing a Denver Broncos gift basket for an avid fan. She had dyed a large bamboo basket just the right vivid orange to match one of the team's colors. Now she was braiding a navy blue ribbon through the weave of the basket.

The braiding task left her mind free to review the potential suspects in Kyle's and Gil's murders. The most likely one, and the one Detective Wilson was pursuing, was Oscar Vargas, the immigrant smuggler. He had demonstrated the ruthlessness to kill at least once before. Claire could see him going after Gil, if he thought Gil had seen him kill Kyle. Or if he found out that Gil had threatened to take information about his smuggling ring to ICE. But as Brittany had said, Vargas had no reason to kill Kyle, and he valued Kyle's work for his ring.

Claire cut the ribbon and tucked the loose end into the weave. She pulled a clear box labeled "Ribbons" off a plastic shelf. The shelving lining two walls of the workroom contained baskets, packing and wrapping materials such as Spanish moss and colored cellophane, fabric remnants, nonperishable foodstuffs, and Colorado-themed gift items and trinkets. She pulled a white ribbon spool out of the box and started weaving it through the basket alongside the navy. Her mind went to work on weaving a case for another suspect.

Claire doubted that Nancy Schwartz had the upper arm strength to deliver the fatal hammer blow to Kyle's head. But if Gil's suicide note was correct and he had struck Kyle, Nancy could have come upon Kyle's unconscious body in the barn and seized the opportunity to eliminate her daughter's unworthy suitor. Dragging him into Gunpowder's stall and poking the horse with the hay fork would have been an easy way to keep Kyle from wooing Brittany. Or to discredit Jessica's nonprofit by making it seem like a dangerous horse was kept on the property.

Nancy had the opportunity, but she was also a horse lover. Would she have injured Gunpowder to force the horse to cover her tracks? Maybe. If she was incensed enough at Kyle—or Jessica. Nancy had a temper, but she also seemed truly indignant when Claire accused her.

Then there was Kyle's rival for Brittany's affections, Vince Donahue, who had wasted no time moving into her life after Kyle was killed. He worked with horses, so he would have had no qualms about going into Gunpowder's stall. And he was a hunter, so was familiar with guns and likely owned a rifle. Lastly, he worked for

Tom Lindall, who resented Charley's intrusion into the Garden of the Gods, which he viewed as his private domain for trail rides.

Claire snipped off the second ribbon and began stuffing white and navy blue shreds into the bottom of the basket. If Hank Isley was the spy she suspected he was, he was working for Tom Lindall, too. Also, he had benefited financially from Kyle's death by becoming the trail guide lead. He was pocketing large tips from the tourists, especially the women whom he enjoyed buttering up.

Of course, Tom Lindall could have killed Kyle himself, hoping to discredit Charley's stable by making it look like Gunpowder did it and Charley kept dangerous horses. Unlike the others, Lindall probably had nothing against Kyle personally. Kyle may have just been unlucky to be the last worker at the stable that night if Tom came by looking to sabotage Charley's business. But there were certainly easier and less lethal ways to sabotage a business.

Claire stopped and tapped her scissors against the table. Why would any of these four kill Gil? If the killer was the one who both hit Kyle with a hammer and finished him off by dragging him into Gunpowder's stall, maybe he or she suspected Gil saw what happened to Kyle. If Gil was still on the grounds at the time, that was likely. But why take the chance of killing Kyle with Gil still around? Claire didn't think Gil really saw anything, because as Charlie said, he would have told the police, if only for self-preservation.

A new thought popped into her brain. What if the two deaths were totally unrelated? Maybe one of these people killed Kyle and another killed Gil, each for their own reasons. And was anyone else capable of committing either murder that she wasn't even considering?

She rubbed her aching head. *Oh, God, this is just too complicated!*

Refocusing on the task at hand, she pulled over the stack of Broncos gear she had gathered for the basket. She had bought a Broncos official team hat, T-shirt, scarf, and socks. And since the woman receiving the basket was also a foodie and wine lover, Claire was including a Broncos salt and pepper set, cake decorating kit, wineglasses, corkscrew and wine stoppers. For an edible item, she had a bag of orange and blue raspberry-flavored Broncos-blend popcorn from the Pikes Peak Gourmet Popcorn Factory.

She started arranging the items in the basket, and her mind wandered back to the murders. The next step in the case was to find the rifle that was used to kill Gil Kaplan. Whoever owned that rifle was likely his killer, and maybe also Kyle's. Detective Wilson was the best one to go after Oscar Vargas, but maybe she could sniff around, see if Tom Lindall or Nancy Schwartz owned any rifles. Of course, Wilson could do that, too.

In fact, she chided herself, why did she think she could help solve these murders anyway? It was his job, after all, not hers.

Just then her home phone rang, making her jump and knock over the half-filled basket, spilling her careful arrangement and scattering her thoughts along with it.

One of the wineglasses rolled off the table, hit the carpet and bounced. Claire lunged for it, but before she could catch it, the glass knocked against the table leg and cracked.

"Damn it!" She snatched up the phone. "Hello?"

"Mrs. Hanover? This is Frank Wilson calling."

Not Detective Wilson, but Frank Wilson. *Interesting.* "What can I do for you?"

"Well, um, that's why I'm calling. I have a favor to ask you."

Something in his tone said that this was difficult for him. Admitting that he needed help from her. What in the world could she possibly do for him?

"What favor?"

"As you know, we're trying to find out where Oscar Vargas lives so we can get a warrant to search his place for the rifle that killed Gil Kaplan." He paused and something rustled near the receiver.

Claire envisioned him pulling on his shirt collar. "Ye—es?"

"Both ICE and Colorado Springs PD have exhausted all our means, including quizzing our street informers. And we have nothing. No one can tell us, or is willing to tell us, where Vargas holes up. Here's where you come in. I know you and Leon Fox have a relationship. I was wondering if you could ask him."

Claire thought about the flamboyant Colorado Springs drug boss who had helped her solve the murder Roger had been accused of in February. Leon had admired her spunk and the two had developed a strange friendship, based on the exchange of favors. And he was always looking for ways to secretly eliminate his competition. But...

"Why would Leon know where Vargas is?"

"There's quite an overlap between drug smuggling and immigrant smuggling gangs. So Fox may have some contacts who know Vargas—or he may know the man himself."

"Okay, I'll try him." *God help me. I wonder what favor Leon's going to ask for in return.*

"Now, don't put yourself in any danger."

Claire pshawed. "I'm safer with Leon than anywhere else."

"Thanks. I appreciate it. *We* appreciate it."

Claire knew that was hard for him to say. "I'm happy to help."

After finishing the conversation with him, she righted the Broncos gift basket. She replaced the spilled items, except for the wineglasses etched with the Broncos logo, one of which was now cracked. She stood with it in her hand and thought about what to do. She didn't have time to order another pair. With a sigh, she pulled a bottle of Colorado wine off her shelves and put that in the basket instead. Tying some orange and blue curling ribbon around its neck might make it look more team-oriented. It was the best she could do.

She threw the cracked glass in the trash and wondered what she would do with one Broncos wineglass. She found Leon's cell phone number in her directory and called him.

Leon's deep voice boomed through the connection. "Claire, my favorite white woman. What you up to, lady?"

"Right now, making a Broncos-themed gift basket. But I have a favor to ask." She explained the deaths at Charley's stable and Detective Wilson's search for Oscar Vargas. "Do you know the man?"

"Not personally, but I know his rep. He's a mean mother. A business associate used one of his guys to run some product across the border awhile back. But he broke that connection when Vargas wanted a bigger share of the take."

"Does your associate know where Vargas lives?"

"Don't rightly know. I suppose I could ask him. Poke around a little. So what's in this for me?"

"You mean besides eliminating more of your competition?"

Leon let out a belly laugh. "Yeah, woman."

Claire looked at the tumbled basket on her work table. "Anyone you know have a birthday coming up? I could make a gift basket for you."

Leon laughed. "I bet you could. You remember Condoleza, right?"

The girlfriend of the massage therapist who had been shot dead while giving Claire a massage. "Oh yeah."

"She's laid up with a broke arm."

"Oh, God, did she get involved with another abusive guy?"

"No, nothing like that. You know I watch out for that girl. She fell on her arm while salsa dancing a couple nights ago. Probably had one too many mojitos." He chuckled. "I was gonna take her some flowers or something, but a gift basket from you would be better."

"Sure, I can do that. Tell me what kinds of things she likes." Claire had already pulled over a pen and a pad of paper and written "salsa how-to DVD?" on it.

She and Leon brainstormed on items for Condoleza's basket, then Leon said, "Think you could have it ready tomorrow? We could slam down some lunch at my rib-joint and do the trade. I should be able to make some calls by then and find out Vargas's hidey-hole for you."

So soon? Claire's mind raced. She had invited Charley and Jessica over for dinner, and she still had the Broncos basket to finish and deliver. But maybe she could delay delivery of that one. She would have to spend the rest of the day buying items for Condoleza's basket locally. It would be tough, but the sooner she could help Wilson close the case, the sooner Charley's business could start to recover.

"Okay, I'll meet you there at noon."

———

At six that evening, Claire opened her front door to Charley and Jessica and invited them in. They would be eating a store-bought cake for dessert, and chips and salsa for an appetizer instead of the seven-layer-dip she had originally planned to make. But she had succeeded in buying most of the items she had listed for Condoleza's gift basket. Roger fixed drinks while she finished putting a salad together, then she could finally relax for a few minutes.

She plopped on the couch in the living room and gladly accepted a margarita from Roger.

"You look a little frazzled, Claire," Jessica said. "I hope having us over wasn't too much trouble."

Claire waved her hand. "No, it's not that. I've been busy working on a gift basket that I'm trading for information on where Oscar Vargas is." When the other three showed their surprise, she explained Wilson's request and her deal with Leon.

Roger frowned. "You know I don't like you associating with him. He's a drug dealer, for God's sake."

"I trust him." Claire patted his arm. "And it's just lunch. If I can do anything to help Charley, I will."

Charley's eyes widened. "I don't want you putting yourself in danger for me."

"It's hard to explain," Claire replied, "But Leon's a friend. He won't hurt me—or let anyone else hurt me either."

Charley studied her for a moment then said, "Okay, but only if you're sure you'll be safe."

"I'm sure." Claire sipped her margarita and savored the perfect blend of tangy lime, peppery tequila, and sweetness. "Now tell me about your day."

"I've been busy today, too," Charley said. "First, Jorge called his former boss in Oaxaca. The man contacted a friend with a tourist horseback riding business in Puerto Vallarta, whose English was excellent. Jorge talked to him about Pedro, then I got on the phone. He said Pedro sounds ideal for his operation and that he should come talk to him once he's deported back to Mexico."

"That's great news." Roger raised his glass in a toast and took a sip.

Charley joined him and smacked his lips. "You make a great margarita, Roger. I also had a meeting with an immigration lawyer about Jorge."

"What did he say?" Claire asked.

Charley shook his head sadly. "He told me that, legally, since I now know that Jorge's not a legal immigrant, I can no longer employ him. If I do, not only will I have to pay a fine, I can be criminally prosecuted."

"Damn," Roger muttered.

Claire leaned forward. "Is there any way you can help him become a legal immigrant?"

"I asked. The lawyer said there's a form I could fill out, a Petition for an Alien Worker." Charley took a gulp of his drink. "But it won't do any good, because the only kinds of workers that are being approved are temporary agricultural workers like crop-pickers, health care workers like nurses, and special categories like highly educated PhD types where no U.S. equivalent exists. There's basically no way an employer can sponsor someone who is just a skilled worker."

Roger polished off his margarita. "What a shame. So Jorge's screwed, then?" He stood and reached out a hand for Charley's empty glass. "Another?"

"Sure." Charley handed him the glass, and as Roger went to the pitcher to pour more, he said, "About the only way immigrants are legally getting in from Mexico these days is if they have a family member who is already legally in the U.S. and who fills out a Petition for an Alien Relative. And even then, the wait is at least sixteen years."

Claire sat up straight. "Sixteen years? You have got to be kidding me!"

"No he's not." Jessica shook her head. "It's absolutely ridiculous."

Charley took the drink Roger offered him. "The lawyer says that's why we have so many illegal immigrants, because there's no realistic way they can get in legally. And the conditions are too deplorable in Mexico for them to stay. There's no work, no way for them to feed their families. That's why we need immigration reform. He said Jorge's best chance was to keep delaying court dates while we wait for politicians to reinstate Reagan's Immigration Act or some equivalent."

Roger resettled on the couch next to Claire. "What's that?"

"It offered temporary amnesty to immigrants who were already in the country and filed for legal status. It allowed them to keep on working and living here while they waited for their paperwork to go through. If we get some kind of immigration reform like that, it should open up more job categories for employers like me to legally petition for someone."

Jessica, who had been slouching in her chair and looking sadder by the minute, piped in. "So what's the delaying tactic?"

Charley looked at her. "Well first, the lawyer told me that I should have Jorge come in and talk to him and hire him as his legal counsel."

"But he can't afford a lawyer," Jessica replied.

Charley held up a hand. "I'll pay for it."

Jessica made as if to speak, then stopped. Claire's thoughts filled in the unspoken words, *Charley can't afford it either.*

"The next step," Charley said, "is to have me, or preferably a relative, file a petition for his legal status, and for Jorge to file for a green card. At that point, he'll be arrested for being in the country illegally."

"But that's no good," Claire began.

Charley held up a hand. "Hear me out. I'll bail Jorge out, and the lawyer will ask the judge to schedule a formal hearing of Jorge's case. Hopefully the judge will agree to a hearing, and it will take many months to schedule it. Also, the lawyer will try to keep on delaying the date. In the meantime, I ask for a temporary work authorization, pending the hearing. Hopefully that won't take as long."

Roger frowned. "And until then, Jorge can't legally work and earn any money."

Charley nodded dolefully. "Right. He could volunteer for me in exchange for room and board, maybe."

"And Jorge's not the only one this hurts," Jessica said. "We'll be paying for the lawyer and bail out of our pocket just on the chance that reform will take place before his case comes up."

"But I'm still going to do it," Charley said fiercely. "Not just for Jorge, but for me. I need him."

"Have you explained all this to Jorge?" Claire asked. "What's he think of it?"

Charley shook his head. "I'll talk to him tomorrow morning at the stable." He straightened. "And speaking of the stable, I've got definite proof now that Tim Lindall has a spy on my property."

"How so?" Roger asked.

"Lindall called me today and said he knows I've got illegal immigrants working for me." Charley made a sour face like he had just bitten into a crabapple. "He said that if I can't follow the law, I don't deserve to be in business. Figuring the news about Pedro must have gotten out, I said I didn't know Pedro was illegal when I hired him. Lindall said, 'He's not the only one,' and told me he was going to file a written complaint with the city Parks and Rec director."

Jessica nibbled on her lip. "Do you think he knows about Jorge?" Charley nodded.

Claire gripped her drink glass tighter. "Remember when I thought Hank Isley may have been listening to our conversation yesterday? And that he was talking to Tom Lindall like he knew him well at Jessica's charity event? I bet that's how Tom found out."

Charley exhaled deeply. "Hank's been a good employee. Stepped right into Kyle's role of leading most of our trail rides. I can't fire him, too."

"But if you know Hank's feeding Tom information, and Hank doesn't know you know, maybe you can use that to your advantage." Claire raised her eyebrow.

A sly grin spread across Jessica's face. "Oooh, sneaky."

"How?" Charley asked.

"What kind of false information could we feed Hank that would create havoc for Tom?" Claire tapped a finger on her lip while her mind raced. "Something that would unbalance his business as much as yours is now, and would let us know once and for all that Hank's the spy?"

"Maybe tell Hank that ICE is going to search Tom's records, too?" Roger offered.

"If Tom's got a lick of smarts," Charley said, "he's already figured out that's going to happen."

Claire stood and walked to the window, then turned to the group. "What about something that could affect his horses instead of his staff?"

"Like a disease?" Charley nodded. "That could work. Something like strangles that could mean your whole herd has to be quarantined."

"What's strangles?"

"Equine distemper. Highly contagious. If Tom heard one of his horses had it, he'd cancel that day's rides and set all of his wranglers to work sterilizing equipment and stalls. It would drive him batty." Charley rubbed his hands together.

"So how do we spread the rumor?" Claire asked.

Charley looked at Jessica. "Outlaw's come up lame, right?"

She nodded. "Just started limping this afternoon. Jorge treated him, though. He thinks the swelling in his hoof will come down in a day or two."

"And today was Hank's day off, so he doesn't know." Charley stood and started pacing. "If I remember right, Roger, you were riding Outlaw when your group met up with Vince's on the trail."

Roger nodded.

"Jessica, you and I could have a conversation in the barn within earshot of Hank tomorrow." Charley rubbed his hands together. "You tell me that the vet said Outlaw has equine distemper. When I ask where he could have gotten it from, you say that you questioned Roger, who was riding him when the two trail rides met up. And Roger said Outlaw had contact with one of Lindall's horses. I'll say that I'm glad we caught it in time and Outlaw should stay quarantined."

Jessica stood. "We could trailer Outlaw to our house before Hank comes in," she said excitedly, "and let him recover from his lameness in our fenced yard. With Outlaw gone, Hank won't be able to see if he really has strangles or not."

"You can keep a horse in your yard?" Roger asked.

Jessica nodded. "It's why we picked the house. It's zoned for up to three horses, and we figured we could use it to quarantine stock if we needed to."

"I'll tell Hank that I told Park and Rec about the contact with Tom's herd," Charley continued, "that I think that's where Outlaw got it from, and that they'll probably want to test all of Tom's herd. That'll drive Tom into a tizzy." Charley chuckled and slapped his thigh.

"Brittany was on that ride," Claire said. "Will she back up your story? Remember she's dating Vince Donahue."

"She's not scheduled to work tomorrow," Jessica said.

"By Thursday, the damage will be done. Tom will have wasted a day sanitizing his stable and trying to figure out which horse or horses are sick." Charley grinned. "He'll be madder than a wet cat, but he won't be able to do anything about it, because then he'd have to admit Hank is his spy."

Charley returned to his chair and reached out to drag a tortilla chip through the salsa. "Speaking of wasting, I'm wasting away here. When's dinner?" He popped the chip into his mouth.

Claire looked at her watch and gasped. "Oh no, the chicken casserole was supposed to be done twenty minutes ago. I hope it's not burned now." She rushed into the kitchen to check. She hoped Charley wouldn't be burned by his scheme either.

FIFTEEN:
RIBS AND RUMORS

JUST AFTER NOON ON Wednesday, Claire drove into the parking lot of the Southern-style barbecue restaurant in Old Colorado City where Leon invested his cocaine-selling profits. She spotted his long black limo with heavily tinted windows in the back of the lot, but no one was around. Assuming that he, his bodyguard, and driver were all inside, she got out and lifted Condoleza's large gift basket from the trunk. Holding the basket gingerly in front of her, she walked to the restaurant's front door.

She was about to set the basket on the ground to open the door when the door swung out for her. Leon's bodyguard, a tall young white man with huge tattooed biceps and an oiled shaved head, stepped out and held the door open for her. He had never spoken to her, and he didn't this time either, so she just gave him a nod and said, "Thanks," as she walked past him.

Once inside, the familiar aromas of wood-smoked pork and fried chicken enveloped her, and she paused to take an appreciative sniff. Leon's favorite table was in the back room, so she headed straight there, past other customers eating and talking in the large front room. As she passed the doorway to the kitchen, she saw a burly cook taking a steaming pan of fresh-baked cornbread out of the oven. Her knees almost gave out as her stomach growled and her mouth started salivating.

Diet be damned.

She rounded the corner into the small room and spotted Leon and his driver standing in the back. Leon's driver was the same size and height as his bodyguard, but dark-skinned and with curly black hair. Both men were talking to the chubby, gray-haired woman who was the restaurant's hostess. Leon threw his head back to laugh at something she said, showing his gleaming white teeth, and gave her a pat on the fanny. Taller than his two henchmen by a couple of inches, he still sported his hefty paunch, so he had been no more successful with his diet than Claire had.

He spotted Claire and approached her. "Well, looky here. Ain't this purty." He lifted the gift basket out of Claire's arms to study it.

Claire pointed out some of the items behind the cellophane. When he had told her that Condoleza's favorite foods were dried apricots and pistachio nuts, she not only included them, but used their colors in the basket scheme and the huge bow on top. She had also stashed some apricot-scented shampoo and apricot-colored nail polish inside.

Leon nodded his head appreciatively. "You done good, woman. Condoleza's gonna go ape shit when she sees this."

He handed the basket to his driver, who put it on one of the two-top tables lining the walls of the room. He and the bodyguard sat at another two-top, while Leon led Claire to the round table in the center of the room, covered with a familiar red-checked tablecloth.

As she settled herself in a chair, Leon said, "I already ordered for us, since I know you like a good mess o' ribs as much as I do." He patted his stomach and grinned.

Claire smiled. "I've been drooling since I walked through the front door."

Ensconced in his chair, Leon guffawed. He turned to the hostess, who had come in with a pitcher of sweet tea and two glasses. "We've made us a convert, Maybelle."

The hostess smiled at Claire. "Be sure to bring all your friends, then." She poured their glasses and left the pitcher, then went over to chat with Leon's two men.

Claire took a sip of tea. She set the glass down and leaned toward Leon with her hands on the table. "Were you able to find out anything for me?"

He gave a somber nod and pulled a folded slip of paper out of the pocket of a leather jacket draped over the back of his chair. He slid the note across to Claire. "This here's Vargas's address."

Claire reached for the paper, but Leon put one of his massive hands over hers, stopping her. "Now when you give this to Wilson, you need to tell him the rest of what I'm gonna tell you." He peered at her.

A chill ran down Claire's back. "I will."

"You make sure you do, or someone's gonna get their ass shot off." He lifted his hand, allowing her to take the note.

"Vargas has at least four men guarding the place all the time," Leon said, "even in the middle of the night. One at the front door, one at the back, and two walking the grounds. They bring in wetbacks in the middle of the night and stash them in the basement, so they're all used to being awake at night. Get my drift?"

"I think so. What you're saying is that the police shouldn't think they can raid the house at night and find them all asleep."

"Right. Best time is prob'ly morning. My contact tells me the house is real quiet then. If Vargas or anyone else leaves the house, it's usually in the afternoon or evening."

"How's your contact know so much?" Claire asked.

"That ain't none of your concern. Or Wilson's. 'Cept I need to know when this thing's gonna come down, so the guy can get his ass out of there."

"Okay, I'll ask Detective Wilson to tell you. He knows how to reach you?"

"He's got my cell number. I'll tell you one thing, though, if the cops think that taking in Vargas is gonna shut down the inflow of illegals into Colorado Springs, they got another think coming."

"Why? Is someone else ready to move in and take over when Vargas's locked up?" Claire snapped her fingers. "I bet that's who your contact is."

Leon tapped the side of her head. "You got some brains up there, woman, don't cha? No, this guy's a double-dipper. He works for Vargas, and as a spy for a fellow *businessman.*" He grinned. "The man's taking a page out of my own book, feeding information to the cops to get rid of his competition. Now, don't you go telling Wilson that."

"I won't." Claire put the paper in her purse.

"One other thing. My contact says those guards got semi-autos, and Vargas has more inside." Leon shook his head. "Taking that house won't be easy."

"You've told me about the guards, but how many other people are usually in the house?"

"Maybe five or six all the time, more on the weekends when they might bring in a few girls, and more when they got Mexicans stashed in the basement."

"Do they bring in immigrants on a schedule, so Detective Wilson can figure out what days of the week to avoid?"

"Nope. There're too many variables."

Claire pursed her lips. "I'd hate for the police to raid the house when immigrants or girls are there. They might get caught in the crossfire."

Leon crossed his arms and thought for a moment. "Wilson better pick a weeknight. And, he should bring some guys who speak Spanish, so they can tell the wetbacks to drop to the floor, if any are there. My man says they usually find out a day or two before when Mexicans are due in. He can probably tell me if any wetbacks will be there when this thing goes down."

"You know, *wetback* is a derogatory term," Claire said. "I'd think you, of all people, would avoid using it."

"What? Like *nigger*?" Leon snorted. "Just like we can call ourselves that, the Mexicans use *wetback* or *mojo* all the time."

"Mojo. You mean, sexy, like in the Austin Powers movies?"

Leon guffawed. "No way, José. It's short for *mojado*, which means wet. But maybe I'll start using that more, tell 'em it also means their *cojones* are big."

Rolling her eyes, Claire said, "So you don't have anything against Mexicans?"

"Not as long as they know their place," Leon replied. "They ain't legal, like you and me, after all. They're here to take the jobs the rest of us don't want, like picking crops or shoveling out stables—like your brother's."

Claire wasn't sure she should say what she felt, but it came out anyway. "You know, it wasn't that long ago that white people were saying that about blacks."

"Right!" Leon slapped the table. "But we clawed our way outta that, earned the right to do more. Hell, we've been here a lot longer than them. It's their turn now to do the shit work."

Claire didn't accept that point of view, but she knew she shouldn't say anything that would anger Leon. Thankfully, her conundrum was solved when the hostess appeared, followed by a waitress. They bore large platters of ribs, cornbread, and slaw. They served the four of them, and Leon's bodyguard and driver immediately dug in at the other table.

Leon eyed his plate and rubbed his hands together. "Enough jawing. It's time to commence eating now."

Claire couldn't agree more. She tucked her napkin in her lap and reached for a rib. She took a bite, and let out a small moan of pleasure. She would have to work on Leon's attitude another time.

———

Claire decided to stop by Detective Wilson's office to deliver Leon's information rather than call him. She hoped Wilson would share more with her in person than over the phone. And after needing to ask for her help with Leon, maybe he would be more willing to share. She waited in the lobby of the police station for him to return from "an interview," as the desk sergeant put it, then she was led back to his desk in the detective's bullpen.

While Wilson fetched her a cup of coffee, she scanned the labels on a pile of bulging case files on the side of his desk. Two were for Kyle Mendoza and Gil Kaplan, and both were stuffed with papers. A third, though, was for Hector Garcia, the man Pedro had said was killed by Oscar Vargas. She wondered if Wilson had connected Hector's death yet to the other two.

Wilson returned with two cups of coffee and handed the Styrofoam one to her before sitting behind his desk. An oily sheen on the top of Claire's coffee didn't bode well for its taste. She took a cautious sip. The coffee had obviously been sitting on the burner awhile, but it wasn't as bad as she expected.

"Thanks," she said to Wilson. "I need caffeine after that huge lunch I had with Leon Fox. I blew my diet, but it was definitely worth it. Have you tried his rib place?"

Wilson shook his head while blowing on his coffee. "Sounds like I should, though. A couple of the beat cops have eaten there and raved about it. And they were welcomed warmly. Apparently Fox likes having cops hang around his restaurant. So, did he find out anything about Vargas's location?"

"Yes, he did." Claire handed him the paper Leon gave her with Vargas's address written on it.

Wilson read the note eagerly. "What did you have to pay him to get this information? We can reimburse you, you know."

Claire pshawed and waved her hand. "He asked me to make a gift basket for Condoleza. You remember her? Enrique's girlfriend?" When Wilson nodded, she said, "I was happy to do it. God knows he's done a lot for me in the past. So, no, the department doesn't owe me anything. Plus, I got a free lunch out of the deal. Now, along with that address, Leon gave me some more information."

Wilson took detailed notes while she told him everything Leon had said. After she finished, he leaned back and studied what he had written. "This'll be a joint raid by our SWAT team and ICE, just in case there are illegal immigrants in the house. Plus, we'll likely need the extra manpower."

"You'll tell Leon when it will be, so his friend can get his man out of the house? And tell you if any illegals are there or expected?"

Wilson rubbed his chin and made a note. "We should move fast, and I don't want to give away the exact date and time. I'll try to give Fox at least twenty-four hours notice."

"Good. I saw Hector Garcia's file on your desk. Are you the lead detective on that case, too?"

"I am now."

"I take it that means the bullet in Gil Kaplan's head matched the one found in Hector Garcia?"

"Yes, it does. So we'll have no trouble getting a no-knock warrant. And, we've got a strong case for pinning Kaplan's murder on Oscar Vargas. I'm hoping we can make just as strong a one for Mendoza's." Wilson rubbed his hands together. "I'd love to wrap up all three of these cases this week."

Claire smiled. She would, too. And so would Charley and Jessica.

"If we round up some of Vargas's gang with him when we do the raid," Wilson continued, "we can probably get one of them to testify against him in exchange for a plea deal."

"Have you ruled out the other suspects for Kyle's murder?"

Wilson hesitated for a moment, then shrugged and leaned forward on his desk. "The reason you had to wait for me was that I was talking to someone to confirm Vince Donahue's alibi the night Mendoza was killed. He said he was having some beers with a friend that night while watching a rodeo they'd recorded off the TV. The friend confirmed it and showed me a credit card receipt for a delivery pizza they ordered."

This wasn't like Wilson, to share so much with her. Claire figured he was in a magnanimous mood because she had gotten Vargas's address for him, and he could see the light at the end of the tunnel. "Until how late?"

"Until the wee hours, the friend said. Between one and two. They kept stopping the recording to play back the roping events in slow-motion. Apparently the two of them have aspirations to compete some day."

"I remember Brittany telling me that Vince was practicing to compete in rodeos." So one suspect had been ruled out. Claire tossed her empty coffee cup into Wilson's trash can. "What about her mother, Nancy Schwartz?"

Wilson nodded. "I talked to her, too. She says she has nothing against your sister-in-law's nonprofit, that there are plenty of clients for both." He cocked his head. "Think she's lying?"

Claire snorted. "That woman's sure changed her tune. I guess love will do that."

"Love?"

Claire told him about Nancy and Jorge Alvarez's relationship.

"Regardless of that," Wilson said, "her story about her actions that night matches her daughter's description. She used the port-a-potty behind your brother's trailer office, then went right back to the car. She claims she never went in the barn."

"But she doesn't have someone who saw her, like Vince does."

"No, but I went over the timeline with both her and her daughter separately a couple of times. Their memories weren't real clear, but their stories sync up. I couldn't find enough time in there for Mrs. Schwartz to go into the barn, drag Mendoza into Gunpowder's stall, poke the horse, return the hay fork to its hook, then get back to the car. Even if she was running the whole time. Same goes for Miss Schwartz."

"I know Brittany well enough now that I don't think she could have done it. She really liked Kyle."

Wilson raised a brow. "She could be a great actress, playing a role for you."

"So you think Brittany and her mother were in cahoots or one's providing an alibi for the other?"

"Could be." He shook his head. "But I think it's a long shot. No, my money's on the known criminal here—Oscar Vargas."

He held up the paper with the man's address on it. "Thanks for getting this for me. I owe you." Then he stood.

Claire knew that was a dismissal. She stood, too. "You're welcome. I'm glad I could do something to help solve the case. I'd love to get my brother's stable out from under the dark cloud of suspicion that's been hanging over it. Will you call Charley and me after the raid?"

"Of course." Wilson came around his desk to shake her hand. His step had a real bounce to it. "I know you're both anxious to put this behind you. Hopefully it will be business as usual for your brother by the end of the week."

"That would be wonderful." Claire smiled at Wilson and walked out of the bullpen area.

Her steps weren't so bouncy, though. She didn't feel as hopeful as Wilson. Any number of things could go wrong during the raid. Even if they caught Vargas, was he really the one who killed Kyle? For no good reason?

And it would be awhile before Charley's stable was back to "business as usual." With most of his staff gone, the immigration issues, and the murders on his property, even if someone wasn't deliberately ruining his business, the effect was the same. Trouble kept piling onto Charley's shoulders, almost as if by malevolent design.

SIXTEEN:
MEMORIES AND CONFESSIONS

CLAIRE STOOD NERVOUSLY IN the lobby of the Liberty Heights retirement facility in Colorado Springs late Thursday morning, awaiting her brother Charley's arrival. She hated to bother him in the middle of all his business troubles, but they had a decision to make about their mother. The facility director had called Claire that morning and said they couldn't wait any longer.

Charley strode through the lobby doors. He had changed out of his typical stable wear and was dressed in black jeans, a white pearl-buttoned shirt with black trim, and a black bolo tie. He wore the same fancy maroon-tooled cowboy boots and fawn-colored felt cowboy hat that he had worn to the stable's opening event, just two and a half weeks before.

Relieved to see him, Claire approached and gave him a hug. "Thanks for coming. This is going to be so hard."

He returned the hug, then stepped away but kept a hand on her back. "Seems like today's my day for tough decisions. I had to let Jorge go this morning. I couldn't wait any longer because ICE could show up anytime. The immigration lawyer said it was the only thing I could do right now." He heaved a great sigh.

Looking up, Claire could see how much that decision had cost him. She hoped he had enough emotional reserves left to get through what was yet to come. "I'm sorry. Did he go to Nancy Schwartz's place?"

"Yes, but he said he'd volunteer—" Charley made quotes in the air. "—for me two days a week after ICE is long gone. We agreed to swap his time for the fees I'm paying the lawyer."

"Sounds like a good arrangement."

"For however long it lasts."

"Speaking of arrangements, did you tell Hank that Outlaw has equine distemper?"

Charley grinned. "Oh yeah, and he ate up the whole story. I saw him leave the barn soon after that, and I followed him. He took out his cell phone and made a call. I heard the words Park and Rec before I ducked back inside. I bet Tom Lindall's got all of his wranglers scrubbing stalls now."

"Sounds like Hank's definitely your spy. Are you going to have to fire him?"

"God, I can't do that. He's the best wrangler I've got left. Maybe I can just keep him on and feed him stories that will yank Tom's chain."

Claire grinned. "That's downright evil, Charley."

"Nah, I'm just joshing. I think I've caused enough trouble for Tom. I do plan to keep Hank on for a while, though, until I can hire some new wranglers and get them trained. Then I'll let him go. I'll just be careful about what gets said on the grounds until then." He took off his cowboy hat and ran a hand through his hair. "So what's our agenda here?"

"Lunch with Mom first in the dining room, then we'll meet with the director."

"Think she'll remember us this time?"

"Who knows? If not, hopefully she'll have a nice lunch with two kind strangers." Claire smiled lamely at Charley, but his response was just a worried frown.

She linked her arm in his and steered him toward the elevator. In the semi-twilight of mid-stage Alzheimer's, their mother was currently housed in the Assisted Living section of the complex. Claire had moved her out of an independent living apartment a few months ago. That was when the director had told her that her mother could no longer be trusted with a kitchen after leaving burners or the oven on for hours at a time. Now, she and Charley had another decision to make.

When they arrived at her mother's room, they found her sitting primly on the edge of her favorite easy chair next to her bed. She was dressed in a nautical-themed pantsuit and clutching a purse. A staff member had opened the door for them. She whispered to Claire that her mother was having a pretty good day, then left. Claire surmised that the young woman had helped her mother get bathed and dressed. Otherwise, her hair would have been a mess and her clothes would have been mismatched.

Claire walked over, squatted in front of her mother, and lightly touched her arm. "Hello Mom, it's your daughter Claire."

Her mother tsked. "I know who you are, dear." She peered at Charley, though, with no sign of recognition on her face.

Claire decided to help her mom out. "My brother Charley and I are here to take you to lunch."

Claire motioned him over and he bent to take his mother's hand. "Hi, Mom."

She looked flustered for a moment. "Charley, oh Charley, how nice of you to come so far to see me."

Charley opened his mouth to say something, but Claire shook her head. He had been in to see their mother a week and a half ago, and at least twice a month since he and Jessica had moved from Durango to Colorado Springs. Every time, he'd had to tell her that he was living nearby now. Maybe it was time to just drop it.

Charley nodded at Claire and turned to their mother. "No distance is too far to come to have lunch with my mother." He cupped a hand under her elbow. "Ready to go?"

She let him ease her out of the chair.

When the purse slipped off her lap, Claire grabbed it and rose. "We can just leave this here, Mom. You shouldn't need it."

Her mother put out a hand. "A woman always needs her purse. What if I have to pay for a taxi?"

They weren't leaving the building. Charley's gaze at Claire over their mother's head was tender with sadness.

"Here you go, then, Mom." Claire looped the purse over her mother's arm. She followed her and Charley out of the room and down the hall to the elevator.

Over lunch in the Liberty Heights dining room, Claire realized her mother thought they were at a restaurant, and Claire didn't bother to try to correct her. Also, her mother was treating Charley as a stranger again, which Claire could tell was bothering him.

Finally, her mother took a sip of iced tea and dabbed her mouth with her napkin. "You remind me of my son," she said to Charley.

Before Charley could respond, Claire said, "In what way? What do you remember about Charley?"

Charley shot her a pained look, but Claire gave her head a little shake. Maybe their mother's memories of Charley would help her recognize that he was sitting across the table from her.

"Poor Charley." Her mother shook her head. "Always in the shadow of his big sister, trying to compete with her."

Uh oh, maybe this wasn't a good idea.

But their mother went on. "I remember when Claire brought her first spelling paper home from first grade with a big red A on it. She was so proud. Charley was just four, not even in … what's it called?"

"Kindergarten?" Claire offered.

"Yes. Well, he took a page out of his coloring book and scribbled all over it, like he was writing. He was learning his al … letters … then but couldn't write any words. Then he put a big red A on the top and brought it to me."

She chuckled. "Of course, I had to praise him as much as I did Claire. Or even more. It was so sweet. Charley needed my love more than Claire did."

This was a mistake. Not only had her mother forgotten that Charley was her son, she was talking about Claire in third person now, too. And Charley was blushing and glancing around the crowded dining room awkwardly.

Claire patted her mother's hand. "I'm sure you love both your children."

Before Claire could change the subject, though, her mother said, "Oh, of course, though Charley was harder to love. Claire was easy, with her good grades and smiles. But Charley would...do this—" She made a pout with her lips. "—whenever I praised his sister. Then I'd have to find something good to say about him so he wouldn't act up." She paused. "I guess I should have found more good things to say to him first."

"Like when I lettered in football and baseball the same year in high school," Charley said between gritted teeth.

Their mother waved her hand. "Oh sure, sports are important for boys, keeps them out of trouble, but they're not as important as grades. I wish Charley had been able to make A's like Claire instead of B's. I used to worry how he'd make a living."

"But Charley's doing great now." Claire waved her hand at her brother, whose expression was pained. "Running his stable business and everything."

Now her mother looked pained. "Something's wrong."

Claire leaned over. "What's wrong? Are you feeling sick?"

"No, no, something's wrong with Charley's business. He has to sell it. Right?" Confusion showed on her face, and Claire realized her mother was thinking of the situation with Charlie's old stable in Durango months ago.

"It's fine, Mom, just fine." Charley was gripping his napkin tightly on the tabletop. When Claire looked at him, he shook his head, obviously not wanting to update his mother—again—on the move and to describe the murders and other current problems to her. She would just forget them anyway. "Shall we have some dessert? You like tapioca pudding, right?"

Their mother was looking confused, probably because Charley called her 'Mom,' but then she brightened. "Oh yes, and those red fruits."

"Strawberries?" Claire asked.

"Yes, yes, that's it."

After they had eaten their desserts and taken their mother back to her room, Claire turned to Charley while their mother was in her bathroom. "I'm sorry about pushing Mom to talk about you. I thought it would help her remember who you are."

Charley frowned. "Yeah, the son who always disappointed her, compared to you, who could do no wrong."

"Don't," Claire said. "Don't let her push you into putting yourself down. You are a capable businessman, a good husband, and a good son. You have nothing to be ashamed of."

"But I'll never be as good as you in her eyes or ..."

"Or in your own?" Claire turned on him. "Well in my eyes, Charley, you're better than I am. Better at business, better at sports and more fit, willing to take risks I'm not, and more successful."

"Oh, you've got to be kidding me. No way can you think I'm better—"

The bathroom door opened and their mother stepped out. When she saw them, she said, "Oh hello, are you the ones who're going to take me to lunch?"

Claire and Charley looked at each other.

He reacted first, took her arm, and led her to her easy chair. "We already did, Mom. Your stomach feels full, right?"

She sat and put a hand on her stomach. "Oh, I guess it does. It's time for my nap then."

Claire covered her mother's legs with the afghan that lay folded on the footstool in front of the chair and lifted her mother's feet onto the stool. "Have a good nap, Mom."

They both kissed her and eased out of the room. Claire checked the bathroom on the way out, turned out the light, and flushed the toilet her mother had forgotten to flush.

After she closed the door of the room, she turned to Charley. "God, her doctor said this is likely hereditary, that it could happen to us."

"If it does," Charley said grimly, "I hope Jessica will just take me out back and shoot me."

Claire was silent while they rode the elevator back down to the first floor. If it did happen, she would go first. Would she not recognize Charley—or Roger—when he came to see her? A shudder coursed through her.

When they entered the director's office, they turned down offers of coffee or water.

The director eased his large bulk into his desk chair. "How did lunch with your mother go?"

Charley frowned. "Not good. She didn't recognize me and had forgotten again that I've moved here from Durango."

"She's still pretty functional, though," Claire added.

The director nodded. "Both of your observations match our assessment. We've talked to your mother's doctor, and, unfortunately, there are no other medications he can suggest."

"What about donepezil?" Charley glanced at Claire. "I did some Internet research on it after a friend mentioned his father had taken it and it helped."

The director shook his head. "It's not compatible with her heart disease. As you know, Alzheimer's is a degenerative disease, and she's not going to get any better. She'll just continue to slowly deteriorate, and we'd like to make sure she's in a safe environment and getting proper care."

He shuffled a few pages in a file on his desk, probably their mother's file. "In Assisted Living, we make sure your mother eats all her meals and we administer her medications. So that's all taken care of. But, she's been found wandering the halls alone a few times. And that's not safe, because her balance is shaky, and she's fallen a few times."

"What do you do when she falls?" Claire asked.

"If a staff member is present when it happens, we keep her still until we've checked for injuries. If she has any pain, we x-ray the area. Thank goodness she hasn't broken anything yet, but the last thing we want to happen is for her to break a hip. And we certainly don't want her to wander outside at night." He nodded at Claire. "As I told you on the phone, these are signs that a client is ready to move on to the next level of care—our secure memory care unit."

Charley leaned forward. "How expensive is this next level?"

"It is more costly, because of the additional staff requirement, but I've reviewed your mother's long-term care policy, and it will cover most of the expense for two years."

"Then what?"

The director looked from Charley to Claire, his gaze softening. "With her heart disease, the, ah, prognosis is that she won't last that long."

Claire gasped. "Oh, God."

Charley reached out to squeeze her hand.

"Mom's dying, Charley."

Charley swallowed hard. "I think we've known that for a while. We just didn't want to admit it." He looked at the director. "We'll do what's best for Mom. What papers do we need to sign?"

The director pulled out some forms. The two of them initialed and signed all of them, Claire as the primary, with her power of attorney for her mother's affairs, and Charley as a family witness. By the time they were through, the words were running together in Claire's mind and her emotions ran away with her thoughts. When they left the office, Claire was choking back tears.

She turned to Charley. "I'm scared, Charley. Scared for Mom, and scared for me. I'm next, you know. Your older sister is going to become a babbling idiot."

Charley pulled her into a hug. "Kind of puts my childhood jealousy into perspective, doesn't it? It's pretty darn stupid compared to this." He pulled back and looked at her. "No matter what happens, you'll be my big sister and I'll love you. And I won't think of you as an idiot any more than I already do." His chest rumbled with a chuckle.

Claire gave him a trembling smile and took a deep breath. "But will you take me out back and shoot me?"

———

The phone rang in Claire's house late that evening while she and Roger were watching TV after dinner. When she picked it up, Detective Wilson said, "I'm headed for your brother's house. Can you meet me there? I have some things to tell you all, and I'd rather not have to say them twice."

"Sure, Roger and I will head over there now." She hung up.

Wilson had sounded stressed out and wired up. What was so important that he had to convene a meeting at Charley's house? She rounded up Roger and they hustled into the car. After a tense drive, they were soon at Charley's house. Wilson's car sat outside. When they rang the doorbell, Jessica let them in.

"Oh good," she said. "Detective Wilson hasn't been here long. I just brewed a pot of coffee, because he asked for some. Want some too?"

After they both said yes, she waved a hand toward the living room. "He and Charley are in there. Claire, could you help me bring in the cups and cookies?"

When Claire and Jessica entered the living room a few minutes later with trays, the men were standing around awkwardly. They were making half-hearted comments about the Broncos' running game, which Claire knew Charley couldn't care less about. But Wilson obviously hadn't wanted to dive into what they were all waiting to hear until everyone was in the room.

As Jessica bustled around serving, he settled into a chair, took a gulp of coffee, then ate a peanut butter cookie and took another. "Thanks, Mrs. Gardner. I haven't had dinner, and this hits the spot."

"It's after nine," Roger said. "You must have been really busy."

This was Wilson's opening cue. He swallowed the second cookie, took another gulp of coffee, then put the cup down. "We raided Oscar Vargas's home this morning. Took him and four others into custody, and ICE took a dozen illegal immigrants to detention."

"Was anyone hurt?" Claire asked.

"It went down pretty well," Wilson replied, "thanks to the information you gave us. Most everyone in the house was asleep, so we caught them napping—literally. One of Vargas's guys got a hand on a gun and fired it, but the shot went wild. He got a bullet in his leg in response and quit firing after that."

"Thank God," Jessica said.

"Since then, I've been questioning Vargas," Wilson said.

Charley shifted forward on the sofa, his elbows on his knees and his hands clenching his coffee cup. "Did he kill Gil and Kyle?"

"Yes and no." Wilson frowned. "Our lab tested the guns and rifles we collected from the raid. One rifle matched the bullets found in Hector Garcia and Gil Kaplan."

"Was it Vargas's?" Claire asked.

"It was found under his bed," Wilson answered, "and we were able to get two of the other men in the house to identify it as his personal weapon. Plus, his personal gang sign was etched onto the barrel." He shook his head. "Dumb ass probably didn't want anyone lifting it, but forgot how that might implicate him."

He rubbed his hands together as he got into his tale. "I took that evidence into the interview room. After making him sweat a bit, I told him he'd likely get the death penalty for one if not both of those murders."

"I bet he wanted to cut a deal," Roger said.

Wilson nodded. "He immediately asked what kind of plea bargain he could make. After a lot of wrangling, the DA traded the death penalty for a maximum of life on both murder charges and immunity on his other illegal activities. That was in exchange for full disclosure."

"Wow," Jessica said. "You let him off easy."

"Not really," Wilson replied. "Back to back life sentences will keep him in prison for the rest of his life. Anyway, once the paperwork was signed, Vargas started spilling the beans. He said he killed Hector Garcia because Garcia told a supposed friend that if he was ever picked up by ICE, he'd trade information about Oscar Vargas's operation for a green card."

Claire put down her coffee cup, too engrossed with Wilson's tale to drink or eat anything. "Can ICE do that?"

Wilson shook his head. "Wouldn't have happened. ICE doesn't have that authority. Anyway, that supposed friend told Vargas, and Garcia was a dead man."

"What about Gil Kaplan?" Charley asked.

"Apparently Kaplan started spying on Pedro Trujillo a few weeks ago. He was following him, probably trying to dig up information that proved he was undocumented. Trujillo got scared and told Vargas."

"Uh oh, bad news for Gil," Roger said.

With a nod, Wilson continued. "Vargas told Trujillo to just act normal, that he had nothing to fear from Kaplan. Vargas thought Kaplan was just blowing hot air and didn't do anything at first. But then after that fight between them that you witnessed," he pointed to Claire, "Trujillo talked to Vargas again. This time Vargas realized Kaplan was dangerous—to Trujillo and to his operation. He told Trujillo he'd handle it."

He paused and finished the last of his coffee. "Could I get a refill?" Wilson held out his cup to Jessica, since the pot was nearest to her. She filled it and handed it back to him while the rest of them waited, literally on the edge of their seats.

Wilson took a sip then resumed his tale. "I sent a man to the ICE detention facility to interview Trujillo and confirm all this. He did—after getting multiple assurances that Vargas was locked up and couldn't get to him."

Jessica shook her head. "Poor Pedro."

"He's still a lawbreaker," Wilson said to her. "Anyway, he had apparently begged Vargas not to kill Kaplan, but Vargas brushed him off. He told Trujillo to go home and spend the evening with friends. Vargas drove over to the Kaplan's home, knowing what Kaplan looked like and where he lived. He tailed Kaplan back to the stable around ten and watched him through binoculars from a distance write the suicide note and take out the gun."

Claire put her fingers to her mouth. "So Gil actually *was* suicidal."

Wilson nodded. "Vargas was chuckling while he told me this. He said he thought Kaplan was going to save him the trouble of knocking him off and kill himself. But an hour went by and nothing happened. Then Kaplan reached over and turned on the car's ignition, so Vargas thought he was chickening out. He marched over and put a bullet in Kaplan's head."

Jessica gasped.

"Then the cold SOB reached in and turned off the ignition." Wilson's mouth turned down in distaste. "We're checking for his fingerprints on the car keys now."

"Sounds like you've got everyone in the police department working on this now," Roger said.

"It's the biggest case we've had in a while." Wilson took another gulp of coffee. "And we've got a list of all the illegals Vargas brought into the country, from his payment records. ICE is having a field day rounding them all up." He looked at Charley. "Pedro Trujillo was the only one who went to your stable."

"That's good." A slow smile split Charley's face. "Any go to Peak View Stables?"

Wilson returned the smile. "Now that you mention it, yes, a couple."

"Hot damn." Charley slapped his thigh. "Now Tom Lindall's in as much hot water as I am."

Claire realized her coffee had grown cold and put it aside. "Did Oscar Vargas admit to killing Kyle Mendoza, too?"

Wilson leaned back and shook his head. "Funny thing is, he never admitted to that. We even wired him up to a polygraph, and the technician said he was telling the truth. We have no physical evidence to tie him to Mendoza's murder. And given how forthcoming he was on all the other crimes he's committed, I really don't think he did it."

Charley flopped back against the sofa cushions. "Damn. So we're back to square one. We have no idea who killed Kyle Mendoza."

Wilson took another peanut butter cookie and eyed it. Before he popped it in his mouth, he said, "That's the main reason I'm here. To let you know that a killer is still on the loose."

SEVENTEEN:
LOVE AND RELATIONSHIPS

"Two points!" Claire clapped her hands, her enthusiasm spontaneous.

Donny, the energetic nine-year-old boy with autism, held up his arms in victory and grinned. He was back in Daisy's saddle Friday morning, with Claire and Brittany on either side. Today, he had been trying to throw a small Nerf basketball into a hoop from his perch, and he had just succeeded a third time.

Brittany retrieved the ball, but before she could hand it to him, Jessica said, "Hold onto the ball for a minute, Brittany. Donny, I want you to turn Daisy around and try throwing the ball from the other side."

Donny said, "Walk," to Daisy and kicked her in the sides.

The horse patiently plodded forward, and Claire kept pace alongside, with Brittany on the other side. They meandered around the corral while Donny tried to figure out how to turn Daisy so that when they reached the basket hoop hanging on its post, the horse would be facing the other direction. Claire realized Jessica was remaining silent to see if Donny could work this problem out on his own.

Finally, as Donny's smile faded and his shoulders slumped in frustration, Jessica said, "You've got a good start, Donny. Just turn Daisy to the right now. Perfect. Now straighten her out. Great job. Now turn her left." She kept up the directions until Daisy was approaching the hoop again from the opposite direction. "You tell her when to stop."

Donny concentrated, his tongue clamped between his teeth, until Daisy's head was next to the hoop. "Whoa!"

Daisy stopped.

"Well done, Donny!" Jessica said.

Brittany gave him the ball, and Claire joined Brittany in clapping for him. After three throws and misses, with Claire and Brittany taking turns chasing down the ball and handing it back to him, he made another basket.

"Two points again," Claire yelled. "You're a basketball star."

Donny punched a fist up in the air and turned to grin at her. "I'm a star!"

When he threw back his head and laughed, Claire felt a warm glow infuse her. It wasn't a perimenopausal hot flash, though. It was the good feeling of accomplishment, of helping a little boy feel confident and proud of himself.

She held up a hand. "High five, Donny."

He slapped her hand and giggled.

Jessica caught Claire's eye and gave her a satisfied smile. To Donny, she said, "Okay, Mr. Basketball Star, we've run out of time. Your session is finished today."

He grabbed Daisy's reins. "Aw, do I hafta stop?"

Claire knew that transitions were hard for many of their clients, including Donny.

Jessica pointed to the nearest picnic table. "I know you're having a good time. But that little girl is waiting for her turn, and your mom is waiting to take you to buy new shoes, remember? You'll have fun doing that. Now, take Daisy over to the fence."

Reluctantly, he followed her directions. Jessica helped him dismount and together they walked over to talk to his mother. Claire heard the word 'basketball' and figured Jessica was suggesting that he practice the hoops on the ground at home.

While she and Brittany gave Daisy some water and rubbed her down, Claire figured this was a good time to quiz her about one of the people Claire still suspected might have killed Kyle Mendoza—Brittany's mother. Searching for an opening, she lit on the topic of Jorge.

"So Jorge's working at your mother's stable now. How's that going?"

"Super," Brittany said. "He's really nice and good with the horses. He's trying to break Juniper of her habit of nipping at the other horses, and she's already not doing it as much."

Claire raised an eyebrow. "I'm kind of surprised your mom was willing to take the risk of hiring him."

"Oh, he's not on the books. Officially, he's a volunteer, and she's giving him cash under the table. At least until ICE finishes here and things quiet down. Mom asked me to let her know what they're doing here."

"Is she worried they might start investigating all the stables in the area and want to see her employee records?"

Brittany's hand stilled on Daisy's neck. "I think she's more worried about Jorge. She's really fallen for him."

"Has she told you she loves him?"

"No, but I can tell." Brittany's brow furrowed. "And something's going on. The two of them were gone all day yesterday, and she's being real secretive. Won't tell me where they went. And she left the house even earlier than I did today."

"Maybe they've got a special date planned."

"I swear, it's like she's the one sneaking out to see her boyfriend, not me. She doesn't seem to mind anymore that I'm seeing Vince."

"And how's that going?"

A shy smile teased Brittany's lips. "Fantastic."

Claire couldn't help being a mom. She brought up the topic she always did with her own daughter about her boyfriends. "I hope he respects you and values your opinions."

"Of course he does." Brittany said with a smile. "He's really nice, and even though we don't agree on every political issue, he listens to what I have to say. And he lets me choose the movies we see. I know he doesn't like chick flicks, though, so I usually choose an action one."

Claire reviewed in her mind the confrontation on the Garden of the Gods trail between the group Vince was leading and theirs. "He did seem pretty patient with Hank and the rest of us when we held up his group on the trail. Until his horses and customers started getting antsy, that is."

Something nagged at the edge of her memory. She focused on what Vince had looked like on his horse, backlit by the sun that warmed his work shirt in a bright yellow, red, and black checked pattern. The wheels turned in her mind and the cogs clicked into place.

The shirt had the same pattern as the fabric scrap found on Gunpowder's hoof!

Shocked, Claire flushed and grabbed onto Daisy's saddle horn.

Daisy's head came up and Brittany peered at her. "You okay, Claire?"

Claire took a deep breath to still her racing heart. "Yes, yes, just a hot flash. I'll be fine. Maybe I just need some water, too."

Brittany handed her a water bottle, and Claire took a long drink. As she handed it back, she tried to keep her voice casual. "I remember the colorful yellow-and-red-checked shirt Vince was wearing that day. Is it a favorite of his?"

Brittany waved her hand. "Oh no, that's one of his old company shirts. They've got a Peak View Stables logo sewn on the pocket. He can't wait to take them off after work. Mr. Lindall gives a couple to all of his wranglers at the beginning of each summer."

"The same pattern every year?"

With a shake of her head, Brittany said, "Mr. Lindall changes the colors every year, so if someone stops working for him and wears the old shirts, they don't look like a current employee. He asks his wranglers to wear the current year's shirts whenever they can, and if they're dirty, to wear past years' shirts. If he had his way, they'd wear them on their days off all over town to advertise the stable."

"But Vince doesn't do that?"

"No. He says he hates being a walking billboard."

"What year was the yellow and red one from?"

"Last year, I think. Why do you want to know all this stuff about shirts?"

At that point, Jessica called out and asked them to bring Daisy over for the little girl.

"I'll tell you later," Claire said to Brittany. As she untied Daisy's reins from the fence, her mind raced. The killer must be someone who worked at Peak View Stables last year, maybe even Tom Lindall himself. If all of his wranglers had the same attitude as Vince, Tom was the most likely to be wearing the shirt late at night.

She had to talk to Detective Wilson.

———

The morning hippotherapy sessions flew by, with no real break for Claire to contact Wilson. They were in the middle of their last session with Robin, the young woman with Down syndrome who had been smitten with Petey, when ICE arrived.

Sam Unger with his black-rimmed glasses climbed out of the unmarked car, followed by his young, athletic fellow officer. They headed for the trailer. Claire had seen Charley go in there after the morning trail ride left with Hank and Kat, the new wrangler.

She looked at Jessica. "Do you need to go talk to them with Charley?"

Jessica gave the men a worried glance. "No, Charley's ready for them. He thought they'd be here yesterday, so the employee paperwork's all been checked. I'll go in after we finish with Robin."

Hoping they didn't find anything wrong other than Pedro, Claire decided she would go in with Jessica. For the remainder of the session, the two of them frequently glanced at the trailer as if they could see through the walls. Claire didn't know if ICE could arrest employers or just fine them. She tensed with dread as she envisioned the men walking out with Charley in handcuffs between them.

After they finished, Jessica talked quickly with Robin's father, and Claire asked Brittany if she could return Daisy to the barn and take care of the mare herself. Brittany assured her it was no problem, and Claire sprinted after Jessica to the trailer.

When they went inside, Charley was using the computer at the reception desk, having given the back office over to the ICE officials. He looked up as Claire closed the door and pointed with his head toward the closed door to the back room.

"How's it going?" Jessica asked.

Charley shrugged. "I asked once. They said they'd let me know when they were done and tell me what they found then."

Jessica sat on the sofa. "Did you ask them about Pedro?"

Charley nodded. "He was put on the bus to Mexico this morning. Since Detective Wilson got a signed statement about Oscar Vargas from him yesterday, they no longer needed to hold him in the U.S."

Claire joined Jessica on the sofa. "Were you able to tell him about the possible job in Puerto Vallarta before he left?"

"Oh, I forgot to tell you." Charley pushed back from the computer. "I went to see Pedro yesterday after our lunch with Mom. I gave him the stable owner's contact information. The money I put in his backpack should be enough to get him there. He was very grateful for the help but kept apologizing for getting me in trouble."

Jessica turned to Claire. "Charley told me Pedro kept saying he'd find a way to send money to pay the fine, but Charley refused." She smiled at Charley. "I'm so glad you did. The last thing poor Pedro needs is to try to start a new life in Mexico with a huge debt hanging over his head."

Charley looked abashed. "Two thousand dollars is not chump change for me, but it's a huge amount for him."

"You should be proud of what you did for him," Jessica said. "I am."

Claire saw the flash of pride in Charley's eyes when he smiled. She was glad that Jessica was finally building up her husband's ego rather than tearing it down.

"If Pedro works as hard for that Puerto Vallarta stable owner as he did for you," she said, "you'll have made a good business contact down there, one who will owe you a favor."

Charley laughed and held up his hands. "Okay, enough already." He glanced back at the back office's closed door. "I just hope that the fine for hiring Pedro is the only one I'll be paying."

As if on cue, the door opened and Sam Unger stepped out. He held a piece of paper in his hand. "So what's the story with this Jorge Alvarez?"

"He no longer works here," Charley replied. Claire could see that he was working hard to keep his voice calm.

"Did you fire him right before we came because you knew he was illegal?"

Charley exhaled. "I didn't know until after you guys took Pedro. Jorge told me about his own circumstances that afternoon. He didn't want me to have to pay a fine for him, too. I had to let him go after that, even though he's worked for me for years. Did a damned fine job, too."

Unger peered at Charley but seemed to believe him. "His social security number is bogus. It's a New York number, just like Pedro Trujillo's."

Holding out his hands, Charley asked, "And how was I supposed to know that?"

Shaking his head, Unger said, "You couldn't, really. But now that *we* know and we have his home address," he held up the paper, "we'll be picking him up."

Jessica clutched the arm of the sofa. "That's so unfair!"

Charley slapped his thigh. "Damn it! Jorge told me he entered the country legally. His case is different than Pedro's."

Unger shrugged. "Well he's not legal now. We contacted the main office, and Mr. Alvarez doesn't have a current green card. Hasn't for years."

Jorge should be warned that ICE is coming for him. Claire decided to try to sneak out and call him. She rose silently and inched toward the outside door while Sam Unger's attention was focused on Charley.

Jessica glanced at her and gave a nod. She walked toward Charley, so Unger's attention would be directed there and away from the door. "We're going to petition for legal status for Jorge as an alien worker."

Unger snorted. "That won't do much good. He's not in any of the special job categories."

Claire gently eased the trailer door open, just as Jessica slapped the reception desk, probably to cover the noise of the door opening. "This is just not fair, not fair to him, or to us. We need him..."

Claire didn't hear the rest, as she eased the door closed, then high-tailed it down the stairs and to the barn. She didn't have

Jorge's cell phone number, but she hoped that Brittany could contact her mother, who would. If they could get word to him, maybe he could hide out, stay away from his apartment.

She ran into the barn and yelled, "Brittany!"

With a startled expression on her face, Brittany came out of the tack room.

"Quick, call your mother," Claire shouted.

"Why?"

"Just do it and give me the phone!"

Brittany pulled out her cell phone, punched a button and handed it to Claire. When Nancy Schwartz answered, Claire said, "Nancy, I need to contact Jorge right away. Do you have his cell phone number?"

"You don't need it."

"What?"

"He's with me now."

"Put him on the phone, then. I'm at Charley's stable and—"

"You can talk to Jorge in person in a sec. I'm picking up Brittany, and he's with me. We're driving into the parking lot right now." She hung up.

"No, no, no!"

She tossed the phone to Brittany. "Call your mom back and tell her to leave right now!" Claire sprinted out of the barn toward the parking lot.

Sure enough, Nancy Schwartz was turning her car into a spot. Jorge was sitting in the front passenger seat next to her. Nancy cut the engine, and Jorge got out and walked around to her side of the car to open her car door. He offered her a hand as if she was a queen. Nancy stood, ignoring her ringing cell phone.

Claire stopped in front of them, huffing and puffing. "You've got ... to leave ... right now!"

"Not without Brittany," Nancy said. "There she is." She waved at her daughter.

Strolling lazily toward the car, Brittany waved back.

"Run!" Claire shouted at her.

With a puzzled frown on her face, Brittany picked up her pace.

But it wasn't fast enough for Claire. "C'mon, c'mon."

Nancy stared at her. "What's the hurry?"

"It's ICE," Claire said, "They're here."

"They're here?" Jorge asked. "Is Charley okay?"

Brittany finally arrived. Nancy gave her a hug then held up her left hand in front of Brittany's face.

Claire stamped her foot and grabbed Jorge's arm. "Damn it, it's not Charley we're worried about, it's you! They—"

Brittany shrieked. "Mom! What's this?"

Nancy wiggled her left hand, showing off the shiny new gold ring. She sidled up next to Jorge and clutched his arm. "We got married this morning."

He put his hand over hers and stood proudly, with a huge grin showing his white teeth.

Brittany looked from her mother to Jorge and back again. "Ohmigod!"

Rendered speechless, Claire stared at them, too apoplectic with worry to think of congratulating them.

The smile started to fade from Jorge's face. "Are you okay with this, Brittany?"

She flung her arms around his neck. "Yes, yes, yes. I'm just so surprised. This is all so sudden."

"Sorry we didn't tell you or take you with us," Nancy said. "We figured we had to move fast. When Jorge and I talked to the immigration lawyer, he said Jorge's best hope for getting a green card was for a close relative to petition for him. When we asked how close, he said like a parent, child, or sibling—which Jorge doesn't have in the U.S.—or a spouse. We just looked at each other and said, 'That's it!'"

Jorge put an arm around Nancy and smiled at her. "We went straight to the courthouse to get a marriage license and had the official there marry us right away."

Nancy returned his smile. "We were as giddy as two teenagers."

Brittany let her arms slide off of Jorge. "Oh, so this is just so he can become legal?"

He reached out and put a hand on her shoulder. "No, Brittany, your mother and I love each other. This is forever."

Looking worried, Nancy gave Brittany a one-armed hug and peered at her daughter's face. "So you're sure you're okay with having Jorge as a stepfather?"

"Of course, Mom! I really like him, and even better, I like how you are with him." She turned to Jorge and stage-whispered. "She's been really bitchy since the divorce."

"Brittany!" Nancy gave her a playful slap, then the three of them embraced in a group hug.

Claire had had enough. "Okay, this is all very nice, folks, but we have a problem. ICE is going to lock up Jorge in detention if he doesn't get out of here right away."

Jorge looked at Nancy. "We knew this would happen. Maybe I should just let them take me now."

"On our wedding day?" She clutched his arm.

He sighed. "As the lawyer said, you can bail me out after you file for a hearing. Then I will be free while we wait for the hearing."

"What if it's too late for all that to happen today?"

"I can handle one night in detention, especially if I can look forward to being with you after that."

The trailer door opened, and Sam Unger stepped out. He scanned the property as if looking for Claire. He turned and his gaze bored into them.

"Your decision has just been made for you," Claire said.

EIGHTEEN:
A HORSE KNOWS

CLAIRE TURNED HER CAR into the parking lot in front of the business office on the Glen Eyrie castle grounds Saturday morning and stepped out. A cool breeze ruffled the nearby Ponderosa pines and carried their crisp scent to her. Her gaze rose to the top of the sandstone formation looming behind the building. She spotted the outline of a bighorn sheep standing on the ridge. It seemed to be watching her. She did the same for a while until it turned its massive curled horns and headed north along the ridge.

Back to business, Claire pulled a barbecue-themed gift basket out of her trunk while thinking back on her early morning phone call with Charley. He and Nancy Schwartz were splitting the cost of Jorge's bail. He said the immigration lawyer thought they would be able to get Jorge out of ICE detention that morning. If not, he would be out Monday at the latest. Then the slow and uncertain process of trying to get him a green card would begin. Both Nancy and Charley were filing petitions, but Nancy's, for an alien relative, had the best chance of ultimately succeeding, though it could take months or even years.

Claire hoped the newlyweds would be able to enjoy each other's company that evening. Brittany was right. Nancy was a different person with Jorge. Claire could no longer imagine Nancy killing Kyle Mendoza.

Besides, all of the signs now pointed to Tom Lindall. She had called Detective Wilson the night before to tell him about the Peak View Stable company shirts and that she thought the scrap from Gunpowder's hoof matched last year's pattern. He remembered they had searched Charley's employees' closets for a shirt with a matching pattern, but not Lindall's. Given that Tom and Vince were potential suspects, Wilson ruefully admitted that was an oversight. After thanking her, he said he would obtain a search warrant to check Lindall's, and all of his last year's employees' shirts, for a hole that matched the cloth fragment found on Gunpowder's hoof.

As Claire hefted the basket and walked toward the small office building, a flutter of hope rose in her heart. Hope that the case would be solved, that the dark cloud of suspicion over Charley's stable finally would be lifted. And hope that her brother's life could return to some semblance of normal. But then she worried her lip. She had been hopeful before and been proven wrong.

Juggling the basket, and avoiding the sharp barbecue fork and tongs poking out of the top, she pushed the door open and walked into the foyer. She found the office for the Executive Assistant to the Development Officer and knocked on the doorframe.

The middle-aged black woman inside looked up from her desk and rose. She waved Claire in and focused her gaze on the basket.

"Oh that's lovely, just lovely. Here, put it on my desk and let me look at it."

Claire set it down and stepped back. "You said your boss was a gourmet griller, so I worked with a barbecue theme."

The woman peered through the cellophane. "I see some interesting spice rubs and marinades in there."

"And a few local hot sauces for zip." Claire had sorted through her collection of hot sauces to make sure she didn't include any with lewd names. Glen Eyrie Castle was owned and operated by the Navigators, a Christian mission organization. Sauces with names like Ass Blaster, Screaming Sphincter, and Biker Bitch might be fun novelty items for some, but not for this group.

Claire pointed toward the back of the basket. "I included red cedar grilling papers and wine-aged oak strips, too."

"Oh, this is perfect," the woman said while clapping her hands. "He'll be so happy with this birthday gift from the staff. Thank you!"

Claire knew the man's birthday wasn't until Monday. "Should we hide the basket somewhere?"

"No need," the woman said. "He's out all day scouting trails to see which ones might work for horseback riding. Take a load off while I write you a check."

Her interest piqued, Claire sat in the visitor's chair in front of the desk. "Horseback riding? So you're going to allow people to ride horses on your trails as well as hike them?"

The woman took a checkbook out of her desk drawer. "Not quite. We don't want private individuals bringing their horses in and wandering all over the place. We were thinking of offering organized group rides instead, so we can keep the horses on separate trails from the people and control where they go."

"So you're going to build a stable on the property?" Claire was concerned that this could pose even more competition for Charley.

"Oh no." The woman waved a hand. "We want to contract it out, have a local stable bring in horses when we need them." She leaned back in her chair and furrowed her brow. "We don't want a corral on the grounds, but we may have to build one if we can't find a stable willing to work with us. We'd really like to find a way to offer horseback rides on the grounds. Our conference attendees keep asking for them. We're just not sure about all the logistics."

Claire scooted forward in her chair and tried to contain her excitement. "I may have the answer for you then. My brother, Charley Gardner, just opened a stable almost directly across 30th Street from your entrance. He's running trail rides in the Garden of the Gods Park now. Visitors could do all the check-in and be matched with horses at his stable, then he could bring in groups from there."

The woman's eyes widened. "That sounds ideal!"

Claire warmed to the topic. "You wouldn't have to worry about a corral or barn on your grounds, just horses on your trails."

The woman tore the check out of the checkbook. Before handing it to Claire, though, she paused. "Wait. I remember reading about a murder and a suicide happening at a nearby stable. Is that your brother's?"

Damn. "The suicide was really murder, and the police have already apprehended that suspect."

"Oh, dear."

"He wasn't an employee of the stable," Claire added quickly. "And the police are very, very close to solving the other murder. Again, their prime suspect is not a stable employee. My brother's stable has just had the awful bad luck to have been the location where both of these killings occurred. They have no relation to him or his business."

The woman looked thoughtful. "I'll talk to my boss about it."

Claire's heart sank. The phrase was a classic dismissal.

Then the woman smiled. "You know, I'm a firm believer that if you pray about something, God provides the answer. I've been praying about this, and here you are. Not only did you bring us this wonderful gift basket, you may have brought us the answer to our problem."

And to Charley's problems competing with Peak View Stables. Relieved, Claire returned the smile.

She exchanged one of Charley's cards for the check and left the office with a spring in her step. She decided to immediately drive to his stable and deliver the potential good news.

———

While Claire was telling Charley and Jessica the exciting news out on the trailer porch, Tom Lindall's blue pickup truck drove into the parking lot. He got out and swung the door shut with a loud slam. He marched toward the trailer, his body stiff with anger.

"Uh oh," Charley said. "He's probably found out about the trick I played on him and he's mad."

When he moved toward the trailer steps, Claire stopped him with a hand on his arm. "Remember Tom Lindall may be a murderer, Charley. Be careful."

Charley shot her a startled look. Then he studied the older man striding toward them. "He doesn't seem to be carrying a weapon, as far as I can tell, and I can take him in a fight, if it comes to that."

"Still, keep an eye on him." Claire turned to Jessica. "I bet Detective Wilson is looking for Tom Lindall right now. Maybe you should call him and tell him the man's here. We might need reinforcements, too."

"For one sixty-some-year-old man?" Charley's look was incredulous.

"For one possible killer," Claire answered. She nodded at Jessica, who bit her lip and went inside to make the call.

By then, Tom had reached the porch and stomped up the steps. "I've got a bone to pick with you." He stabbed a finger in Charley's chest.

Charley stepped back. "What's the problem, Tom?"

"You made me cancel a whole day's worth of trail rides and waste my staff's time cleaning my stable top to bottom."

"And how did I make you do that?"

"By spreading the rumor that Parks and Rec thought one of your horses caught strangles from one of mine. Then I find out today that your horse isn't even sick."

"We brought Outlaw back to the stable this morning," Charley said to Claire. He put his hands on his hips and stared at Lindall. "And where did these rumors come from, Tom?"

Red-faced, Tom waved his hands. "People talk."

"No, you planted a spy here." Charley poked a finger in Tom's chest this time. "Hank Isley has been feeding you information about my operation the whole time he's been working here, and it finally backfired on you."

Tom stiffened, his hands clenched at his side. "You've got no proof of that!"

"Oh, yes I do. He's the only one I told that story to, and yes, I did it deliberately to prove once and for all that he's your spy. And here you come striding in this morning and confirm it."

"I don't even know the man!"

"Bullshit. I know Hank used to work for you. And Claire here saw you talking to him at Jessica's fundraiser event." He pointed toward the corral. "In fact, it's about time I confront the spy himself about this. You can come along or not—your choice. Since no trail ride went out this morning, Hank's over there replacing a couple of broken boards."

Charley pushed past Tom, clattered down the steps and strode toward the corral without bothering to check if anyone was following. Tom stood scowling for a moment, then took off, his shorter legs pumping hard as he tried to catch up with Charley.

Claire followed Tom, a shiver crawling up her spine. Had Charley just turned his back on a killer?

When the three of them reached the far side of the corral where Hank was hammering in a fresh board, he stopped and glanced at each of them in surprise.

Claire stepped back to where she could keep an eye on Tom and stay out of his reach in case she needed to run for help.

"What's up, boss?" Hank said to Charley, though his gaze slid to Tom and back.

Charley snorted. "That's a laugh, Hank. We all know who your real boss is. Tom here has been paying you to spy on me, and I just caught you red-handed at it."

Hank's eyes narrowed. "I don't know what you're talking about."

Tom exhaled and put his hands on his hips. "Might as well give it up, Hank. Charley here's sussed us out. You're the only one he talked to about that case of strangles, and I just blew up at him about it."

Hank hefted the hammer and glowered at Tom. "Thanks a whole hell of a lot for blowing my cover. You promised you'd keep whatever information I gave you to yourself."

"That was before Charley pulled that dirty trick on me. Cost me a bundle."

Charley grinned. "C'mon, Tom, you lost only one day's worth of rides, and I bet you've already rescheduled most of them. And you've got a shiny clean stable to boot."

"Fuck off," Tom and Hank said to him in unison.

"And you're fired," Tom said to Hank. "You should've checked the facts before telling me anything."

Hank stepped menacingly toward Tom. "You bastard! How the hell was I supposed to check on it when the horse wasn't even here? This is all your fault for coming over here. If you hadn't, my cover wouldn't have been blown."

"No matter whose fault it is, you're no good to me anymore."

Hank aimed a wad of spit at Tom's boots. "Good riddance. Charley's a better boss anyway."

As Hank slapped the hammer head against his other palm, Claire flashed back on the fact that Gil had hit Kyle in the head with one. She peered at Hank, whose pretty-boy face was now twisted in rage. Could he be driven to use the lethal tool in anger, too?

"I'm firing you, too, Hank," Charley said.

Hank reeled to glare at him. "Fuck why? I've been working my tail off for you!"

"Because I can't trust you. You've already lied to me, shown me that I can't rely on your loyalty." Charley shook his head. "No, you screwed yourself, Hank, by dipping your hand into two tills at once."

Hank swung his hammer against the board he had just nailed in, cracking it. His expression got even darker and meaner, and Claire could swear steam was blowing out of his ears.

Then something clicked in her brain. Since Hank used to work openly for Tom, he probably owned one of those yellow and red checked shirts. And Kyle Mendoza's death helped him in two ways. First, by moving Hank into the lead guide spot, where he made more money in tips. And second, by ingratiating him with Tom Lindall, by discrediting Charley's stable. That is, if Tom had asked him to do it, or if he told Tom about it later. The question was, how involved was Tom?

Yes, all of the signs pointed to Hank, who looked ready to kill someone now. Claire had to warn her brother. "Charley?"

"Not now, Claire." Charley glowered at Hank and waved a hand toward the stable. "Get your things and report to me at the trailer. I'll get your back pay ready."

He turned and walked toward the trailer.

Hank's face turned absolutely livid, and a low-throated growl rose in his throat.

Eyes wide, Tom stepped back.

"Charley, watch out!" Claire screamed, just as Hank threw the hammer.

Turning at her scream, Charley ducked. The hammer missed his head and hit his shoulder. He spun, roared with pain and grabbed his shoulder.

Before he could recover, Hank leapt on him, throwing him to the ground. He pummeled Charley with his fists.

Tom ran over and grabbed one of Hank's arms, spinning him around. "Stop that!"

Hank swung at Tom, connecting with his jaw and sending him reeling. He turned back to Charley.

But Charley had used the diversion to scramble to his feet, wincing as he put pressure on his sore shoulder. He was ready for Hank and threw a punch into his gut.

Letting out an "oof," Hank doubled over.

Charley swept a boot against the back of Hank's legs, crumpling them so he slammed down onto his knees. Then he and Tom worked in tandem to pin Hank's arms behind him.

Hank struggled and cursed, but hobbled and on his knees, he couldn't escape.

Tom kicked him in the rear. "That's for sucker-punching me!"

"I'll get some rope," Claire yelled and ran for the barn.

"I don't think we'll need it," Charley said. "We'll just hold him, maybe get a few licks in, till he cools down."

Oh yes, they'll need it, Claire thought as she chugged for the barn. Charley didn't realize he and Tom were holding onto a killer. She yelled over her shoulder, "Don't let go of him, no matter what!"

Then she had another gut-sinking thought. If Hank did the killing at Tom's behest, would Tom turn on Charley, too? But why would Tom have grabbed Hank in the first place, if Hank had killed for him? She needed to tell Charley he couldn't trust either of them. But she didn't have time to explain it yet. And why weren't the cops here yet? Jessica was supposed to have called them.

Claire ran into the barn, where Brittany stood in the alley between the stalls with Gunpowder. She was tightening the girth on Gunpowder's saddle.

"I need rope," Claire said between huffs.

"In the tack room," Brittany replied. "What's going on? I heard yelling outside." She swung onto Gunpowder's back and took the reins.

Claire ran to the tack room, grabbed a lariat, and ran out. "Follow me," she said. "We may need your help."

She ran out of the barn. Brittany kicked Gunpowder into a trot to follow her.

When Claire arrived back at the corral, Charley and Tom were holding Hank down on the ground, face down with his arms still pinned behind his back. Charley glanced at her. "I told you we didn't need that."

Claire started unwinding the lariat while she caught her breath. "Yes, you do. I think Hank's the one who killed Kyle."

"What?" Charley raised a brow at Claire.

"The hell, I did!" Hank yelled.

Tom gaped at her. That look of surprise seemed genuine, but maybe he was just surprised she had found out.

She opened her mouth to explain what she meant to Charley and to warn him about Tom, but Brittany had arrived on Gunpowder. The horse let out a piercing scream. He reared up, his eyes rolling back in his head.

Brittany held on to Gunpowder's mane for dear life.

Charley let go of Hank and ran to Gunpowder's head. Saying "Whoa, whoa, boy," he pulled down on Gunpowder's bridle until the horse was back on four hoofs.

Brittany slid off Gunpowder's back and backed away, confusion showing on her face. "Why'd he do that?"

Claire realized Gunpowder was scared of Hank, the man who had gored him with the hay fork. She yelled, "Get Gunpowder away from Hank!"

In the meantime, Hank had twisted out of Tom's grasp and leapt to his feet. He threw a roundhouse punch that landed in Tom's gut and toppled the older man to his knees. Instead of running away from Gunpowder, though, as Claire expected, Hank ran for Brittany. He threw an arm around her chest, yanked a buck knife out of his pocket, and held it to her neck.

Brittany's eyes went wide, but she didn't struggle.

Smart girl, Claire thought. *Don't make him hurt you.*

"What the hell are you doing?" Charley yelled at Hank.

"Get that fucking horse away from me," Hank yelled back. He stepped back, yanking Brittany with him. The action caused the knife to nick her neck, drawing blood.

Claire didn't think it was possible, but Brittany's eyes got even wider.

"Careful!" Claire yelled at Hank. She grabbed Gunpowder's reins. Between her pulling on the reins and Charley tugging on the harness, they turned the horse so he was facing away from Hank. They led Gunpowder a few yards away.

Gunpowder snorted and pawed the ground. He kept trying to turn his head to look at Hank, as if making sure his former tormentor was still far away from him.

Charley faced Hank again. "What's going on here?"

Hank ignored him and yelled at Tom, "Get over there with them."

Tom pushed himself to his feet while holding onto his stomach. His face was greenish pale, and he was sweating, but his mouth was set in a determined hard line. He gingerly stepped toward Charley and Claire.

Hank started walking backward toward the parking lot, dragging Brittany with him while the rest of them watched warily.

"Hank's already killed once," Claire whispered to Charley, once Hank was out of earshot. "He could very well kill Brittany."

"What makes you say that?" Charley's quiet voice was tinged with confusion and anger.

"I'll explain later," Claire said. "Right now, we've got to figure out how to get Brittany away from him."

Brittany stumbled and almost fell, but Hank yanked her to his chest. He quickly had the knife back against her throat.

They were far enough away by then that Claire couldn't see Brittany's expression clearly. She wondered if the young woman had really tripped or was testing Hank. *Careful, girl.*

Charley's brow furrowed. "Jessica must have called the police by now."

"How do you know she saw all this?" Tom asked through gritted teeth, his hand still clutching his stomach.

"We don't." Claire rested a gentle hand on his shoulder. "I thought you were the killer, and I told her to call them when you drove up. Sorry."

"Hey, I don't care," Tom said. "As long as they get here in time to keep Hank from hurting Brittany."

"They won't. He's almost to his car," Charley said. "It's up to us. What can we do?"

"Got any weapons?" Tom asked.

Charley shook his head, but then Claire remembered the new wrangler, Kat, and her concealed carry permit. "Where's Kat?"

Charley nodded in understanding. He pointed toward the back pasture. "Out bringing in some mares."

"Start talking to Hank," Claire inched around Gunpowder, so the horse blocked her view of Hank and Brittany out in the parking lot, and theirs of her. "Slow him down, try to convince him to let go of Brittany, and I'll get Kat."

Claire hunched down and ran for the barn. Charley moved Gunpowder to continue to screen her, then handed the reins to Tom.

"Let her go," Charley yelled at Hank while walking toward the parking lot. "She's got no part in this."

"Fuck you," Hank yelled back.

Tom pulled Gunpowder into the corral and latched the gate, then followed Charley.

"You don't need her," Tom yelled. "We're not stopping you—"

Claire rounded the barn and couldn't make out the rest. Her heart lifted, though, as she spotted a wiry, dark-haired woman approaching the pasture gate on horseback with three unsaddled mares ahead of her.

Claire ran toward her. "Are you Kat? Do you have a gun?"

Kat slid off her mount and put a hand on the gate. Looking confused, she said, "Who are you?"

"Charley's sister, and we've got a situation. I need you to come with me."

Kat pushed the unsaddled mares aside, then opened the gate and led her horse through it and reclosed the gate. She looped her horse's reins over the pasture fence rail and ran behind Claire to the back of the office trailer. "What's going on?"

Between huffs, Claire said, "Hank's the killer, and he's got Brittany at knifepoint."

Kat gasped.

"Jessica called the police," Claire continued, "but they aren't here yet. We can't let Hank get away with Brittany. So, where's your gun?"

Kat pulled a small pistol out of a concealed holster under her shirt and tucked into the back waistband of her jeans. "I'm not a great shot. I don't want to hurt Brittany."

"We'll hope for an opening. Maybe when they're getting in Hank's car." Claire signaled for Kat to follow her.

They ran along the back of the trailer until they reached the other end. Claire peeked around the side and signaled Kat to do the same. They could see most of the parking lot. Both the driver's door and the rear passenger door of Hank's car were open. Hank pulled Brittany off the hood of his car, and Claire could see he had tied her hands behind her back with his belt.

Charley and Tom were still hollering at him. Their voices were nearer, so they had gotten closer to the parking lot, probably hoping to rush Hank as soon as he was distracted and away from Brittany.

"Get back or I cut her," Hank yelled at them while pulling Brittany toward the open rear car door, the knife still at her neck.

"Okay, okay, we're moving back," Charley yelled, frustration and fear in his voice. "Don't hurt her."

Hank told Brittany to get in and slide over. He pushed her head down toward the seat, then whacked her head with the butt of his buck knife. Brittany's whole body slumped.

"Shit!" Kat said between clenched teeth.

"Oh, God. I hope she's just unconscious." Claire clutched Kat's free arm. "As soon as he steps away from her, shoot him!"

Kat stared at her and licked her lips. "My aim's not that good, and I've never shot a person."

Claire gave a grim nod. "Do your best."

Footsteps clattered toward the parking lot.

"I can still kill her!" Hank hollered while holding his knife against Brittany's throat. "Get back."

While Charley and Tom backtracked, Kat squinted at the parking lot and raised the pistol in her right hand. Her hand shook. She transferred the pistol to her left hand, wiped her right on her jeans then transferred the gun back. She sighted on Hank.

Seemingly satisfied that Charley and Tom were far enough away, Hank slammed Brittany's door shut and rushed toward the open driver's door.

"Now!" Claire yelled at Kat.

Nothing. Hank jumped into the driver's seat and shut the door. "Shoot him!"

Nothing. Kat was frozen in fear.

Hank started the car engine.

Impressions flooded Claire's senses as time slowed. Heavy steps thudded in sync with her rapid heartbeat. Those and a shout of "Get him!" told her that Charley and Tom were running for the car. But they were too far away.

A bead of sweat trickled down her hairline. A horsefly buzzed her ear.

Claire's whole body snapped to attention. She grabbed the gun out of Kat's hand and fired it toward where Hank sat, reversing the car out of the parking spot.

Blam!

The bullet pinged off the hood.

Blam!

A low hiss signaled that that bullet had gone through a tire. The car was still moving.

Blam!

That bullet slammed into the car door just below Hank's arm.

"Shit!" Hank braked and threw the buck knife out the open car window onto the pavement. He raised his hands. "I give up! Don't shoot!"

Claire stopped. In the silence that followed, she heard Kat gasping beside her. Or was that herself?

"You done shooting, Annie Oakley?" Charley yelled at Claire. Now in view, he and Tom had both stopped running and were staring at her.

She stood shakily and walked toward Hank's car, holding the gun as steadily as she could on the panic-faced man. "I hope so."

NINETEEN:
THE WRAP-UP

CHARLEY AND TOM HELD Hank down on the parking lot pavement while Claire quickly wound the rope Tom had brought down from the corral around Hank's wrists. Digging up old memories of Girl Scout knots, she tied it securely while Hank kept up a steady stream of curses aimed at sending her straight to hell.

She ignored his invectives and calmly pulled the remaining length down to his ankles and began wrapping it around them. After she finished cinching the knot on Hank's ankles, she walked to the back of Hank's car.

"How's Brittany?"

Brittany lay on the back seat, her hand holding a compress against her head, while Jessica wrapped tape around it. A bandage covered the knife nick on Brittany's neck. Kat had untied Brittany's hands and was kneeling next to her legs, anxiously watching Jessica administer to the girl. Jessica had run out of the trailer after hearing shots. When she found out what had happened, she rushed back inside and came running down to the parking lot with the first-aid kit.

"This bump's pretty nasty," Jessica said. "And she's got a cut on it, much worse than the one on her neck. But the bleeding's slowed down. It will be okay until the ambulance gets her to the hospital and they stitch it up." Jessica stood and looked over her handiwork. "I'm more worried about concussion. Do you hurt anywhere else, Brittany?"

"I'm just banged up some, from when he threw me in the car." Brittany flung her arm over her face, shielding her eyes from the sun. "I thought he was going to kill me for sure. Thank God you guys rescued me!"

When she made a move to sit up, Jessica pressed down on her shoulder. "Stay there until the paramedics come. We don't want you to get dizzy and black out again."

Kat looked up at Claire, a sheepish expression on her face. "Sorry I froze back there. I've just had the gun a few weeks, and I'm still not comfortable with it."

"I've been there," Claire said. "I don't think you can ever get truly comfortable with using one, especially against a person."

Kat pursed her lips and nodded. "But if I'm going to conceal-carry, I should try. I'll work on it."

Claire knelt next to Brittany's head and put a hand on her shoulder. "You're going to be okay."

Brittany nodded then winced. "I hope so. My head hurts. A lot. And I feel shaky, like I'm going to puke."

"That's adrenaline shock, most likely," Claire replied. "Take some slow, deep breaths."

"Why did Hank do this?"

"Hank's the one who dragged Kyle into Gunpowder's stall and poked the horse," Claire said. "That's why Gunpowder's afraid of him—and vice versa."

"How the hell did you know that?" Charley asked while still keeping watch over the finally quiet and defeated-looking Hank.

She turned to Tom. "Your trademark stable shirt. You gave one to Hank last year when he worked for you, didn't you?"

Tom's brow furrowed in a puzzled frown. "I gave him two. What's that got to do with this?"

"It's got everything to do with this." Claire looked at Charley. "Remember that scrap of cloth we found on Gunpowder's hoof?"

Charley nodded, then his eyes widened. "I didn't get a good look at it. Does it match the pattern on Tom's official stable work shirts from last year?"

"Yes, and I think Hank was wearing one when he tortured Gunpowder. And it got torn, maybe when he slipped in the stall."

Hank pivoted his head to glare at her. "You've got no proof for any of this."

Claire turned toward the sound of a siren. Two cars pulled up in the parking lot. One was a patrol car, and the other was Detective Wilson's. He and the patrolman got out and slammed their doors shut.

"Maybe not yet," she said to Hank. "But we will soon."

Wilson walked up and surveyed the scene. "Sorry it took us so long. We were on a call on the other side of town. Does someone want to explain all this?"

"I will." Claire told him everything that had happened and pointed out where the three bullets she'd fired had hit. One had pinged off the hood leaving a divot, one was in the flat tire, and the third had plowed through the driver's door and the cushion of the driver's seat. That was the one that had shocked Hank into surrendering.

When the ambulance drove in, Wilson interrupted Claire to get a short statement from Brittany before she was taken to the hospital. Jessica called Nancy and relayed a message to Brittany that her mother would meet her at the hospital. Kat excused herself to return Gunpowder, her horse, and the mares she had been herding in from the pasture to the barn.

After the ambulance drove off, Wilson nodded approvingly at the patrolman, who had secured Hank in cuffs but left the rope on the man's wrists and ankles.

"Told him we were taking him in for kidnapping and bodily harm," the patrolman said, "and I read him his rights."

"I heard," Wilson replied. "Good work. We'll let him stew a bit on the concrete. Start taking photos of the crime scene." Wilson returned his attention to Claire.

She explained why she suspected Hank now rather than Tom of killing Kyle.

Tom shook his head while staring at Hank. "I'm no killer. Can't believe he is either."

Claire studied him. "I still don't know if you told Hank to do it, or if he did it on his own."

"There's no way in hell I'd do that," Tom said vehemently. "A business rivalry is no reason to kill someone."

With a sullen expression, Hank muttered against the concrete, "It's that damn crazy horse who's a killer."

Wilson studied Hank. He pulled a piece of paper out of his inside sport coat pocket, opened it, and bent down to show it to him.

"This is a search warrant authorizing me to search the homes and vehicles of the listed people and to confiscate any Peak View Stables shirts that I find."

Tom peered over Wilson's shoulder at the warrant. "How come my name's on there?"

Wilson returned the warrant to his coat pocket. "Because you own shirts that match the scrap we found, as do all of your employees. I'll start with both of your vehicles." He held out his hand. "Car keys?"

"I've got nothing to hide." Tom dug his keys out of his jeans pocket and gave them to Wilson. "It's the blue truck."

One side of Hank's mouth twitched. "You'll have to get my keys from these damn vigilantes who shot up my car and tied me up. Even better, how 'bout charging them all with assault, especially that crazy bitch who tried to kill me?"

"Sounds to me like it was the other way around." Wilson took Hank's car keys from Charley and tossed them casually in the air. "Is someone tied up here? Sorry, can't see it."

Hank cursed under his breath and squirmed against his bonds while Charley looked amused.

Wilson opened Hank's trunk and bent over the back bumper to look inside.

Curious, Claire sidled up next to him.

Wilson peeked out from under the lid. "Hold it right there. I don't want anyone but me touching these vehicles."

Claire stepped back. "I'll stay out of your way."

He waved the patrolman over to take photos while he snapped on a pair of latex gloves. Then he removed some tools and a plastic crate full of crumpled beer cans from the back of Hank's car trunk. He straightened and retrieved a large paper bag out of the trunk of his police car. After returning with the bag, he reached far back into Hank's trunk and carefully pulled forward a balled-up yellow, red, and black checked shirt. He held it up to the camera.

Jessica came up next to Claire and whispered, "Is that it?"

"Probably."

Wilson spread the shirt out and whistled. The hem on the left side of the shirt front was torn at least six inches and a small piece of cloth was missing. He pulled a baggie out of his pocket and held it up to show Claire.

"Picked this up from the evidence room this morning."

The baggie held the scrap of cloth taken off of Gunpowder's hoof. Wilson held it against the tear. It seemed to match the hole perfectly. He raised an eyebrow at Claire.

She nodded. "Will this be enough to prove Hank did it?"

"The lab will have to confirm the match with a microscope." Wilson leaned over the shirt and studied it. "I can't believe he didn't throw this away."

He pointed to a small dried brown stain on the shirt. "That looks like blood. And there's another spot here. If the DNA matches Kyle Mendoza's, then we've got him fair and square." He opened the paper bag and placed the shirt inside.

Claire let out the breath she hadn't realized she had been holding. "I sure hope so. Charley needs this case to be solved."

Wilson stapled the paper bag shut and dated and signed it. He stowed it in his car trunk and returned the crate and tools to Hank's trunk. After pulling off the latex gloves, he stuffed them in his pocket and wiped his hands against each other. "I think it's time to take

Hank Isley down to the station. See what he has to say for himself after we lay out all the charges against him."

Wilson and the patrolman walked over to Hank and untied the ropes. Then the two of them lifted Hank to his feet. While they escorted him to the patrolman's squad car, Claire and Jessica joined Charley and Tom.

After Charley apologized to Tom for the trick he played on him, Tom said, "I guess you had a good reason, to suss out Hank as a spy. Who knew he'd turn out to be a killer, too? I suppose it's partly my fault, if Hank thought he was doing me a favor by making it look like you had a killer horse on the property."

They watched while Wilson put a hand on the top of Hank's head as he slid awkwardly into the back seat of the police car.

"We still don't know what motivated him," Charley said. "He and Kyle could have had some disagreement, or maybe he was jealous of Kyle being my top hand. After Kyle died, Hank led most of the trail rides, and I'm sure his tips increased."

"Whatever." Tom stuck out a hand. "I hope you'll accept my apology, too, for having him spy on you."

Charley shook it. After the two exchanged a promise to cooperate better together in the future, Tom got in his truck. As the three vehicles drove off, Jessica, Claire and Charley silently watched them leave.

Charley exhaled. "I'm sure glad we finally caught the guy who killed Kyle."

"Yeah, me too," Jessica said while Claire nodded. "But there goes another employee."

The side of Charley's mouth twisted up in a sour grin. He put an arm around each of the two women. "Now, how the hell am I going to run a stable with only one and a half wranglers?"

———

Hours later, Claire, Charley, and Jessica were sitting on the front porch of the office trailer brainstorming about just that over glasses of homemade lemonade, when a car pulled into the parking lot. The waning rays of the late afternoon sunlight glinted off its windshield, so they couldn't see who was inside. Vince Donahue got out and walked around to the passenger side. He helped ease Brittany out of the car, then put an arm around her waist to support her.

She slowly made her way up to the porch, while Vince assisted her. She finished the walk up from the parking lot with sweat on her face and a look of pride.

But when they reached the steps, Vince swept Brittany up in his arms. He mounted the steps, deposited her on a bench next to Claire, then sat next to Brittany on her other side.

"I can't believe you're up and about, Brittany." Claire gave her a hug and pulled back to inspect the bruised face of her young friend. "Especially after such a trauma."

Jessica offered them both some lemonade from a large glass pitcher stuffed with lemon slices and chunks of ice. "I'm so glad to see you, Brittany. But not that goose egg on your head. What did the doctors say about concussion?"

"They didn't see any signs of bleeding in the CT scan," Brittany said, after taking a gulp of lemonade. "But Mom's going to have to wake me up every couple of hours tonight and check my eyes. It took two stitches to close the cut, so I might end up with a scar."

"I'm surprised you're here instead of home in bed," Charley said.

"I will be soon." Brittany put down her glass and looked at Vince. "But Vince and I had something important to talk to you about first."

Vince leaned forward toward Charley. "Mr. Gardner, I'd like to apply for a position as wrangler."

Charley's eyes widened. "But you work for Tom."

"I hear you pay better," Vince said with a nod to Brittany, then he smiled. "And I like the rest of your staff."

Charley's eyes narrowed. "I can't have the two of you flirting with each other at work."

Claire crossed her fingers but kept quiet. This was Charley's decision to make. Then she noticed that Jessica's fingers were crossed, too.

Brittany held up her hands. "No, sir. We know it's important to be professional, especially in front of the tourists. And we'll both work hard for you. We won't let our relationship get in the way of that."

Charley looked from one to the other. "God knows I need the help. And if Tom has you leading rides, you must be good." He held out a hand to Vince. "You're hired."

Vince shook it. "I have a friend who's looking for work, too. Comes from a family dude ranch in Wyoming, so he's used to pampering tourists. I was going to recommend he talk to Tom, but if you want, I can suggest he interview with you."

"Please do," Charley said, rubbing his hands together. "I'd love to talk to him. Okay, let's go fill out some paperwork. And please tell me both you and your friend are legal."

They all laughed.

"Congratulations, Charley," Claire said after the guffaws died down. "It looks like your problems are getting solved."

Charley gave her a wry smile. "I've still got at least one left. How the hell am I going to break this news to Tom?"

TWENTY:
A FAREWELL AND
A CELEBRATION

EARLY SUNDAY AFTERNOON CLAIRE sat next to Roger on a polished wooden pew in the whitewashed adobe Sacred Heart Catholic Church in Old Colorado City. While she and Roger hadn't known Kyle Mendoza well, she had gotten to know his mother and brother from Petey's hippotherapy sessions. She wanted to attend his funeral to support the family while they said a final farewell to the young man on whom they had leaned so much.

Charley and Jessica were attending, too, and sitting in the same pew.

Claire looked at the closed coffin up front, draped with white lilies and dark green ferns. Another young person whose life had been taken much too soon. Way too many young people she had known had died recently, and she almost wished the next death would be someone older. Until she remembered her mother teetering on the brink of mental incapacity.

No, not her, not yet, she prayed.

A rustle and murmur passed through the attendees, making Claire look around for the source. The Mendoza family was walking down the aisle to take their seats in the front. Ana and her husband, Emilio, came first, followed by Petey holding the hand of a young woman. With her long silky black hair and beautiful features, she was a female incarnation of handsome Kyle.

Claire realized this must be the missing Sophie, Kyle and Petey's sister who had been estranged from the family. Somehow, she must have been convinced to come from California for the service. Maybe that's why there had been such a delay between Kyle's death and the service. Crossing her fingers, Claire hoped this would be the beginning of a reconciliation between Sophie and her family. Petey needed his big sister.

Throughout the service and in between genuflecting for prayers and rising for hymns, Claire tried to catch glimpses of Sophie in front of them, until Roger shot her a puzzled look. Before she stopped peering she had seen Sophie's hand ruffling Petey's hair and took that to be a good sign. Another good sign was that she held his hand again as the family left the chapel first after the end of the service.

In the parish friendship hall afterward, Claire waited her turn in line to express her condolences. She gave Ana a hug and whispered in her ear, "I see Sophie came."

"Yes," Ana replied, her eyes shining with unshed tears of grief and her mouth upturned in happiness at the same time. "We've talked, gotten over some old hurts. She tells me she'll watch over Petey when Emilio and I are gone."

Claire returned Ana's smile. "I'm very happy for you, but I'm also sad that Kyle is gone."

Ana bit her lip and nodded. "Thank you."

Claire took that as a cue to move on. After shaking Emilio's hand and exchanging some well-wishes, she introduced herself to Sophie and explained, "I'm Charley's sister. Kyle worked for Charley, and I help his wife, Jessica, with her hippotherapy sessions. I've gotten to know Petey through them."

Hearing his name, Petey, who was standing next to his sister, leaned forward and smiled at Claire. She gave him a little wave, and he waved back.

"Mom's told me how helpful the sessions are for Petey," Sophie responded. "I'm so glad Mrs. Gardner can offer something like that in Colorado Springs."

"Speaking of Colorado Springs, how long will you be here?"

Sophie put an arm around her brother's shoulders. "As long as I need to be. I plan to start looking for work in the area Monday. Hopefully I'll find a job here and can stay permanently."

"I'm glad," Claire said. "I know Ana is very relieved you've come back—to Colorado Springs and the family."

Roger tapped her shoulder, and she glanced behind her. She realized she was holding up the line. "Find me later," Claire said to Sophie. "With my gift basket delivery business, I know a lot of businesspeople in town. Maybe I can help."

She moved on to give Petey a hug, then waited for Roger to finish. As they walked over to the punch table, she said, "I'm glad that sibling rivalry problem was solved, though it's too bad Kyle had to die for Sophie to return to her family."

Roger handed her a cup of punch and took a sip of his. "Hopefully your own sibling rivalry problem is being solved, too."

Claire peered at him. "I didn't know you noticed."

"Charley's been jealous of his big sister for years. He hasn't said anything to me outright, but I could tell he felt like he was living in your shadow."

"One he imagined," Claire said, turning to look at Charley and Jessica across the room. "Certainly not one of my own making." She sighed. "But yes, hopefully with the two murderers in jail and his staff level back up with the two new hires, his stable will recover. And hopefully he'll realize then that he's the one running the most successful business in the family, not his big sister."

———

As Roger drove into the parking lot of Gardner's Stables the next evening, Claire had a sense of déjà vu, thinking back on the opening celebration they had attended three weeks before. They were attending a celebration here again, this time for Charley's birthday. Once again she held a gift basket on her lap. So far, though, she had resisted the urge to fidget.

The basket was filled with books about the geology of Colorado Springs and the Garden of the Gods, local rock and mineral samples, a membership card for the Colorado Springs Mineralogical Society that she had signed up Charley for, and rock collecting tools. She had even put in some rock candy and chocolate rocks for fun. She couldn't wait to see his face when he unwrapped the cellophane.

She remembered her brother's fascination with rocks when they were children, though when he was very little, they usually went in his mouth. Later, he collected those he found with interesting colors and shapes. Still later he learned their names—granite, feldspar, quartz, mica. If Charley hadn't been fascinated even more by horses, she was sure he would have become a geologist.

After parking the BMW, Roger came around to her side and collected the basket from her so she could get out of the car. A whisper of a breeze teased their hair, and puffy white clouds drifted across the sky. Claire was grateful they hadn't developed into rain clouds, though Charley and Jessica had rented and erected a large dining tent just in case. They headed for the tent, out of which came a murmur of conversations and tinkling of glasses.

Claire spied a couple of large grills pumping smoke beside the tent and pulled on Roger's arm. "I want to say hi to Leon first."

She spotted the large black man holding a plastic cup of beer in one hand and a long barbecue fork in another. He wore a tall white chef's hat and a jaunty red-checked apron stretched across his rounded belly. He grinned and posed as someone took his photo.

Claire couldn't help laughing as she approached. "I didn't know you did the cooking, too, Leon."

"Claire!" He stepped out from behind the grill and gave her a big hug. He pulled back and nodded to Roger. "Roger, my man. I'd shake your hand, but I see they're full of one of Claire's creations."

Roger acknowledged Leon's greeting, then said, "I see the gift table, so I'm going to drop this off. I'll be back."

While he walked away, Leon handed his fork to a young man and took off the hat and apron. "I was just posing for some shots we're going to put in our catering brochure. Hell, I don't know nothing 'bout birthing ribs, to misquote that famous movie, but these talented young people do."

He clapped a hand on the young man's shoulder. Then he leaned down to say quietly to Claire, "Thanks for lining up this gig for me. I've already talked to three people here about bringing our barbecue operation to their next party."

"That's great news, and I was happy to do it. Charley loves barbecue, so it was a natural fit. Have you met him yet?"

"Sure have. Nice man. Takes after his sister." Leon nudged her with his elbow. "Speaking of which, Condoleza loved that basket you made her. Earned me some nice brownie points." He puffed out his chest and waggled his eyebrows.

Claire smiled. "And I'm sure you took advantage of those brownie points."

Leon guffawed and gave her a salacious wink. "You bet I did!"

"And I need to thank you, too, for the information you gave me. It was very important in solving the case, and in helping my brother keep his business from going under."

"Always glad to help a fellow businessman, especially one related to a good friend."

Roger returned and put an arm around Claire. "I'm parched. Let's go find the beer keg."

"It's up on the porch." Leon pointed. "And last I saw, your bro' was there, too."

A woman Claire recognized as his restaurant manager waved to him.

He held up a 'just a minute' finger. "Looks like I'm being called to duty. That uppity woman's got me fetching and carrying for her."

Claire and Roger said their goodbyes and moved toward the trailer. They said hello to Dave and Ellen and Brittany and Vince as they passed both couples. They were sitting at picnic tables and digging into ribs, chicken, beans, and slaw heaped onto sturdy disposable plates. Baskets of cornbread and rolls and wire condiment holders with sauces, butter packets, salt and pepper sat on each table. Leon's catering business seemed well-organized, and people were raving about the food.

After mounting the steps to the trailer porch, Roger filled two plastic cups with beer at the keg and handed one to her. They gently tapped the glasses so as not to spill the precious contents, and drank deeply. Claire leaned on the railing and looked out over the much larger gathering than was present at the opening. She sighed in contentment.

Just then Charley came out of the trailer, talking with the Executive Assistant to the Development Officer from Glen Eyrie Castle whom Claire had delivered her gift basket to on Saturday. Jessica followed with a tall, thin, middle-aged man. Claire recognized him from the photo on his assistant's desk as being the Development Officer. Charley gave Claire a hug and introduced Roger and her to the man.

He pumped her hand enthusiastically. "So I have you to thank for that wonderful gift basket I received from my employees this morning. I can't wait to start using all those grilling rubs and spices."

Claire smiled at him and his beaming assistant. "I'm so glad you liked it."

The man sniffed the fragrant smoke coming from the grills and rubbed his hands together. "Smells like some true experts are working the fires here, though."

"Get yourself some food," Charley said. "I'll be along to keep you company after I talk to my sister."

While the two Glen Eyrie representatives headed for the serving line, Claire turned to Charley and raised an eyebrow. "So, is their being here a good sign?"

"An excellent sign," Charley said. "We shook hands this afternoon on a deal for my stable to provide trail rides on the castle grounds. He's going to write up a contract and send it over tomorrow."

Roger clapped a hand on Charley's back. "Excellent news indeed!"

"Oh, Charley, I'm so happy for you." Claire gave him another hug, then hugged Jessica, who had been hopping with excitement behind him.

After returning Claire's hug, Jessica hooked her arm in one of Charley's and beamed up at him. "I'm so proud of him. He kept his cool and negotiated a really good deal for us. Then he topped it all off by inviting them to come to this birthday barbecue—the perfect invitation for a man who loves barbecue. That was the *coup de grâce*."

Charley beamed back at Jessica, basking in her praise. Claire caught her eye and gave her a thumbs-up then ladled on more praise herself. "Before you know it, Charley, you may need to start making expansion plans! See, I told you that you were the one in the family with the business smarts."

He smiled. "Maybe you're right. But you've been a huge help, Claire. Thank you."

"Anything for my little brother." She meant it, but she also realized that she didn't need to keep trying to rescue Charley. He could manage just fine on his own.

"Now, if you could just get that Tom Lindall off your back," Roger said, "your life would be perfect."

Charley laughed. "Life's perfect, then. I called Tom after negotiating the Glen Eyrie deal to let him know that I'd be happy to juggle my Garden of the Gods trail ride schedule, even reduce it or stay off certain trails, to suit him. Then, while he was in a good mood, I broke the news to him about Vince coming to work for me. He took it pretty well, considering. Said he knew the attraction was Brittany, because he'd seen the two of them together."

The news surprised Claire. "That was certainly nice of him."

"Well, as he said, he's had lots of staff come and go over the years that he's been managing Peak View Stables, so he can handle it." He took Jessica's hand and headed for the stairs. "And now I have one more thing to show you before we get some chow. Follow us."

Claire glanced at Roger, who shrugged, then the two of them walked behind Charley and Jessica into the barn. Once they reached the rear, they heard the clopping of a horse's hooves and the murmur of two voices. A horse neighed softly.

Jorge walked into the back of the barn from the pasture, leading Gunpowder. Nancy sat in a saddle on top of the horse. Both of them were whispering sweet nothings to the horse—and to each other, Claire suspected.

When Jorge saw them, he said, "Whoa" to Gunpowder, who stopped placidly. Jorge waved the group over.

"When did ICE release you?" Claire asked him as they approached.

"Saturday," Jorge replied and blushed.

Claire wondered why he was blushing, until Charley laughed and added, "Yeah, and the sneak didn't tell me until this morning that he was out."

Atop Gunpowder, Nancy smiled. "You wouldn't begrudge us our honeymoon, would you?"

"Of course not," Charley said. "I was just worried about Jorge."

"Sorry I didn't call you," Jorge said. "I had other things on my mind." His gaze at Nancy was full of love.

Jessica laughed and winked at Nancy. "I wonder what!"

Roger put an arm around Claire's waist and whispered in her ear, "Well that's one honeymoon we know went well."

Charley rubbed Gunpowder's neck. "And how's my favorite horse?"

"As you know, I have been working with him all day with Nancy's help," Jorge said. "He didn't already know her scent, but he still accepted having her on his back. And with Hank gone, he's calmed down a lot. I think we can try him on a trail ride tomorrow, as the rear *vaquero*'s horse."

"That's great news!" Charley rubbed Gunpowder's forehead. "You ready to hit the trail, fella?"

As if he knew what Charley was saying, Gunpowder nudged him with his head and gave a soft whinny. The 'killer horse' had truly been redeemed.

"You two ready for some chow?" Charley asked Jorge and Nancy.

"Soon," Jorge said. "We will put Gunpowder in his stall first."

"How about you?" Charley asked Roger and Claire.

"I thought you'd never ask," Roger said. "My stomach's been growling since we arrived."

They all laughed. Charley looped an arm around Jessica's waist and headed for the barn door. "Time for some of this Leon guy's barbecue then. I hope it's as good as you say it is, Claire."

"Oh. it is. Leon may drive a hard bargain, but he never disappoints." She followed with Roger, smiling to herself. Yes, all was right with the world.

THE END

Neil Groundwater

ABOUT THE AUTHOR

Beth Groundwater writes two mystery series for Midnight Ink, the Claire Hanover series and the RM Outdoor Adventures series. This book is the third book in the Claire Hanover gift basket designer series. The first, *A Real Basket Case*, was nominated for the 2007 Best First Novel Agatha Award after it was published in hardcover. Beth lives in Colorado and enjoys its many outdoor activities, including skiing and whitewater rafting. Contrary to what some readers think, she does not have a gift basket business of her own, but she enjoys creating gift baskets for family, friends, and charity auctions. Beth loves speaking to book clubs about her books in-person or via speakerphone or Skype. To find out more, please visit her website at bethgroundwater.com and her blog at bethgroundwater.blogspot.com.

WWW.MIDNIGHTINKBOOKS.COM

From the gritty streets of New York City to sacred tombs in the Middle East, it's always midnight somewhere. Join us online at any hour for fresh new voices in mystery fiction.

At midnightinkbooks.com you'll also find our author blog, new and upcoming books, events, book club questions, excerpts, mystery resources, and more.

MIDNIGHT INK ORDERING INFORMATION

Order Online:

• Visit our website www.midnightinkbooks.com, select your books, and order them on our secure server.

Order by Phone:

• Call toll-free within the U.S. and Canada at
  1-888-NITE-INK (1-888-648-3465)

• We accept VISA, MasterCard, and American Express

Order by Mail:

Send the full price of your order (MN residents add 6.875% sales tax) in U.S. funds, plus postage & handling to:

> Midnight Ink
> 2143 Wooddale Drive
> Woodbury, MN 55125-2989

Postage & Handling:

Standard (U.S. & Canada). If your order is:
> $25.00 and under, add $4.00
> $25.01 and over, FREE STANDARD SHIPPING

AK, HI, PR: $16.00 for one book plus $2.00 for each additional book.

International Orders (airmail only):
> $16.00 for one book plus $3.00 for each additional book

Orders are processed within 12 business days. Please allow for normal shipping time.
Postage and handling rates subject to change.

BETH GROUNDWATER

~A Real~
Basket Case

A CLAIRE
HANOVER MYSTERY

A Real Basket Case
Beth Groundwater

Feeling neglected by her workaholic husband, forty-something gift basket maker Claire Hanover joins an aerobics class. In a moment of weakness, Claire agrees to let charming aerobics instructor Enrique come to her house to give her a massage. She realizes she has made a deadly mistake when Enrique is shot and killed in her bedroom and her husband, Roger, is arrested for the murder.

Determined to clear Roger's name and save her marriage, Claire sets out to find the real killer, encountering drug dealers, jealous ex-girlfriends, and angry cops along the way.

978-0-7387-2701-1, 312 pp. $14.95

To Hell in a Handbasket
Beth Groundwater

Gift basket designer Claire Hanover is reluctantly enjoying a spring ski vacation with her family in Breckenridge, Colorado, when a bloodcurdling scream cuts the frigid air. Claire is appalled to find the sister of her daughter's boyfriend, dead on the slopes. Others assume the girl's death was an accident, but Claire notices another pair of ski tracks veering dangerously into the victim's path. To protect her daughter as incriminating clues surface, Claire unravels a chilling conspiracy.

978-0-7387-2702-8, 312 pp. $14.99